"I don't like men, I never did."

[PAGE 100]

*The*
# LAUGHING GIRL
*A Novel*

BY

## ROBERT W. CHAMBERS
AUTHOR OF "THE RESTLESS SEX," "BARBARIANS," ETC.

ILLUSTRATED BY
## HENRY HUTT

## D. APPLETON AND COMPANY
NEW YORK          LONDON
### 1918

Printed in the United States of America

TO

MY SON

BOB

AT PLATTSBURGH BARRACKS

# FOREWORD

## I

Here's a pretty tale to tell
All about the beastly boche—
How the Bolsheviki fell
Out of grace and in the wash!
—How all valiant lovers love,
How all villains go to hell,
Started thither by a shove
From the youth who loved so well,
Virtue mirrored in the glass
Held by his beloved lass.

## II

*He who grins in clown's disguise*
*Often hides an aching heart—*
*Sadness, sometimes worldly-wise,*
*Dresses for a motley part—*
*Cap, and bells to cheat the ears,*
*Chalk and paint to hide the tears*
*Lest the world, divining pain,*
*Turn to gape and stare again.*

### III

You who read but may not run
Where the bugles summon youth,
You who when the day is done
Ponder God's eternal Truth
Ere you fold your hands to rest,
Sheltered from the fierce huns' ruth,
Here within the guarded West
Safe from swinish tusk and tooth
Laugh in God's name, if you can!—
Serving so the Son of Man.

### IV

*Gorse is growing, poppies bloom*
*Where our bravest greeted Christ.*
*Is His dwelling, then, the tomb?*
*Has the sacrifice sufficed?*
*What is all we have then worth*
*In Thy sight, Lord, in Thy sight?*
*Take our offered heart-sick mirth—*
*Let our laughter fight Thy fight.*

R. W. C.

# TABLE OF CONTENTS

CHAPTER                                               PAGE

I. AN INHERITANCE . . . . . . . . 1

II. AL FRESCO . . . . . . . . 17

III. IN THE CELLAR . . . . . . . . 26

IV. MODUS VIVENDI . . . . . . . . 44

V. AN ODD SONG . . . . . . . . 67

VI. MASTER AND MAID . . . . . . . 81

VII. CONSERVATION AND CONVERSATION . 94

VIII. THE KNEES OF THE GODS . . . . . 108

IX. REX, REGIS . . . . . . . . 123

X. CLELIA . . . . . . . . . 133

XI. A PYJAMA PARTY . . . . . . . 153

XII. ROYALTY . . . . . . . . . 170

XIII. IN THE RAIN . . . . . . . . 188

XIV. THE MYSTERIOUS MR. SMITH . . . 209

XV. A TRAVELING CIRCUS . . . . . 225

XVI. THE COUNTESS . . . . . . . 239

XVII. MORE MYSTERY . . . . . . . 250

XVIII. THE GANGSTERS . . . . . . . 271

# Table of Contents

CHAPTER                                                       PAGE

XIX. CONFIDENCES . . . . . . . . . . 282

XX. A LOCAL STORM . . . . . . . 289

XXI. SUS SCROFA . . . . . . . . . 300

XXII. PARTICEPS CRIMINIS . . . . . . 314

XXIII. THUSIS . . . . . . . . . . 332

XXIV. RAOUL . . . . . . . . . . 345

XXV. THE DUCHESS OF NAXOS . . . . 356

# LIST OF ILLUSTRATIONS

"I Don't Like Men, I Never Did" . . *Frontispiece*

FACING
PAGE

She Was Peeling Potatoes in the Kitchen . 26

"Go to the Devil!" She Whispered Softly . 168

"I Seen the Bomb a-Sizzlin' and a-Fizzlin' on
the Floor" . . . . . . . . . . . 272

# THE LAUGHING GIRL

## I

THERE was a red-headed slattern sweeping the veranda—nobody else visible about the house. All the shutters of the stone and timber chalet were closed; cow-barn, stable, spring-house and bottling house appeared to be deserted. Weeds smothered the garden where a fountain played above a brimming basin of gray stone; cat-grass grew rank on the oval lawn around the white-washed flag-pole from which no banner flapped. An intense and heated silence possessed the place. Tall mountains circled it, cloud-high, enormous, gathered around the little valley as though met in solemn council there under the vast pavilion of sky.

From the zenith of the azure-tinted tent hung that Olympian lantern called the sun, flooding every crested snow-peak with a nimbus of pallid fire.

In these terms of belles-lettres I called Smith's attention to the majesty of the scene.

1

"Very impressive," remarked Smith, lighting a cigarette and getting out of the Flivver;—"I trust that our luncheon may impress us as favorably." And he looked across the weedy drive at the red-headed slattern who was now grooming the veranda with a slopping mop.

"Her ankles might be far less ornamental," he observed. I did not look. Ankles had long ceased to mean anything to me.

After another moment's hesitation I handed Smith his suit-case, picked up my own, and descended from the Flivver. The Swiss officer at the wheel, Captain Schey, and the Swiss officer of Gendarmerie beside him, Major Schoot, remained heavily uninterested in the proceedings. To think of nothing is bovine; to think of nothing at all, and do that thinking in German, is porcine. I inspected their stolid features: no glimmer of human intelligence illuminated them. Their complexions reminded me of that moist pink hue which characterizes a freshly cut boiled ham.

Smith leisurely examined the buildings and their surroundings, including the red-headed girl, and I saw him shrug his shoulders. He was right; it was a silly situation and a ridiculous property for a New Yorker to inherit. And the longer I surveyed my new property the more worried I became.

I said in English to Major Schoot, one of the ample, pig-pink gentlemen in eye-glasses and the

2

uniform of the Swiss Gendarmerie: "So this is Schwindlewald, is it?"

He blinked his pale little eyes without interest at the low chalet and out-buildings; then his vague, weak gaze flickered up at the terrific mountains around us.

"Yes," he replied, "this is now your property, Mr. O'Ryan."

"Well, I don't want it," I said irritably. "I've told you that several times."

"Quite right," remarked Smith; "what is Mr. O'Ryan going to do with a Swiss hotel, a cow-barn, a bottling factory, one red-headed girl, and several large mountains? I ask you that, Major?"

I was growing madder and madder; and Smith's flippancy offended me.

"I'm an interior decorator," I said to Major Schoot. "I've told you that a dozen times, too. I don't wish to conduct a hotel in Switzerland or Greenland or Coney Island or any other land! I do not desire either to possess kine or to deprive them of their milk. Moreover, I do not wish to bottle spring water. Why then am I not permitted to sell this bunch of Swiss scenery and go home? What about my perfectly harmless business?"

Major Schoot rolled his solemn fish-blue eyes: "The laws of the canton and of the Federal Government," he began in his weak tenor voice, "require that any alien inheriting property in the Swiss Republic,

3

shall reside upon that property and administer it for the period of not less than one year before offering the said property for sale or rent——"

He already had told me that a dozen times; and a dozen times I had resisted, insisting that there must be some way to circumvent such a ridiculous Swiss law. Of what use are laws unless one can circumvent them, as we do?

I now gazed at him with increasing animosity. In his uniform of Major of Swiss Gendarmes he appeared the personification of everything officially and Teutonically obtuse.

"Do you realize," I said, "that my treatment by the Swiss Confederation and by the Federal police has been most extraordinary? A year ago when my uncle's will was probated, and that German attorney in Berne notified me in New York that I had inherited this meaningless mess of house and landscape, he also wrote that upon coming here and complying with the Swiss law, I could immediately dispose of the property if I so desired? Why the devil did he write that?"

"That was a year ago," nodded Major Schoot. Captain Schey regarded me owlishly. "A new law," he remarked, "has been since enacted."

"I have suspected," said I fiercely, "that this brand new law enacted in such a hellofa hurry was enacted expressly to cover this case of mine. Why? Why does your government occupy itself

4

with me and my absurd property up here in these
picture-book Alps? What difference does it make to
Switzerland whether I sell it or try to run it? And
another thing!—" I continued, madder than ever at
the memory of recent wrongs—"Why do your police
keep visiting me, inspecting me and my papers, trail-
ing me around? Why do large, moon-faced gentlemen seat themselves beside me in restaurants and
cafés and turn furtive eyes upon me? Why do they.
open newspapers and punch holes in them to scrutin-
ize me? Why do they try to listen to my conversation addressed to other people? Why do strange
ladies lurk at my elbow when hotel clerks hand me
my mail? Dammit, why?"

Major Schoot and Captain Schey regarded me in
tweedle-dum-and-tweedle-dee-like silence: then the
Major said: "Under extraordinary conditions extraordinary precautions are necessary." And the
Captain added: "These are war times and Switzerland must observe an impartial neutrality."

"You mean a German neutrality," I thought to
myself, already unpleasantly aware that all the banks
and all the business of Switzerland are owned by
Teutons and that ninety per cent of the Swiss are
German-Swiss, and speak German habitually.

And still at the same time I realized that, unless
brutally menaced and secretly coerced by the boche
the Swiss were first of all passionately and patriot-
ically Swiss, even if they might be German after that

fact. They wished to be let alone and to remain a free people. And the Hun was blackmailing them.

Smith had now roamed away through the uncut grass, smoking a cigarette and probably cursing me out—a hungry, disconsolate figure against the background of deserted buildings.

I turned to Major Schoot and Captain Schey:

"Very well, gentlemen; if there's no immediate way of selling this property I'll live here until your law permits me to sell it. But in the meanwhile it's mine. I own it. I insist on my right of privacy. I shall live here in indignant solitude. And if any stranger ever sets a profane foot upon this property I shall call in the Swiss police and institute legal proceedings which——"

"Pardon," interrupted Major Schoot mildly, "but the law of Switzerland provides for Government regulation of all inns, rest-houses, chalets, and hotels. All such public resorts must remain open and receive guests."

"I won't open my chalet!" I said. "I'd rather fortify it and die fighting! I hereby formally refuse to open it to the public!"

"It *is* open," remarked Captain Schey, ' theoretically."

"Theoretically," added Major Schoot, "it never has been closed. The law says it must not be closed. Therefore it has not been closed. Therefore it is

6

open. Therefore you are expected to entertain guests at a reasonable rate——"

"What if I don't?" I demanded.

"Unhappily, in such a case, the Federal Government regretfully confiscates the property involved and administers it according to law."

"But I wish to reside here privately until such time as I am permitted to sell the place! Can't I do that? Am I not even permitted privacy in this third-rate musical comedy country?"

"Monsieur, the Chalet of Schwindlewald has always been a public 'Cure,' not a private estate. The tourist public is always at liberty to come here to drink the waters and enjoy the climate and the view. Monsieur, your late Uncle, purchased the property on that understanding."

"My late Uncle," said I, "was slightly eccentric. Why in God's name he should have purchased a Swiss hotel and bottling works in the Alps he can perhaps explain to his Maker. None of his family know. And all I have ever heard is that somebody interested him in a plan to drench Europe with bottled spring-water at a franc a quart; and that a further fortune was to be extracted from this property by trapping a number of Swiss chamois and introducing the species into the Andes. Did anybody ever hear of such nonsense?"

The Swiss officers gaped at me. "Very remarkable," said Major Schoot without any inflection in his voice or any expression upon his face.

Smith, weary of prowling about the place, came over and said in a low voice: "Cut it out, old chap, and start that red-headed girl to cooking. Aren't you hungry?"

I was hungry, but I was also irritated and worried.

I stood still considering the situation for a few moments, one eye on my restless comrade, the other reverting now and then to the totally emotionless military countenances in front of me.

"Very well," I said. "My inheritance appears to be valuable, according to the Swiss appraisal. I shall, therefore, pay my taxes, observe the laws of Switzerland, and reside here until I am at liberty to dispose of the property. And I'll entertain guests if I must. But I don't think I'm likely to be annoyed by tourists while this war lasts. Do you?"

"Tourists tour," observed Major Schoot solemnly.

"It's a fixed habit," added Captain Schey,—"war or no war. Tourists invariably tour or," he added earnestly, "they would not be tourists."

"Also," remarked Schoot, "the wealthy amateur chamois hunter is always with us. Like the goitre, he is to be expected in the Alps."

"Am I obliged to let strangers hunt on my property?" I asked, aghast.

"The revenue to an estate is always considerable," explained Schoot. "With your inn, your 'Cure,' your bottling works, and your hunting fees your income should be enviable, Mr. O'Ryan."

I gazed angrily up at the mountains. Probably every hunter would break his neck. Then a softer mood invaded my wrath, and I thought of my late uncle and of his crazy scheme to stock the Andes with chamois—a project which, while personally pursuing it, and an infant chamois, presently put an end to his dashing career upon earth. He was some uncle, General Juan O'Ryan, but too credulous, and too much of a sport.

"Which mountain did he fall off?" I inquired in a subdued voice, gazing up at the ring of terrific peaks above us.

"That one—the *Bec de l'Empereur*," said Captain Schey, in the funereal voice which decency requires when chronicling necrology.

I looked seriously at the peak known as "The Emperor's Nose." No wonder my uncle broke his neck.

"Which Emperor?" I inquired absently.

"The Kaiser."

"You don't mean William of Hohenzollern!"

"The All-Highest of Germany," he replied in a respectful voice. "But the name is in French. That is good politics. We offend nobody."

"Oh. Well, *why* all the same?"

"Why what?"

9

"Why celebrate the All-Highest's Imperial nose?"

"Why not?" retorted the Swiss mildly; "he suggested it."

"The Kaiser suggested that the mountain be named after his own nose?"

"He did. Moreover it was from that peak that the All-Highest declared he could smell the Rhine. Tears were in his eyes when he said it. Such sentiment ought to be respected."

"May I be permitted to advise the All-Highest to return there and continue his sentimental sniffing?"

"For what purpose, Monsieur?"

"Because," I suggested pleasantly, "if he sniffs very earnestly he may scent something still farther away than the Rhine."

"The Seine?" nodded Captain Schey with a pasty, neutral smile.

"I meant the United States," said I carelessly. "If William sniffs hard enough he may smell the highly seasoned stew that they say is brewing over there. It reeks of pep, I hear."

The two neutral officers exchanged very grave glances. Except for my papers, which were most perfectly in order and revealed me as a Chilean of Irish descent, nothing could have convinced them or, indeed, anybody else that I was not a Yankee. Because, although my great grandfather was that celebrated Chilean Admiral O'Ryan and I had been born in Santiago and had lived there during early boyhood, I looked like a typical American and had resided in New York for twenty years. And there also I practiced my innocent profession. There were worse interior decorators than I in New York and I was, perhaps, no worse than any of them—if you get what I am trying not to say.

"Gentlemen," I continued politely, "I haven't as yet any lavish hospitality to offer you unless that red-headed girl yonder has something to cook and knows how to cook it. But such as I have I offer to you in honor of the Swiss army and out of respect to the Swiss Confederation. Gentlemen, pray descend and banquet with me. Join our revels. I ask it."

They said they were much impressed by my impulsive courtesy but were obliged to go back to barracks in their flivver.

"Before you go, then," said I, "you are invited to witness the ceremony of my taking over this impossible domain." And I took a small Chilean flag from the breast pocket of my coat, attached it to the halyards of the white-washed flag pole, and ran it up, whistling the Chilean national anthem.

Then I saluted the flag with my hat off. My bit of bunting looked very gay up there aloft against the intense vault of blue.

Smith, although now made mean by hunger, was decent enough to notice and salute my flag. The

11

flag of Chili is a pretty one; it carries a single white star on a blue field, and a white and a red stripe.

One has only to add a galaxy of stars and a lot more stripes to have the flag I had lived under so many years.

And now that this flag was flying over millions of embattled Americans—well, it looked very beautiful to me. And was looking more beautiful every time I inspected it. But the Chilean O'Ryans had no business with the Star Spangled Banner as long as Chili remained neutral. I said this, at times to Smith, to which he invariably remarked: "Flap-doodle! No Irishman can keep out of this shindy long. Watch your step, O'Ryan."

Now, as I walked toward Smith, carrying my suitcase, he observed my advent with hopeful hunger-stricken eyes.

"If yonder maid with yonder mop can cook, and has the makings of a civilized meal in this joint of yours, for heaven's sake tell her to get on the job," he said. "What do you usually call her—if not Katie?"

"How do I know? I've never before laid eyes on her."

"You don't know the name of your own cook?"

"How should I? Did you think she was part of the estate? That boche attorney, Schmitz, at Berne,

12

promised to send up somebody to look after the place until I made up my mind what I was going to do. That's the lady, I suppose. And Smith—did you ever see such very red hair on any human woman?"

I may have spoken louder than I meant to; evidently my voice carried, for the girl looked over her shabby shoulder and greeted us with a clear, fresh, unfeigned, untroubled peal of laughter. I felt myself growing red. However, I approached her. She wore a very dirty dress—but her face and hands were dirtier.

"Did Schmitz engage you and are you to look out for us?" I inquired in German.

"If you please," she replied in French, leaning on her mop and surveying us out of two large gray eyes set symmetrically under the burnished tangle of her very remarkable hair.

"My child," I said in French, "why are you so dirty? Have you by chance been exploring the chimney?"

"I have been cleaning fireplaces and pots and pans, Monsieur. But I will make my toilet and put on a fresh apron for luncheon."

"That's a good girl," I said kindly. "And hasten, please; my friend, Mr. Smith, is hungry; and he is not very amiable at such times."

We went into the empty house; she showed us our rooms.

13

"Luncheon will be served in half an hour, Messieurs," she said in her cheerful and surprisingly agreeable voice, through which a hidden vein of laughter seemed to run.

After she had gone Smith came through the connecting door into my room, drying his sunburned countenance on a towel.

"I didn't suppose she was so young," he said. "She's very young, isn't she?"

"Do you mean she's too young to cook decently?"

"No. I mean—I mean that she just seems rather young. I merely noticed it."

"Oh," said I without interest. But he lingered about, buttoning his collar.

"You know," he remarked, "she wouldn't be so bad looking if you'd take her and scrub her."

"I've no intention of doing it," I retorted.

"Of course," he explained, peevishly, "I didn't mean that you, personally, should perform ablutions upon her. I merely meant——"

"Sure," said I frivolously; "take this cake of soap and chase her into the fountain out there."

"All the same," he added, "if she'd wash her face and fix her hair and stand up straight she'd have—er—elements."

"Elements of what?" I asked, continuing to unpack my suitcase and arrange the contents upon my dresser. Comb and brushes I laid on the left; other toilet articles upon the right; in the drawers

14

I placed my underwear and linen and private papers.

Then I took the photograph which I had purchased in Berne and stood it up against the mirror over my dresser. Smith came over and looked at it with more interest than he had usually displayed.

It was the first photograph of any woman I had ever purchased. Copies were sold all over Europe. It seemed to be very popular and cost two francs fifty unframed. I had resisted it in every shop window between London and Paris. I nearly fell for it in Geneva. I did fall in Berne. It was called "The Laughing Girl," and I saw it in a shop window the day of my arrival in Berne. And I could no more get it out of my mind than I could forget an unknown charming face in a crowded street that met my gaze with a shy, faint smile of provocation. I went back to that shop and bought the photograph labeled "The Laughing Girl." It traveled with me. It had become as necessary to me as my razor or toothbrush.

As I placed it on the center of my dresser tilted back against the looking-glass, for the first time since it had been in my possession an odd and totally new sense of having seen the original of the picture somewhere—or having seen somebody who resembled it—came into my mind.

"As a matter of fact," remarked Smith, tying his tie before my mirror, "that red-haired girl of yours downstairs bears a curious resemblance to your lady-love's photograph."

"Good Lord!" I exclaimed, intensely annoyed. Because the same distasteful idea had also occurred to me.

# II

OUR luncheon was a delicious surprise. It was served to us on a rustic table and upon a fresh white cloth, out by the fountain. We had a fragrant omelette, a cool light wine, some seductive bread and butter, a big wooden bowlful of mountain strawberries, a pitcher of cream, and a bit of dreamy cheese with our coffee. The old gods feasted no more luxuriously.

Smith, fed to repletion, gazed sleepily but sentimentally at the vanishing skirts of my red-headed Hebe who had perpetrated this miracle in our behalf.

"Didn't I tell you she'd prove to be pretty under all that soot?" he said. "I like that girl. She's a peach."

In point of fact her transfiguration had mildly amazed me. She had scrubbed herself and twisted up her hair, revealing an unsuspected whiteness of neck. She wore a spotless cotton dress and a white apron over it; the slouch of the slattern had disappeared and in its place was the rather indolent, unhurried,

17

and supple grace of a lazy young thing who has never been obliged to hustle for a living.

"I wonder what her name is?" mused Smith. "She deserves a pretty name like Amaryllis——"

"Don't try to get gay and call her that," said I, setting fire to a cigarette. "Mind your business, anyway."

"But we ought to know what she calls herself. Suppose we wanted her in a hurry? Suppose the house caught fire! Suppose she fell into the fountain! Shall I go to the pantry and ask her what her name is? It will save you the trouble," he added, rising.

"*I'll* attend to all the business details of this establishment," said I, coldly. Which discouraged him; and he re-seated himself in silence.

To mitigate the snub, I offered him a cigar which he took without apparent gratitude. But Shandon Smith never nursed his wrath; and presently he affably reverted to the subject:

"O'Ryan," he remarked, leaning back in his chair and expelling successive smoke rings at the Bec de l'Empereur across the valley, "that red-haired girl of yours is a mystery to me. I find no explanation for her. I can not reconcile her extreme youth with her miraculous virtuosity as a cook. I cannot coordinate the elements of perfect symmetry which characterize her person with the bench show points of a useful peasant. She's not formed like a 'grade';

18

she reveals pedigree. Now I dare say you look upon her as an ordinary every-day, wage-earning pot-wrestler. Don't you?".

"I do."

"You don't consider her symmetrical?"

"I am," said I, "scarcely likely to notice pulchritude below stairs."

Smith laughed:

"For that matter she dwells upstairs in the garret, I believe. I saw her going up. I'm astonished that you don't think her pretty because she looks like that photograph on your dresser."

What he said again annoyed me,—the more so because, since her ablutions, the girl did somehow or other remind me even more than before of that lovely, beguiling creature in my photograph. And why on earth there should be any resemblance at all between that laughing young aristocrat in her jewels and silken negligée and my slatternly maid-of-all-work— why the one should even remotely suggest to us the other—was to me inexplicable and unpleasant.

"Smith," I said, "you are a sentimental and romantic young man. You shyly fall in love several times a day when material is plenty. You have the valuable gift of creative imagination. Why not employ it commercially to augment your income?"

"You mean by writing best sellers?"

"I do. You are fitted for the job."

"O'Ryan," he said, "it would be wasted time.

19

Newspapers are to-day the best sellers. Reality has knocked romance clean over the ropes. Look at this war? Look at the plain, unvarnished facts which history has been recording during the last four years. Has Romance ever dared appropriate such astounding material for any volume of fiction ever written?"

I admitted that fiction had become a back number in the glare of daily facts.

"It certainly has," he said. "Every day that we live—every hour—yes, every minute that your watch ticks off—events are happening such as the wildest imagination of a genius could not create. You can prove it for yourself, O'Ryan. Try to read the most exciting work of fiction, or the cleverest, the most realistic, the most subtle romance ever written. And when you've yawned your bally head off over the mockery of things actual, just pick up the daily paper."

He was quite right.

"I tell you," he went on, "there's more romance, more excitement, more mystery, more tragedy, more comedy, more humanity, more truth in any single edition of any French, English, Italian, or American daily paper published in these times than there is in all the fiction ever produced."

"Very true," I said. "Romance is dead to-day. Reality reigns alone."

"Then why snub me when I say that your red-

headed maid is a real enigma and an actual mystery?
She might be anything in such times as these. She
might be a great lady; she might be a scullion. Have
you noticed how white and fine and slim her hands
are?"

"I notice they're clean," said I cautiously.

He laughed at me in frank derision, obstinately
interested and intent upon building up a real romance
around my maid-of-all-work. His gayety and his
youth amused me. I was a year his senior and I
felt my age. The world was hollow; I had learned
that much.

"Her whole make-up seems to me suspiciously like
camouflage," he said, "her flat-heeled slippers, for
example! She has a distractingly pretty ankle, and
have you happened to notice her eyes, O'Ryan?"

In point of fact I had noticed them. They were
gray and had black lashes. But I was not going to
give Smith the satisfaction of admitting that I had
noticed my housemaid's eyes.

"Her eyes," continued Smith, "are like those wide
young eyes in that pretty photograph of yours. So
is her mouth with its charmingly full width and the
hint of laughter in its upcurled childish corners——"

"Nonsense!——"

"Not at all. Not at all! And all you've got to do
is to put a bunch of jewels on her fingers and a thin,
shimmery silk thing showing her slender throat and

21

shoulders, and then some; and then you can fix her hair like the girl's hair in your photograph, and hand her a guitar, and drop one of her knees over the other, and hang a slipper to the little naked foot that swings above its shadow on the floor——"

"I shall do none of those things," said I. "And I'll tell you some more, Smith: I believe it's your devilish and irresponsible chatter which has put the unpleasant idea into my head that my red-headed domestic resembles that photograph upstairs. I don't like the idea. And I'd be much obliged if you wouldn't mention it again."

"All right," he said cheerfully.

But what he had said about this resemblance left me not only vaguely uncomfortable, but also troubled by a sort of indefinite curiosity concerning my cook. I desired to take another look at her immediately.

After a while I threw aside my cigarette: "I'm going into the pantry," said I, "to discuss business with my housekeeper. Here's the key to the wine-cellar. There's more of that Moselle there, I understand."

And I started toward the house, leaving him to twiddle his thumbs and stare at the Bec de l'Empereur. Or he could vary this program by smoking his head off if he chose. Or investigate the wine-cellar. But my cook he could not flirt with as long as I was on the job.

He seemed to be a very nice fellow in his way, but

he had put a lot of nonsense into my head by his random talk.

Yet he was certainly an agreeable young man. I had first met him in Berne—that hot-bed of international intrigue, where every other person is a conspirator and every other a boche.

Now Smith's papers and passport revealed him as a Norwegian; his reason for being in Switzerland a purely commercial one. He had arrived in Berne, he told me, with a proposition to lay before the Federal Government. This was a colossal scheme to reforest parts of Switzerland with millions and millions of Norway pines and hardwoods—a stupendous enterprise, but apparently feasible and financially attractive.

So far, however, he had made little headway. But somewhere in the back of my head I had a lively suspicion that Shandon Smith was no more a Norwegian than was I; and that he could tell a very interesting story about those papers and passports of his if he cared to. I had lived too long in New York not to recognize a New Yorker no matter what his papers showed.

Anyway we seemed to attract each other and during my enforced and bothersome sojourn in Berne we became companionable to the edge of friendship.

And when I told him about my ridiculous inheritance and the trouble I was having in trying to get rid of it, he offered to come up here with me and keep me company while the Swiss Government was making up its composite mind about his offer to reforest such cantons as required it.

That is how we came to be here in Schwindlewald together. I was to stay until the prescribed time elapsed when I should be allowed by law to sell the place: he was willing to remain with me until his offer to the Swiss Government had been either accepted or rejected.

I had begun to like Smith very much. We were on those terms of easy and insulting badinage which marks the frontier between acquaintances and friends.

Now as I entered the house I turned on the threshold and glanced back to see what Smith was doing. His hat was off; the Alpine breeze was ruffling his crisp, blond hair. He sat at ease beside the fountain, a fresh cigar balanced between his fingers, a corkscrew in the other hand. Beside him on the grass stood a row of bottles of light Moselle. He had investigated the cellar. And as I watched what appeared to me a perfectly characteristic type of American from Manhattan Island, his voice came across the grass to me, lifted in careless song:—

—"My girl's a corker,
She's a New Yorker,

She plays the races,
Knows the sporty places
Uptown, downtown,
Always wears a nifty gown."—

"Yes," said I to myself, "you're a Norwegian—aye don' t'ank!" which is good Norwegian for "I don't think."

And I smiled subtly upon Smith as he drew the first cork from the first bottle of that liquid sunshine called Château Varenn, and with which one may spend a long and intimate afternoon without fear of consequences.

As I entered the house his careless song came to me on the summer wind:

"My girl's a corker,
She's a New Yorker——"

"Such a saga," said I to myself, "could be sung only by that sort of Viking. Now why the deuce is that young man in Switzerland?"

But it didn't matter to me, so I continued along the wide hallway toward the kitchen in the rear.

# III

SHE was peeling potatoes in the kitchen when I entered;—she did it as daintily, as leisurely as though she were a young princess preparing pomegranates—But this sort of simile wouldn't do and I promptly pulled. myself together, frowning.

Hearing me she looked up with a rather sweet confused little smile as though aroused from thoughts intimate but remote. Doubtless she was thinking of some peasant suitor somewhere—some strapping, yodling, ham-fisted, bull-necked mountaineer——

"I have come to confer with you on business," said I, forestalling with a courteous gesture any intention she might have had to arise out of deference to my presence. I admit I observed no such intention. On the contrary she remained undisturbed, continuing leisurely her culinary occupation, and regarding me with that engaging little half-smile which seemed to be a permanent part of her expression—I pulled myself together.

"My child," said I pleasantly, "what is your name?"

"Thusis," she replied.

26

"Thusis? Quite unusual, — hum-hum — quite exotic. And then—hum-hum!—what is the remainder of your name, Thusis?"

"There isn't any more, Monsieur."

"Only Thusis?"

"Only Thusis."

"You're—hum-hum!—very young, aren't you, Thusis?"

"Yes, I am."

"You cook very well."

"Thank you."

"Well, Thusis," I said, "I suppose when Mr. Schmitz engaged you to come up here, he told you what are the conditions and what vexatious problems confront me."

"Yes, he did tell me."

"Very well; that saves explanations. It is evident, of course, that if I am expected to board and feed any riff-raff tourist who comes to Schwindlewald I must engage more servants."

"Oh, yes, you'll have to."

"Well, where the deuce am I to find them? Haven't you any friends who would perhaps like to work here?"

"I have a sister," she said.

"Can you get her to come?"

"Yes."

"That's fine. She can do the rooms. Could you get another girl to wait on table?"

"I have a friend who is a very good cook——"

"You're good enough!——"

"Oh, no!" she demurred, with her enchanting smile, "but my friend, Josephine Vannis, is an excellent cook. Besides I had rather wait on table—with Monsieur's permission."

I said regretfully, remembering the omelette, "Very well, Thusis. Now I also need a farmer."

"I know a young man. His name is Raoul Despres."

"Fine! And I want to buy some cows and goats and chickens——"

"Raoul will cheerfully purchase what stock Monsieur requires."

"Thusis, you are quite wonderful."

"Thank you," she said, lifting her dark-fringed gray eyes, the odd little half-smile in the curling corners of her lips. It was extraordinary how the girl made me think of my photograph upstairs.

"What is your sister's name?" I inquired—hoping I was not consciously making conversation as an excuse to linger in my cook's kitchen.

"Her name is Clelia."

"Clelia? Thusis? Very unusual names—hum-hum!—and nothing else—no family name. Well—well!"

"Oh, there was a family name of sorts. It doesn't matter; we never use it." And she laughed.

It was not what she said—not the sudden charm

28

of her fresh young laughter that surprised me; it was her effortless slipping from French into English—and English more perfect than one expects from even the philologetically versatile Swiss.

"*Are* you?" I asked curiously.

"What, Mr. O'Ryan?"

"Swiss?"

Thusis laughed and considered me out of her dark-fringed eyes.

"We are Venetians—very far back. In those remote days, I believe, my family had many servants. That, perhaps, is why my sister and I make such good ones—if I may venture to say so. You see we know by inheritance what a good servant ought to be."

The subtle charm of this young girl began to trouble me; her soft, white symmetry, the indolent and youthful grace of her, and the disturbing resemblance between her and my photograph all were making me vaguely uneasy.

"Thusis," I said, "you understand of course that if I am short of servants you'll have to pitch in and help the others."

"Of course," she replied simply.

"What do you know how to do?"

"I understand horses and cattle."

"Can you milk?"

"Yes. I can also make butter and cheese, pitch

hay, cultivate the garden, preserve vegetables, wash, iron, do plain and fancy sewing——"

I suppose the expression of my face checked her. We both laughed.

"Doubtless," I said, "you also play the piano and sing."

"Yes, I—believe so."

"You speak French, German, English—and what else?"

"Italian," she admitted.

"In other words you have not only an education but several accomplishments."

"Yes. But in adversity one must work at whatever offers. Necessitas non habet legem," she added demurely. That was too much for my curiosity.

"Who are you, Thusis?" I exclaimed.

"Your maid-of-all-work," she said gravely—a reproof that made me redden in the realization of my own inquisitiveness. And I resolved never again to pry into her affairs which were none of my bally business as long as she made a good servant.

"I'm sorry," said I. "I'll respect your privacy hereafter. So get your sister and the other girl and the man you say is a good farmer——"

"I told them in Berne that you'd need them. They ought to arrive this evening."

"Thusis," I said warmly, "you're a wonder. Go ahead and run my establishment if you are willing.

You know how things are done in this country. You also know that I don't care a rap about this place and that I'm only here marking time until the Swiss Government permits me to sell out and get out."

"Do you wish to leave the entire responsibility of this place to me, Mr. O'Ryan?"

"You bet I do! How about it, Thusis? Will you run this joint and look out for any stray tourists and keep the accounts and wait on table? And play the piano between times, and sing, and converse in four languages——"

We both were laughing now. I asked her to name her monthly compensation and she mentioned such a modest salary that I was ashamed to offer it. But she refused more, explaining that the Swiss law regulated such things.

So that subject being settled and her potatoes pared and set to soak, she picked up a youthful onion with the careless grace of a queen selecting a favorite pearl.

"I hope you will like my soup to-night," said this paragon of servants.

I was for a moment conscious of a naïve desire to sit there in the kitchen and converse with her— perhaps even read aloud to her to relieve the tedium of her routine. Then waking up to the fact that I had no further business in that kitchen, I arose and got myself out.

Smith, lolling in his chair by the fountain with half a dozen empty Moselle bottles in a row on the grass beside his chair, was finishing another Norse Saga as I approached:

—The farmer then to that young man did say:
"O treat my daughter kindly,
Don't you do her any harm,
And I will leave you in my will
My house and barn and farm;—
My hay in mows,
My pigs and cows,
My wood-lot on the hill,
And all the little chick-uns in the ga-arder!"

The city guy he laffed to scorn
    What that old man did say:
"Before I bump you on the bean
    Go chase yourself away.
Beat it! you bum blackmailing yap!
I never kissed your daughter's map
Nor thought of getting gay!
I'm here on my vacation
And I ain't done any harm,
I do not want your daughter, Bill,
Nor house and barn and farm,
Nor hay in mows
Nor pigs and cows
Nor wood-lot on the hill.
Nor all them little chick-uns in the ga-arden!"

Them crool words no sooner said
Than Jessie fetched a sob:
"I'll shoot you up unless we're wed!"
Sez she—"You prune-fed slob!
Get busy with the parson——"

Here Smith caught sight of me and ceased his saga.

"Yes," I said, "you're a Norwegian all right. Three cheers for King Haakon!"

"You speak in parables, O'Ryan."

"You behave in parabolics. I don't care. I like you. I shall call you Shan."

"Your companionship also is very agreeable to me, Michael. Sit down and have one on yourself."

We exchanged bows and I seated myself.

"By the way," I remarked carelessly, "her name is Thusis." And I filled my glass and took a squint at its color. Not that I knew anything about Moselle.

"What else is her name?" he inquired.

"She declines to answer further. Thusis seems to be her limit."

"I told you she was a mystery!" he exclaimed with lively interest. "What else did she say to you, Michael?"

"Her sister is coming to-night. Also a lady-friend named Josephine Vannis; and a farmer of sorts called Raoul Despres."

"Take it from me," said Smith, "that if truth is stranger than fiction in these days, this red-haired girl called Thusis is no more Swiss than you are!"

"No more of a peasant than you are a Norwegian," I nodded.

"And whoinhell," he inquired, keeping his countenance, "ever heard of a South American named O'Ryan?"

"It's a matter of Chilean history, old top."

"Oh, yes, I know. But the essence of the affair is that an Irish family named O'Ryan have, for several generations, merely been visiting in Chili. Now one of 'em's in Switzerland as close to the big shindy as he can get without getting into it. And, the question is this: how long before he pulls a brick and starts in?"

"Chili is neutral——"

"Ireland isn't. Sinn Fein or Fusiliers—which, Michael?"

"Don't talk nonsense," said I, virtuously. "I'm no fighter. There's no violence in me. If I saw a fight I'd walk the other way. There's none of that kind of Irish blood in me."

"No. And all your family in the army or navy. And you practically a Yankee——"

I stared at him and whistled the Chilean anthem.

"That's my reply," said I. "Yours is:

34

# In the Cellar

"My girl's a corker,
She's a New Yorker——"

"What piffle you talk, you poor prune," said this typical Norwegian.

So we filled our glasses to our respective countries, and another round to that jolly flag which bears more stars and stripes than the Chilean ensign.

It being my turn to investigate the cellar I went. Down there in one of the alleys between bins and casks I saw Thusis moving with a lighted candle—a startling and charming apparition.

What she might be doing down there I could not guess, and she was so disturbingly pretty that I didn't think it best to go over and inquire. Maybe she was counting the bottles of Moselle to keep reproachful tabs on us; maybe she was after vinegar. No; I realized then for the first time that the girl was far too pretty for any man to encounter her by candle-light with impunity.

She did not see me—wouldn't have noticed me at all in the dim light had not my bunch of bottles clinked—both hands being loaded, and a couple of extra ones under each arm.

The sound startled her apparently; she turned quite white in the candle-light and stood rigid, listening, one hand pressing her breast.

"It is I, Thusis," I said. "Did I frighten you?"

She denied it rather faintly. She was distractingly pretty in her breathless attitude of a scared child.

I ought to have said something cheerful and matter of fact, and gone out of the cellar with my cargo of bottles. Instead I went over to her and looked at her—a silly, dangerous proceeding. "Thusis," I said, "I would not frighten you for one million dollars!"

Realizing suddenly the magnitude of the sum I mentioned I pulled myself together, conscious that I could easily make an ass of myself.

So, resolutely expelling from voice and manner any trace of sex consciousness, I said in the spirit of our best American novelists: "Permit me, Thusis, to recommend a small glass of this very excellent Moselle. Sipped judiciously and in moderation the tonic qualities are considered valuable as a nourishment to the tissues and nerves."

"Thank you," she said, slightly bewildered.

So I knocked off the neck of the bottle in medieval fashion—which wasted its contents because she was afraid of swallowing glass, and said so decidedly. I then noticed a row of corkscrews hanging on a beam, and she, at the same moment, discovered a tasting porringer of antique silver under one of the casks.

She picked it up naïvely and polished it with a corner of her apron. Then she looked inquiringly at me.

So I drew the cork and filled her porringer.

"It is delicious Moselle," she said. "Is it Château Varenn?"

"It is. How did you guess?"

"I once tasted some."

"Another of your accomplishments," said I, laughing. She laughed too, but blushed a little at her expert knowledge of Moselle.

"I have rather a keen sense of taste and a good memory," she explained lightly; and she sipped her Moselle looking at me over the rim of the silver porringer—a perilous proceeding for me.

"Thusis," said I.

"Yes, Monsieur O'Ryan."

"Did you ever, by chance, see that photograph they sell all over Europe called 'The Laughing Girl'?"

Her dark-fringed eyes regarded me steadily over the cup's silver edge:

"Yes," she said, "I've seen it."

"Do you think that b-b-beautiful c-creature resembles you?"

"Do you?" she inquired coolly, and lowered the cup. There ensued a little silence during which I became vaguely aware of my danger. I kept repeating to myself: "Try to recollect that your grandfather was an Admiral."

After a moment she smiled: "Thank you for the tonic, Monsieur. I feel better; but I am afraid it was a presumption for me to drink in your presence. . . . And no cup to offer you."

"I'll use yours," said I, taking it. She was still smiling. I began to feel that I ought to pull myself together and invoke the Admiral more earnestly. But when I remembered him he bored me. And yet, could it be possible that an O'Ryan was drinking Moselle in his own cellar with his cook? In no extravagance of nightmare had I ever evoked such a cataclysmic scene. I have dreamed awful dreams in the course of my life:—such grotesqueries as, for example, finding myself on Fifth Avenue clothed only in a too brief undershirt. I have dreamed that I was wedded to a large Ethiopian who persisted in embracing me passionately in public. Other horrors I have dreamed after dining incautiously, but never, never, had I dreamed of reveling in cellars with my own cook!

A slight perspiration bedewed my brow;—I said in a strained and tenor voice not my own, but overmodulated and quite sexless: "Thusis, I am gratified that the slight medicinal tonic of which you have partaken in moderation has restored you to your normal condition of mental and bodily vigor. I

38

trust that the natural alarm you experienced at encountering me in the dark, has now sufficiently subsided to enable you to return to your culinary duties. Allow me to suggest an omelette for luncheon. . . . I thank you."

The girl's bewildered eyes rested on me so sweetly, so inquiringly, that I knew I must pull myself together at once or never. But, when I evoked the image of that damned Admiral he was grinning.

"Thusis," I said hoarsely, "you *do* look like that girl in my photograph. I—I can't help it—b-but you do!"

At that her perplexed expression altered swiftly and that bewitching smile flashed in her gray eyes.

"Good heavens," I exclaimed, "you look more like her than ever when you smile! Don't you know you do?"

Instantly the hidden laughter lurking in the curled corners of her mouth rippled prettily into music.

"Oh, Lord," I said, "you *are* 'The Laughing Girl' or her twin sister!"

"And you," she laughed, "are so much funnier than you realize,—so delightfully young to be so in earnest! You consider the world a very, very serious place of residence,—don't you, Mr. O'Ryan? And life a most sober affair. And I am afraid that you also consider yourself quite the most ponderous proposition upon this tottering old planet. Don't you?"

Horrified at her levity I tried to grasp the amazing fact that my cook was poking fun at me. I could not compass the idea. All I seemed to realize was that I stood in my cellar confronting a slender laughing stranger by candle-light—an amazingly pretty girl who threatened most utterly to bewitch me.

"I'm sorry!—are you offended?" she asked, still laughing, and her dark-fringed eyes very brilliant with mischief.—"Are you very angry at me, Mr. O'Ryan?"

"Why do you think so?" I asked, wincing at her mirth.

"Because I suppose I know what you are thinking."

"What am I thinking?"

"You're very, very angry with me and with yourself. You are saying to yourself in pained amazement that you hav business in a cellar exchanging persiflage with a presumptuous servant! You are chagrined, mortified! You are astonished at yourself—astounded that the solemn, dignified, distinguished Cabalero Don Michael O'Ryan y Santiago de Chile y Manhattaños——"

I turned red with surprise and wrath—and then slightly dizzy with the delicious effrontery of her beauty which daring had suddenly made dazzling in the candle-light.

For a minute my brain resembled a pin-wheel;

then I pulled myself together, but not with the aid of the Admiral. No! The Admiral made me sick. In my sudden rush of exhilaration I derided him.

"Thusis," said I, when I recovered power of speech, "there's just one thing to do with you, and that is to kiss you for your impudence."

"Your own *cook!* Oh, shocking! Oh, Señor! Oh Don Michael——"

——"And I'm going to do it!——" said I solemnly.

"Remember the seriousness of life!" she warned me, retreating a step or two as I set all my bottles upon the ground. "Remember the life-long degradation entailed by such an undignified proceeding, Don Michael."

That was too much. She saw trouble coming, turned to escape what she had unloosed: and I caught her near the cellar stairs.

Then, under the lifted candle, I saw her face pale a little, change, then a flush stain the white skin to her throat.

"Don't do that," she said, still smiling, but in a quiet and very different voice. "I invited it by my silly attitude;—I know it perfectly well. But you won't do it—will you, Mr. O'Ryan?"

"You deserve it, Thusis."

"I know I do. But don't."

My arms slipped from her. I released her. She was still smiling faintly.

"Thank you," she said. "I'm sorry I offered you provocation. I don't know why you seem to tempt me to—to laugh at you a little—not unkindly. But you *are* so very young to be so solemn——"

"I tell you I *will* kiss you if you repeat that remark again!"

It was on the tip of her tongue to retort that I dared not: I saw defiance in her brilliant eyes. Something in mine, perhaps, made her prudent; for she suddenly slipped past me and fled up the stairs.

Half way up she turned and looked back. There was an odd silence for a full minute. Then she lifted the candle in mocking salute:

"I defy you," she said, "to tell Mr. Smith what you've been about down here in the cellar with your cook!" I said nothing. She mounted the stairs, her head turned toward me, watching me. And, on the top step:

"Try always to remember," she called back softly, "that the world is a very, very solemn and serious planet for a ponderous young man to live in!"

I don't remember how long after that it was before I picked up my bottles and went out to the fountain where Smith sat awaiting me. I don't know what he saw in my face to arouse his suspicion.

"You've been in the kitchen again!" he exclaimed.

I placed the bottles on the grass without noticing the accusation.

"What was it this time—business as usual?" he inquired sarcastically.

"I have not been in the kitchen," said I, "although I did transact a little business with my cook." I did not add:—"business of making an outrageous ass of myself."

As I drew the first cork I was conscious of Smith's silent and offensive scrutiny. And very gradually my ears revealed my burning guilt under his delighted gaze.

Calm, but exasperated, I lifted my brimming glass and bowed politely to Smith.

"Go to the devil," said I.

"A rendezvous," said he.

And we drank that friendly toast together.

# IV

SMITH'S luggage and mine, and my other effects—trunks, boxes, and crates—arrived very early the next morning; and several large, sweating Swiss staggered up the stairs with the impedimenta until both they and their job were finished.

When I left New York, not knowing how long this business of my ridiculous inheritance might detain me in Switzerland, I packed several trunks with clothing and several crates with those familiar and useful—or useless—objets-d'art which for many years had formed a harmless and agreeable background for my more or less blameless domestic career in New York.

Rugs, curtains, furniture, sofa-pillows, books, a clock mantel set, framed and unframed pictures and photographs including the O'Ryan coat-of-arms—all this was the sort of bachelor stuff that Smith and I disinterred from the depths of trunks, crates, and boxes, and lugged about from corner to corner trying effects and combinations.

Before we had concluded our task I think he had

44

no opinion at all of me as an interior decorator. Which revealed considerable insight on his part. And although I explained to him that interior decorators became so fed up on gorgeous and sumptuous effects that they themselves preferred to live amid simpler surroundings reminiscent of the Five and Ten Cent Store, he remained unconvinced.

"It's like a lady-clerk in a candy shop," I insisted. "She never eats the stuff she sells. It's the same with me. I am surfeited with magnificence. I crave the humble what-not. I long for the Victorian. I need it."

He gazed in horror at a framed picture of my grandfather the Admiral.

"Oh God," he said, "what are we to do with this old bird?"

Intensely annoyed I took it from him and hung it over my mantel. It wasn't a Van Dyck, I admit, but it demanded no mental effort on my part. One can live in peace with such pictures.

"Some day, Smith," said I, "you'll understand that the constant contemplation of true Art is exhausting. A man can't sleep in a room full of Rubens. When I put on my dressing gown and slippers and light a cigarette what I want is relaxation, not Raphael. And these things that I own permit me to relax. Why," I added earnestly, "they might as well not be there at all so little do they distract my attention. That's the part of art suitable for domestic purposes,—something that you never look at, or, if you do, you don't want to look at it again."

He said: "I couldn't sleep here. I couldn't get away from that old bird over the mantel. However, it's your room."

"It is."

"Doubtless you like it."

"Doubtless."

"On me," he remarked, "it has the effect of a Jazz band." And he went into his own apartment. For half an hour or so I fussed and pottered about, nailing up bunches of photographs fanwise on the walls, arranging knickknacks, placing brackets for curtain-poles and shoving the poles through the brass rings supporting the curtains. They had once belonged to the Admiral. They were green and blue with yellow birds on them.

After I finished draping them, I discovered that I had hung one pair upside down. But the effect was not so bad. In domestic art one doesn't want everything exactly balanced. Reiteration is exasperating; repetition aggravating to the nerves. A chef-d'œuvre is a priceless anæsthetic: duplicated it loses one hundred per cent of its soporific value. I was glad I had hung one pair of curtains upside down. I went into Smith's room. He was shaving and I had him at my mercy.

"The principal element of art," said I to Smith, "is beauty—or rather, perhaps, the principal ele-

46

ment of beauty is art—I am not very clear at this moment which it is. But I do know that beauty is never noisy. Calm and serenity reign where there is no chattering repetition of effects. Therefore, as an interior decorator, I always take liberties with the stereotyped rules of decoration. I jumble periods. I introduce bold innovations. For example: Old blue plates, tea-pots and sugar-bowls I do not relegate to the pantry or the china-closet where they belong. No. I place them upon a Louis XV commode or a Victorian cabinet, or on a mantel. A clock calms the irritating monotony of a side-board. A book-case in the bath-room produces a surprisingly calm effect amid towels and tooth-mugs. A piano in the dining room gives tone . . . if played. And so, in my profession, Smith, I am always searching for the calm harmony of the inharmonious, the unity of the unconventional, and the silence of the inexplicable. And, if I may venture to say so, I usually attain it. This is not a business card."

And having sufficiently punished Smith, I returned to my own room.

Lovingly, and with that unerring knowledge born of instinct, I worked away quite happily all the morning decorating my room, and keeping one eye on Smith to see that he didn't drift toward the kitchen. He betrayed a tendency that way once or twice but desisted. I think he was afraid I might decorate his room in his absence. He need not have worried: I wanted all my things in my own room.

While I was busy hanging some red and pink curtains in my dressing-room and tacking a yellowish carpet to the floor—a definitely advanced scheme of color originating with me—I heard voices in the rear court and, going to the window, beheld my consignment of brand new servants arriving from Berne by diligence.

Smith, who had come up beside me to peer out through the blinds, uttered an exclamation.

"That girl in Swiss peasant dress!—she looks like the twin sister to your cook!"

"She is her sister. But she isn't nearly as pretty."

"She's infinitely prettier!" he asserted excitedly. "She's a real beauty!—for a peasant."

I corrected him in my most forbearing manner: "What you are trying to convey to me," said I, kindly, "is that the girl is flamboyantly picturesque, but scarcely to be compared to Thusis for unusual or genuine beauty. That's what you really mean, Smith; but you lack vocabulary."

"Whatever I lack," he retorted warmly, "I mean exactly what I said! For a peasant, that girl is beautiful to an emphatic degree,—far more so than her sister Thusis. Be kind enough to get that."

I smiled patiently and pointed out to him that the hair of the newcomer was merely light golden, not that magnificent Venetian gold-red of Thusis' hair;

and that her eyes were that rather commonplace violet hue so much admired by cheap novelists. I don't know why he should have become so animated about what I was striving to explain to him: he said with unnecessary heat: "That's what I'm trying to drive into your Irish head! That girl is beautiful, and her red-headed sister is merely good-looking. Is my vocabulary plain?"

I began to lose my temper: "Smith," said I, "you fell for Thusis before I noticed her at all——"

"I merely called your attention to the resemblance between her and your photograph of 'The Laughing Girl.' And I did *not* 'fall for her'—as you put it with truly American elegance——"

"Confound it!" I exclaimed, "what do you mean by 'American elegance'? Don't hand me that, Smith —you and your 'My girl's a corker!' Of the two of us you'd be picked for a Yankee before I'd be. And I have my own ideas on that subject, too—you and your Sagas about—

" 'She plays the races'——"

"In my travels," he said, looking me straight in the eye, "it has happened that I have picked up a few foreign folk-songs. You understand me, of course."

"Yes," I replied amiably. "I think I get you, Smith. Whatever you say goes; and you're a Viking as far as I'm concerned."

49

The slightest shadow of a grin lurked on his lips. "Good old Michael," he said, patting me on the shoulder. And, reconciled, we looked out of the window again in brotherly accord. Just in time to see the golden-haired sister of Thusis rise and jump lightly from the wagon to the grass.

"Did you see that!" he demanded excitedly. "Did you ever see such grace in a human being? Did you, Michael?"

What was the use? I saw nothing supernaturally extraordinary in that girl or in her flying leap. Of course she was attractive in her trim, supple, dainty, soubrette-like way. But as for comparing her to Thusis!——

"Her name's Clelia," I remarked, avoiding further discussion. "She's to do the rooms; Thusis waits on table and runs our establishment; and that other girl down there—her name is Josephine Vannis, I believe —she is to cook for us. You know," I added, "she also is very handsome in her own way. . . ."

He nodded without interest. She seemed to be of the Juno type, tall, dark-haired, with velvet eyes and intensely white skin,—too overwhelmingly classical to awaken my artistic enthusiasm. In fact she rather scared me.

"And to think that six-foot goddess is my new cook," said I, rather awed. I took another intent survey of the big, healthy, vigorous, handsome girl;

and I determined to keep out of her kitchen and avoid all culinary criticism.

"She'd not hesitate to hand us a few with a rolling-pin," I remarked. "Juno was celebrated for her quick temper, Shan, so don't find fault with your victuals."

"No," he said very earnestly, "I won't."

My new gardener was now carrying in the assorted luggage,—bundles and boxes of sorts done up in true peasant fashion with cords.

He seemed to be a sturdy, bright, good-looking young fellow with keen black eyes and a lively cocksure manner.

"He'll raise jealousies below stairs," remarked Smith. "That young fellow is the beau ideal of all peasant girls. He'll be likely to raise the deuce below stairs with Thusis and Juno."

Somehow or other the idea of such rustic gallantry did not entirely please me. Nor did Smith's reference to Thusis and his cool exclusion of Clelia.

"I don't believe Thusis would care for his type," said I carelessly. "And if he gets too—too——" I hesitated, not exactly knowing what I had meant to say.

"Sure," nodded Smith; "fire him if he bothers Clelia."

I dimly realized then that I didn't care whether he cut up with Clelia or not. In fact, I almost hoped he would.

51

A little later when I was in my room, alone, and agreeably busy, there sounded a low and very discreet knocking at my door. Instantly my pulse, for some unexplained reason, became loud and irregular.

"Come in," said I, laying aside my work—some verses I had been composing—trifles—trifles.

Thusis came in.

As the hostile Trojans rose unanimously to their feet when Helen entered—rose in spite of their disapproval—so I got up instinctively and placed a chair for her. She merely dropped me a curtsy and remained standing.

"Please be seated," said I, looking at her with uneasy suspicion.

"Monsieur O'Ryan forgets himself," she protested in the softest and most winningly demure of voices. But I saw the very devil laughing at me out of her gray eyes.

"I don't know why a man should receive his servants standing," said I. "Sit down," I added coldly, seating myself.

"Pardon, but I could not venture to seat myself in Monsieur's presence——"

Perfectly conscious of the subtle mockery in her voice and manner, I told her sharply to be seated and explain her errand. She curtsied again—a most devilishly impudent little curtsey—and seated herself with the air of a saint on the loose.

"My thisther Clelia, and my friend Jothephine

52

Vannith, and Raoul Dethpreth requetht the honor of rethpectfully prethenting themthelves to Monsieur's graciouth conthideration," she said with an intentional lisp that enraged me.

"Very well," I replied briefly. "You may go back and get rid of your lisp, and then explain to them that you are to be waitress and general housekeeper here, and that they are to take their orders from me through you."

"Yes, Monsieur."

I don't think she relished my dry bluntness for I saw a slight color gather in her cheeks.

I thought to myself that I'd come very close to spoiling the girl by my silliness in the cellar. I'd made a fool of myself, but I'd do it no more in spite of her heavenly resemblance to my photograph.

"That will be all at present, Thusis," I said coldly. "Come back in half an hour for orders. And see that you wear a clean apron."

Her lovely face was quite red as she passed out, forgetting to curtsey. As for my own emotions they were mixed.

One thing was certain; there was going to be a show-down between Thusis and me before very long.

If she were indeed the peasant girl she pretended to be, she'd recover her balance when I did, and learn her proper place. If she were, perhaps, a child of the bourgeoisie—some educated and superior young girl compelled to take service through family misfortune—and I now entertained no further doubt that this was really the case—she had nobody but herself to blame for my present attitude.

But!—but if, by any inexplicable chance, her social circumstances were, or had once been, even better than bourgeoise, then the girl was a political agent in masquerade. But, whoever she was, she had no business to presume on her wit and insolent beauty to amuse herself at my expense. And if she had really been sent by the Swiss police into my household to keep an eye on me she was going about it in a silly and stupid manner.

For such surveillance I didn't care a pewter penny. Spies had lagged after me ever since I entered Switzerland. It was rather amusing than otherwise.

But, as far as Thusis was concerned, I now decided that, no matter what she was or had been, she had voluntarily become my servant; and I intended that she should not again forget that fact.

As I sat there at my desk, grimly planning discipline for Thusis, I chanced to look up at the photograph of "The Laughing Girl"; and stern thoughts melted like frost at sunrise.

How amazingly, how disturbingly the lovely pictured features reminded me of Thusis!

The resemblance, of course, must be pure accident, but what an astonishing coincidence!

Musing there at my desk, possessed by dreamy and pleasing thoughts, I gradually succumbed to the spell which my treasured photograph invariably wove for me.

And I unlocked my desk and took out my verses.

They had been entitled "To Thusis." This I had scratched out and under the canceled dedication I had written: "To a Photograph."

I had quite forgotten that I had told Thusis to report for orders in half an hour: I was deeply, sentimentally absorbed in my poem. Then there came a low knocking; and at the mere prospect of again encountering my exceedingly impudent housekeeper I experienced a little shock of emotion which started my heart thumping about in a most silly and exasperating manner.

"Come in!" I said angrily.

She entered. I kept my seat with an effort.

"Well," said I in an impatient voice, "what is it now?"

Thusis looked at me intently for a moment, then the little devils that hid in her gray eyes suddenly laughed at me, totally discrediting the girl's respectful and almost serious face with its red mouth slightly drooping.

"Monsieur has orders for the household?" she inquired in her sweet, grave voice of a child.

That floored me. I had spoken about giving my

orders through her. I didn't know what orders to give.

"Certainly," said I,—"hum-hum! Let me see!— Let—me—see," I repeated. "Yes—certainly—the orders must be given—hum-hum!——"

But what the devil I was to order I hadn't the vaguest idea.

"We'll have luncheon at one," I said, desperately. She made no observation. I grew redder.

"We'll dine, too," I added. Her gray eyes mocked me but her mouth drooped respectfully.

"For further orders," said I, "c-come b-back in half an hour. No, don't do that! Wait a moment. I—I really don't know what sort of an establishment I have here. Hadn't I better make a tour of inspection?"

"Monsieur will please himself."

"I think I'd better inspect things."

"What things, Monsieur?"

"The—the linen press—er—the *batterie-de-cuisine* —all that sort of thing. Do you think I'd better do it, Thusis?"

"Would Monsieur know any more about them if he inspects these things?" she inquired so guilelessly, so smilingly, that I surrendered then and there.

"Thusis," I said, "I don't know anything about such matters. They bore me. Be a nice child and give what orders are necessary. Will you?"

"If Monsieur wishes."

"I do wish it. Please—take full charge and run this ranch for me and bring me the bills. You see I trust you, Thusis, although you have not been very respectful to me."

"I am sorry, Monsieur," she said with a tragic droop of her lovely mouth. But her eyes belied her.

"Thusis?"

"Monsieur?"

"I won't ask you who you are——"

"Merci, M'sieu."

"Don't interrupt me. What I am going to ask you, is, why do you continually and secretly make fun of me——"

"M'sieu!"

"You do!"

"I, M'sieu?"

"Yes, you, Thu.... Always there is a hint of mockery in your smile,—always the hidden amusement as though, in me, you find something ridiculous——"

"Please!——"

"—Something secretly and delightfully absurd——"

"But you know you *are* funny," she said, looking a trifle scared at her own temerity.

"What!" I demanded angrily.

"Please be just, Mr. O'Ryan. I minded my own business until you tempted me."

57

That was perfectly true but I denied it.

"You know," she said, "when a man finds a girl attractive the girl always knows it, even when she's a servant. . . . And certain circumstances made it much more amusing than you realize. . . . I mean to be respectful. I am your servant. . . . But you know very well that it *is* funny."

"What is funny?"

"The circumstances. You found me attractive. It mortified you. And the way you took it was intensely amusing to me."

"Why?"

"Because you are you; and I am I. Because the fact that you found your cook attractive horrified you. That was intensely funny to me. And when, waiving the degradation, you actually attempted to kiss your own cook——"

Laughter burst from her lips in a silvery shower of rippling notes which enchanted and infuriated me at the same time.

I waited, very red, to control my voice; then I got up and set a chair for her. And she dropped onto it without protest.

"What are you doing in my household?" I asked drily.

At that her laughter ceased and she gave me a straight sweet look.

"Don't you really know?"

58

"Of course not. You're an agent of some sort. That's evident. Are you here to watch me?"

"Dear Mr. O'Ryan," she said, lightly, "have I been at any pains to deceive you? I'm not really a servant; you learned that very easily. And I let you learn it—" She laughed:—"and it was a very pretty compliment I paid you when I let you learn it."

"I don't understand you," I said.

"It's very simple. My name really is Thusis; I wish to remain in your employment. So do my friends. We will prove good servants. You shall be most comfortable,—you and your amusing friend, Mr. Smith—*the Norwegian.*"

I smiled in spite of my suspicion and perplexity, and Thusis smiled too, such a gay little confidential smile that I could not resist the occult offer of confidence that it very plainly implied.

"You are *not* here to keep tabs on me?" I demanded.

"You very nice young man, of course not!"

"Do you really think I'm nice, Thusis?"

"I think you're adorable!"

The rush of emotion to the head made me red and dizzy. I had never been talked to that way by a young girl. I didn't know it was done.

And another curious thing about this perfectly gay and unembarrassed eulogy of hers, she said it as frankly and spontaneously as she might have spoken to another girl or to an attractive child:

there was absolutely no sex consciousness about her.

"Are you going to let us remain and be your very faithful and diligent servants?" she asked, mischievously amused at the shock she had administered.

"Thusis," I said, "it's going to be rather difficult for me to treat you as a servant. And if your friends are of the same quality——"

"It's perfectly easy," she insisted. "If we presume, correct us. If we are slack, punish us. Be masculine and exacting; be bad tempered about your food——" She laughed delightfully— "Raise the devil with us if we misbehave."

I didn't believe I could do that and said so; and she turned on me that bewildering smile and sat looking at me very intently, with her white hands clasped in her lap.

"You don't think we're a band of robbers conspiring to chloroform you and Mr. Smith some night and make off with your effects?" she inquired.

We both laughed.

"You're very much puzzled, aren't you, Mr. O'Ryan," she continued.

"I am, indeed."

"But you're so nice—so straight and clean yourself—that you'd give me the benefit of any doubt, wouldn't you?"

"Yes."

"That's because you're a sportsman. That's be-

60

cause you play all games squarely." Her face became serious; her gray eyes met mine and seemed to look far into them.

"Your country is neutral, isn't it?" she said.

"Yes."

"*You* are not."

"I have my ideas."

"And ideals," she added.

"Yes, I have them still, Thusis."

"So have I," she said. "I am trying to live up to them. If you will let me."

"I'll even help you——"

"No! Just let me alone. That is all I ask of you." Her youthful face grew graver. "But that is quite enough to ask of you. Because by letting me alone you are incurring danger to yourself."

"Why do you tell me?"

"Because I wish to be honest with you. If you retain me as your servant and accept me and my friends as such,—even if you live here quietly and blamelessly, obeying the local and Federal laws and making no inquiries concerning me or my three friends,—yet, nevertheless, you may find yourself in very serious trouble before many days."

"Political trouble?"

"All kinds of trouble, Mr. O'Ryan."

There was a silence; she sat there with slender fingers tightly interlocked as though under some sort of nervous tension, but the faint hint of a smile in the

61

corners of her mouth—which seemed to be part of her natural expression—remained.

She said: "And more than that: if you let us remain as your servants, we shall trust to you and to Mr. Smith that neither one of you by look or word or gesture would ever convey to anybody the slightest hint that I and my friends are not exactly what we appear to be—your household servants."

"Thusis," said I, "what the deuce are you up to?"

"What am I up to?" She laughed outright:— "Let me see! First—" counting on her fingers, "I am trying to find a way to live up to my ideals; second, I am going to try to bring happiness to many, many people; third, I am prepared to sacrifice myself, my friends, my nearest and dearest." . . . She lifted her clear eyes: "I am quite ready to sacrifice you, too," she said.

I smiled: "That would cost you very little," I said.

There was another short silence. The girl looked at me with a curious intentness as though mentally appraising me—trying to establish in her mind any value I might represent to her—if any.

"It's like an innocent bystander being hit by a bullet in a revolution," she murmured: "it's a pity: but it is unavoidable, sometimes."

"I represent this theoretical and innocent bystander?"

"I'm afraid you do, Mr. O'Ryan; the chances are that you'll get hurt."

A perfectly inexplicable but agreeable tingling sensation began to invade me, amounting almost to exhilaration. Was it the Irish in me, subtly stirred by the chance of a riot? Was it a possible opportunity to heave a brick, impartially and with Milesian enthusiasm?

"Thusis," said I, "there is only one question I must ask you to answer."

"I know what it is."

"What?"

"You are going to remind me that, to-day, the whole world is divided into two parts; that the greatest war of all times is being waged between the forces of light and of darkness. And you are going to ask me where I stand."

"I am."

The girl rose; so did I. Then she stepped forward, took my right hand and rested her other upon it.

"I stand for light, for the world's freedom, for the liberties of the weaker, for the self-determination of all peoples. I stand for their right to the pursuit of happiness. I stand for the downfall of all tyranny —the tyranny of the mob as well as the tyranny of all autocrats. That is where I stand, Mr. O'Ryan. . . . Where do you stand?"

"Beside you."

She dropped my hand with an excited little laugh:

"I was certain of that. In Berne I learned all about you. I took no chances in coming here. I took none in being frank with you." She began to laugh again, mischievously: "Perhaps I took chances in being impertinent to you. There *is* a dreadful and common vein of frivolity in me. I'm a little reckless, too. I adore absurd situations, and the circumstances—when you unwillingly discovered that I was attractive—appealed to me irresistibly. And I am afraid I was silly enough—common enough —malicious enough to thoroughly enjoy it. . . . But," she added naïvely, "you gave me rather a good scare when you threatened to kiss me."

"I'm glad of that," said I with satisfaction.

"Of course," she remarked, "that would have been the climax of absurdity."

"Would it?"

"Certainly."

"Why?"

"Fancy such a nice young man kissing his cook in the cellar."

"That isn't what you meant."

"Isn't it?" she asked airily.

"No."

"What did I mean then, Mr. O'Ryan?"

"I don't know," said I thoughtfully.

64

She gave me one of her smiling but searching looks, in which there seemed a hint of apprehension. Then, apparently satisfied by her scrutiny, she favored me with a bewitching smile in which I thought to detect a slight trace of relief.

"You will keep me, then?" she asked.

"Yes."

"Thank you!"

She stretched out her beautiful hand impulsively: I took it.

"Thanks—and good-by," she said a trifle gravely, Then, with a shadow of the smile still lingering: "Good-by: because, from now on, it is to be master and servant. We must both remember that."

I was silent.

"You will remember, won't you?" she said—the laughter flashed in her eyes:—"especially if we ever happen to be in the cellar together?"

I said, forcing a smile and my voice not quite steady: "Suppose we finish that scene, now, Thusis?"

"Good heavens!" she said:—"and the Admiral watching us!" She drew her hand from mine and pointed at the picture over my mantel.

"I'm afraid of that man," she said. "The cellar is less terrifying——"

"Thusis!"

But she laughed and slipped through the door.

"Good-by, Don Michael!" she called back softly from the stairs.

I walked back slowly to the center of my room and for a long time I stood there quite motionless, staring fixedly at the Admiral.

# V

## AN ODD SONG

"THERE'S one thing certain," thought I; "my household personnel is altogether too pulchritudinous for a man like Smith, and it begins to worry me."

Considerably disturbed in my mind I reconnoitered Smith's rooms, and found him, as I suspected, loitering there on pretense of re-arranging the contents of his bureau-drawers.

Now Smith had no legitimate business there; it was Clelia's hour to do his rooms. But, as I say, I already had noticed his artless way of hanging about at that hour, and several times during the last two weeks I had encountered him conversing with the girl while she, her blonde hair bound up in a beguiling dust-cap, and otherwise undeniably fetching, leaned at ease on her broom and appeared quite willing to be cornered and conversed with.

My advent always galvanized this situation; Clelia instantly became busy with her broom and duster, and Smith usually pretended he had been inquiring of Clelia where I might be found.

He attempted the same dishonesty now, and, with

every symptom of delight, cordially hailed me and inquired where I'd been keeping myself since breakfast.

"I've been out doors," said I coldly, "where I hoped—if I did not really expect—to find you."

This sarcasm put a slight crimp in his assurance, and he accompanied me out with docile alacrity, which touched me.

"It's too good a household to spoil," said I. "A little innocent gaiety—a bit of persiflage en passant—that doesn't interfere with discipline. But this loitering about the vicinity of little Clelia's too brief skirts is almost becoming a habit with you."

"She's a nice girl," returned Smith, vaguely.

"Surely. And you're a very nice young man; but you know as well as I do that we can't arrange our social life to include the circle below stairs."

"You mean, in the event of travelers arriving, they might misconstrue such a democracy?"

"Certainly, they'd misjudge it. We couldn't explain why our cook was playing the piano in the living-room or why Clelia laid aside her dust-pan for a cup of tea with us at five, could we?"

"Or why Thusis and you went trout fishing together," he added pleasantly.

A violent blush possessed my countenance. So he was aware of that incident! He had gone to Zurich that day. I hadn't mentioned it.

"Smith," said I, "these are war times. To catch

68

fish is to conserve food. Under no other circumstances——"

"I understand, of course! Two can catch more fish than one. Which caught it?"

"Thusis," I admitted. "Thusis happened to know where these Swiss trout hide and how to catch them. Naturally I was glad to avail myself of her knowledge."

"Very interesting. You need no further instruction, I fancy."

"To become proficient," said I, "another lesson or two—possibly——" I paused out near the fountain to stoop over and break off a daisy. From which innocent blossom, absent-mindedly, I plucked the snowy petals one by one as I sauntered along beside Smith.

Presently he began to mutter to himself. At first I remained sublimely unconscious of what he was murmuring, then I caught the outrageous words: "Elle m'aime—un peu—beaucoup—passablement—pas-du-tout——"

"What's that?" I demanded, glaring at him. "What are you gabbling about?"

He seemed surprised at my warmth. I hurled the daisy from me; we turned and strode back in hostile silence toward the bottling house.

My farmer, Raoul Despres, was inside and the door stood open. We could hear the humming of the dynamo. Evidently, obeying my orders of yesterday, he had gone in to look over and report upon the condition of the plant with a view to resuming business where my recent uncle had left off.

We could see his curly black head, and athletic figure inside the low building. As he prowled hither and thither investigating the machinery he was singing blithely to himself:

> "Crack-brain-cripple-arm
> You have done a heap of harm—
> You and yours and all your friends!
> Now you'll have to make amends."

Smith and I looked at each other in blank perplexity.

"That's a remarkable song," I said at last.

"Very," said Smith. We halted. The dynamo droned on like a giant bee.

Raoul continued to sing as he moved around in the bottling house, and the words he sang came to us quite plainly:

> "Crack-brain-cripple-arm
> Sacking city, town and farm!
> You, your children and your friends,
> All will come to rotten ends!"

"Smith," said I, "who on earth do you suppose he means by 'Crack-brain-cripple-arm'?"

"Surely," mused Smith, "he could not be referring to the All-highest of Hunland. . . . Could he?"

"Impossible," said I. We went into the bottling house. And the song of Raoul ceased.

It struck me, as he turned and came toward us with his frank, quick smile and his gay and slightly jaunty bearing, that he had about him something of that nameless allure of a soldier of France.

"But of course you are Swiss," I said to him with a trace of a grin twitching at my lips.

"Of course, Monsieur," he replied innocently.

"Certainly. . . . And, how about that machinery, Raoul?"

"It functions, Monsieur. A little rust—nothing serious. The torrent from the Bec-de l'Empereur runs the dynamo; the spring flows full. Listen!"

We listened. Through the purring of the dynamo the bubbling melody of the famous mineral spring was perfectly audible.

"How many bottles have we?" I asked.

"In the unopened cases a hundred thousand. In odd lots, quart size, twenty thousand more."

"Corks? Boxes?"

"Plenty."

"Labels? Straw?"

"Bales, Monsieur."

"And all the machinery works?"

For answer he picked up a quart bottle and placed it in a porcelain cylinder. Then he threw a switch; the bottle was filled automatically, corked, labeled, sheathed in straw and deposited in a straw-lined box.

"Fine!" I said. "When you have a few moments to spare from the farm you can fill a few dozen cases. And you, too, Smith, when time hangs heavy on your hands, it might amuse you to drop in and start bottling spring water for me—instead of re-arranging your bureau drawers."

The suggestion did not seem to attract him. He said he'd enjoy doing it but that he did not comprehend machinery.

I smiled at him and made up my mind that he'd not spend his spare time in Clelia's neighborhood.

"Raoul," said I, "that was an interesting song you were singing when we came in."

"What song, Monsieur?"

"The one about 'Crack-brain-cripple-arm.'"

He gazed at me so stupidly that I hesitated.

"I thought I heard you humming a song," said I.

"Maybe it was the dynamo, Monsieur."

"Maybe," I said gravely.

Smith and I walked out and across toward the cow-stables.

There was nothing to see there except chickens; the little brown Swiss cattle being in pasture on the Bec-de l'Empereur.

"If time hangs heavy with you, Smith," I ventured, "why not drive the cows home and milk them in the evenings?"

He told me, profanely, that he had plenty to do to amuse himself.

72

"What, for example, did he tell you?"

"Write letters," he said,—"for example."

"To friends in dear old Norway, I suppose," said I flippantly.

"To whomever I darn well please," he rejoined drily.

That, of course, precluded further playful inquiry. Baffled, I walked on beside him. But I sullenly decided to stick to him until Clelia had done the chamber-work and had safely retired to regions below stairs.

Several times he remarked he'd forgotten something and ought to go to his rooms to look for the missing objects. I pretended not to hear him and he hadn't the effrontery to attempt it.

The words of Raoul's song kept running in my mind.

> "Crack-brain-cripple-arm
> You have done a heap of harm—"

And I found myself humming the catchy air as I strolled over my domain with my unwilling companion.

"I like that song," I remarked.

"Of course *you* would," he said.

"Why?"

"Because you're so bally neutral," he replied ironically.

"I *am* neutral. All Chileans are. I'm neutral because my country is."

"You're neutral as hell," he retorted with a shrug —"you camouflaged Yankee."

"If I weren't neutral," said I, "I'd not be afraid of admitting it to a New York Viking."

That put him out on first. I enjoyed his silence for a while, then I said: "Come on, old top, sing us some more Norse sagas about 'My girl's a corker.'"

"Can it!" retorted that typical product of Christiania.

So with quip and retort and persiflage veiled and more or less merry, we strolled about in the beautiful early summer weather.

"Why the devil don't you find Thusis and take another lesson in angling?" he suggested.

"Because, dear friend, Thusis hitched up our horse and went to Zurich this morning."

"What? When?"

"Ere the earliest dicky-bird had caroled—ere Aurora had wiped night's messy cobwebs from the skies with rosy fingers."

"What did she go for?—that is, what did she *say* she was going for?"

"To purchase various household necessaries. Why?"

"She's a funny girl," he remarked evasively.

"Yes?"

"Rather."

"In what humorous particular do you hand it so generously to Thusis?" I inquired.

"Oh, you know well enough she's odd. You can't explain her. She's no peasant, and you know it. She's not Swiss, either. I don't know what she is. I don't know quite what she's doing here. Sometimes she reminds me of a runaway school girl; sometimes of the humorless, pep-less prude who usually figures as heroine in a best seller. And sometimes she acts like a vixen! . . . I didn't tell you," he added, "but I was amiable enough to try to kiss her that first evening. I don't know where you were—but you can take it from me, O'Ryan, I thought I'd caught hold of the original vestal virgin and that my hour had come for the lions!"

"You beast," said I, not recollecting my own behavior in the cellar. "What did she say?"

"She didn't say anything. She merely looked it. I've been horribly afraid she'd tell her sister," he added naïvely.

"Smith," I said, laying an earnest hand on his arm, "you mustn't frivol with my household. I won't stand for it. I admit that my household is an unusual one. Frankly, I have no more idea than you have that Thusis and Clelia are real servants, or why they choose to take service here with me. Probably they're political agents. I don't care. But you and I mustn't interfere with them, first, because

75

it disorganizes my ménage; second, because I believe they're really nice girls."

"I think so, too," he said.

"Well, then, if they are, we don't want to forget it. And also we must remember that probably they are political agents of some country now engaged in this war, and it won't do for us to become involved."

"How involved?"

"Well, suppose I took Thusis more or less seriously?"

"*Do* you?"

"I didn't say I did. I said suppose I do? Who is she? With all her dainty personality and undoubted marks of birth and breeding—with the irrefutable evidence of manner and speech and presence—with all these ear-marks by which both she and Clelia seem plainly labeled—*who* is Thusis?"

"I don't know," he said soberly.

"Nor I. And yet it is apparent that she has taken no pains to play the part of a peasant or of a servant for our benefit. Evidently she doesn't care—for I venture to believe she's a good actress in addition to the rest of her ungodly cleverness.

"But she seems to think it immaterial as to whether or not you and I wonder who she may be. Mentally, Thusis snaps her fingers at us, Smith. So does Clelia."

"Clelia is gentler—more girlish and immature,"

76

he said, "but she makes no bones about having been in better circumstances. She's sweet but she's no weakling. My curiosity amuses her and she pokes a lot of fun at me."

"Doesn't she tell you anything? Doesn't she give you any hint?"

"No, she doesn't. She's friendly—willing to stop dusting and exchange a little innocent banter with me. . . . Do you know, O'Ryan, I never before saw such a pretty girl. She's only eighteen. Did you know it?"

"No, I didn't."

"And Thusis is twenty."

I thought deeply for a while, then:

"We'd better keep away from them except when business requires an interview," I concluded.

"Why," he pointed out in annoyance, "that leaves *me* out entirely."

"Of course. I shall not think of Thusis at all except on terms of business. That's the safe idea, Smith, business,—strictly business. It neutralizes everything; it's a wet blanket on folly; it paralyzes friskiness; it slays sentiment in its tracks. Become a business man. Engage in some useful occupation. Suppose, for example, I pay you a franc a week to feed my chickens."

"I've plenty to do, I tell you."

"Then do it, old top, and steer shy of that little blue-eyed parlor maid of mine."

He made no answer. We prowled about until nearly lunch-time. But the odd thing was that I had lost my appetite. It may have happened because I'd begun to worry a little about Thusis.

What the deuce had that girl been doing in Zurich all this while? She was too attractive to go about that seething city alone with market-cart and horse. Some fresh young officer—

"Smith?"

He looked up, mildly surprised at my vehemence.

"Where the devil do you suppose Thusis is?" I asked.

"In Zurich, isn't she?"

"Yes, but she's been gone a long time and she ought to be back."

"Probably," he said, "she's gallivanting with some handsome young fellow along the Lake promenade. Possibly she's lunching at the Baur-au-Lac with some fascinating lieutenant. Or maybe they've strolled over to the Café de la Terrasse or to Rupps; or," he went on as though interested in his irritating speculations, "it may be that Thusis has gone out in a motor launch with some sprightly cavalier; or she may be at the Tonhalle, or at Belvoir Park."

"No doubt," said I, exasperated. "You needn't speculate further."

"Business over, why shouldn't Thusis kick up her pretty heels a bit?" he inquired.

"Because Thusis isn't that sort."

"How do *you* know that she isn't that sort?"

I didn't, and his question made me the madder.

"Luncheon ought to be ready," he reminded me presently. I could actually hear the grin in his voice.

"All right," said I. "I'm hungry." Which was a lie. Then, as we turned toward the house, Thusis drove into the yard.

Blue ribbons fluttered from her whip, from the fat horse's head-stall, from his braided tail. There were bows of blue ribbon on her peasant's apron, too, which danced saucily in the wind. I went over to aid her descend from the cart, but she laughed and jumped out with a flash of white stockings and blue garters.

"I've been wondering," said I, "why you were so long."

"Were you worried?"

The demurely malicious glance she flung at me became a laugh. She turned to Smith:

"Did he think somebody might kidnap his young and silly housekeeper?" she inquired. "Pas de chance! I am horridly wise!"—she touched her forehead with the tip of one finger—"and a thousand years old!"—she laid one hand lightly over her heart. And turned to me. "I am a thousand years of age," she repeated, smiling. "Such as I are not kidnapped, Monsieur O'Ryan. Au contraire. I myself am far more likely to kidnap——"

She loowed Smith gaily in the eye "—some agreeable young man—some day." And very slowly her gray eyes included me.

Then she tossed the reins to Raoul who had come up beside the cart:

"A protean moment," she said to me, "and I shall reappear as a very presentable waitress to wait upon you at luncheon."

And off went this amazing housekeeper of mine dancing lightly away across the grass with the buckles on her little peasant slippers twinkling and every blue ribbon a-flutter.

I turned and looked at Raoul. He returned my gaze with an odd smile.

"Of what," said I, "are you thinking?"

"I was thinking," he replied seriously, "that the world is a very droll place,—agreeable for the gay, but hell for those born without a sense of humor."

# VI

I HAD become tired of following Smith about and of trying to keep an eye on Clelia. The little minx was so demure that it seemed difficult to believe she deliberately offered Smith opportunities for philandering. Otherwise my household caused me no anxiety; everything went smoothly. Thusis waited on table and ran the place, Josephine Vannis cooked to perfection, Raoul had started a garden and the bottling works; and no tourists had bothered us by interrupting the régime and demanding food and shelter.

Outwardly ours was a serene and emotionless life, undisturbed by that bloody frenzy which agitated the greater surface of the globe.

Here in the sunny silence of our little valley ringed by snow peaks, the soft thunder of some far avalanche or the distant tinkle of cow-bells were the loudest interruptions that startled us from the peaceful inertia consequent upon good food and idle hours.

Outwardly as I say, calm brooded all about us. True the Zurich and Berne newspapers stirred me

up, and the weekly packages of New York papers
which Smith and I received caused a tense silence in
our rooms whither we always retired to read them.

Smith once remarked that it was odd I never received any Chilean papers. To which I replied that
it seemed queer no Norwegian newspapers came to
him.

We let it rest there. As for my household I never
saw Josephine Vannis at all except by accident in
the early evening when I sometimes noticed her in
the distance strolling with Raoul.

On Clelia, I kept an unquiet eye as I have said.
Thusis I saw only on strictly business interviews.
And Smith thought it strange that there was so
much business to be discussed between us. But
every day I felt it my duty to go over my household accounts with Thusis, checking up every item.
In these daily conferences there were, of course, all
sorts of matters to consider, such as the farm and
dairy reports from Raoul, the bottling reports, daily
sales of eggs, butter, and bottled spring-water—a
cart arriving from Zurich every morning to take
away these surplus items to the Grand Hotel, Baur-
au-Lac, with which Thusis had made a thrifty contract.

This was a very delightful part of the day to me,
—the hour devoted to business with Thusis, while
Smith fumed in his room. Possibly Clelia fumed

with him—I was afraid of that—and it was the only rift in the lute.

Every morning I tried to prolong that business interview with Thusis,—she looked so distractingly pretty in her peasant garb. But though her gray eyes were ever on duty and her winning smile flashed now and then across the frontier of laughter, always and almost with malice, she held me to the matter of business under discussion, discouraging all diversions I made toward other topics, refusing to accompany me on gay excursions into personalities, resisting any approach toward that little spot of unconventional ground upon which we had once stood face to face.

For since that time when, for hours afterward, my hand remained conscious of her soft, cool hand's light contact—since that curious compact between us which had settled her status, and my own, here under this common roof above us, she had permitted no lighter conversation to interrupt our business conferences, no other subject to intrude. Only now and then I caught a glimpse of tiny devils dancing in her gray eyes; only at long intervals was the promise of the upcurled corners of her mouth made good by the swift, sweet laughter always hidden there.

There was no use attempting any less impersonal footing any more; Thusis simply evaded it, remaining either purposely dull and irresponsive or, gathering up her accounts, she would rise, curtsey, and back out with a gravity of features and demeanor that her mocking eyes denied.

Once, as I have said, I discovered a fishing rod in the attic, dug some worms, and started out upon conservation bent. And encountering Thusis digging dandelions for salad behind the garden, explained to her my attire and implements. As it was strictly a matter of business she consented to go with me as far as the brook. There, by the bridge in the first pool, she caught the first trout. And, having showed me how, retreated, resolutely repelling all suggestions that she take a morning off, and defying me with a gaiety that made her eyes brilliant with delighted malice.

"It was my duty to show you how Swiss trout are caught," she called back to me, always retreating down the leafy path—"but when you propose a pleasure party to your housekeeper—oh, Don Michael, you betray low tastes and I am amazed at you and I beg you most earnestly to remember the Admiral."

Whereupon I was stung into action and foolish enough to suppose I could overtake her. Where she vanished I don't know. There was not a sound in the wood. I was ass enough to call—even to appeal in a voice so sentimental that I blush to remember it now.

And at last, discomfited and sulky, I went back

84

to my fishing. But hers remained the only trout in my basket. Smith and I ate it, baked with parsley, for luncheon, between intermittent inquiries from Smith regarding the fewness of the catch.

And now, it appeared, somebody had already told him that Thusis and I had gone fishing together that day. Who the devil had revealed that fact? Clelia, no doubt,—having been informed by Thusis. And no doubt Thusis had held me up to ridicule.

So now, at the hour when our daily business conference approached, instead of seating myself as usual at the table in my sitting-room, I took my fishing-rod, creel, a musty and water-warped leather fly-book, and went into Smith's room.

"Suppose we go fishing," I suggested, knowing he'd refuse on the chance of a tête-à-tête with Clelia the minute I was out of sight.

He began to explain that he had letters to write, and I laughed in derision and sent my regards to all the folks in dear old Norway.

"Go to the deuce," said I. "Flirt with my chamber-maid if you want to, but Thusis will take your head off—"

"Isn't she going with *you?*"

"—When she returns," I continued, vexed and red at his impudent conclusion. It was perfectly true that I meant to take Thusis fishing, but it was not Smith's business to guess my intentions.

"You annoy me," I added, passing him with a
scowl. At which he merely grinned.

In the hallway I encountered Clelia in cap and
apron, very diligent with her duster.

"Clelia," said I pleasantly, "has Raoul brought
the mail?"

"Yes, Monsieur."

"Where is it?"

"There was only a bill from the Grand Hotel for
cartage."

"What!" said I in pretense of dismay, "no letter
yet from Mr. Smith's wife? And seven of his children down with whooping-cough!"

"W-wife!" stammered Clelia, her blue eyes becoming enormous. "S-seven children!"

"Seven in Christiania," I explained sadly, "the
other eleven at school near Bergen. Poor fellow.
His suspense must be dreadful."

I'm no actor; I saw immediately in Clelia's face
that I had overplayed my part as well as the total
of Smith's progeny, for the color came swiftly back
and she shot at me a glance anything but demure.

"The other eleven," I explained, "were by his first
three wives."

Clelia, dusting furiously, looked around at me over
her shoulder.

"At least," she said, "he's done his duty by his
country."

"W-what!" I stammered.

"The population of Norway is so very small," she added gaily. And went on with her dusting.

"Minx," thought I to myself as I marched down stairs and out toward the fountain where, from the servants' wing of the chalet Thusis could not fail to observe me. And she did. She appeared, presently, account books under one arm. Out of the subtle corner of my subtlest eye—the left one—I observed her. And with surpassing cunning I selected a yellow fly from the battered book and tied it on my leader.

"Monsieur!"

"Good-morning, Thusis. We're going fishing. So if you'll ask Josephine to put up some war lunch for us—"

"Has Monsieur forgotten his daily business interview?" she inquired smilingly.

"Not at all. But we're going to conserve time as well as food, Thusis. We can fish and consult at the same time."

"But—"

"All waste must cease," I said firmly. "We musn't waste even a minute in the day. And if we can do two things at the same time it is our economic duty to do them." I smiled at her. "I shall dig worms," said I, "for two, while you prepare lunch for two. That is a wonderful way of economizing time and labor, isn't it, Thusis?"

She smiled, bit her lip, as though regretting an

indiscretion, looked up at the cloudless sky, let her gray eyes wander from one snowy peak to the next, glanced almost insolently at me, then smiled with that delicious impulse characteristic of her.

"You know you have no business to take me fishing," she said. "Your cleverness is not Machiavellian; it is Michael-valian. It doesn't deceive me for one moment, Señor Michael!"

I laughed, picked up a stable-fork that stood against the cow-barn:

"Worms for two; luncheon for two," said I.

"I don't *like* that juxtaposition!" she protested. "Do you really wish me to go with you? Why won't you sit here on the edge of the pool and go over these accounts?"

"Conservation of time and energy forbid doing one thing when two things can be accomplished at the——"

"You are absurd!"

I went over to the barnyard and began to dig.

"Hasten, Thusis," I called to her. "I'll be ready in ten minutes."

"I've a good mind not to go," she said.

"You've a *good* mind," said I, disinterring a fine fat worm.

"I *have* a mind, anyway, and it counsels me not to go fishing with you, Don Michael."

"Argue with it," said I. "It's a reasonable mind,

Thusis, and is open to conviction. Prove to it that
you ought to go fishing."

"Don Michael, you are ridiculous."

"Let it be a modest lunch," said I, "nourishing
and sufficient. But not a feast, Thusis. Don't put
in any wreaths of roses, or any tambourines. But
you can stick a fry-pan into the basket, with a little
lard on the side, and I'll show you how we cook trout
in the woods at home."

"In Chile?"

"In the Adirondacks," said I, smiling.

I went on digging and accumulating that popular
lure for trout not carried in the fly-books of expert
anglers, but known to the neophyte as the "Barn-
yard Hackle."

Once I glanced over my shoulder. Thusis was not
there. Presently, and adroitly dissembling my anxiety by a carefully camouflaged series of sidelong
squints I discovered her near the kitchen-wing of
the chalet talking earnestly to Josephine.

And so it happened that, having garnered a suffi-
ciency of Barn-yard hackles, I went to the fountain
pool to wash my hands.

And when, with playful abandon, I stood drying
them upon my knickerbockers, I saw Thusis emerge
from the house carrying my pack-basket.

She came up rather slowly.

"Here is your lunch," she said, looking at me
with an inscrutable expression suggesting amuse-

ment and annoyance in an illogical combination.

"You mean *our* lunch," said I.

"I mean *your* lunch."

"Aren't you coming, Thusis?"

I looked into the pack-basket and discovered her account books in it.

"An oversight," she said, calmly. "Give them to me."

I started to fish them out and caught sight of the package of lunch.

"Good heavens!" said I, "there is twice too much for one!"

She appeared to be greatly disturbed by the discovery.

"Josephine has made a dreadful mistake," she said. "She has put up lunch enough for two!"

"It mustn't be wasted," said I, gravely. "I'm afraid you'll have to come fishing with me after all, Thusis."

There appeared to be no other way out of it. At least neither of us suggested any other way.

"Oh, dear," she said, looking up at me, and the very devil was in her gray eyes.

Which discovery preoccupied me when she went back to the house for her hat and for another rod which she had, it seemed, discovered in the laundry, all equipped for business.

The agreeable tingle of subdued excitement per-

meated me as she returned with the rod but without
any hat.

"I don't need one," she said, calmly, pulling out
several hair pins.

And then I saw a thick mass of molten gold tumble
down; and the swift white fingers of Thusis dividing
it into two heavy braids—a thrilling sight—and
once, in the thrall of that enchantment where I stood
motionless to watch her at this lovely office, I became aware of her lifted eyes—two celestial assas-
sins intent on doing me deep harm.

Then, still busy with her hair, she moved slowly
forward across the grass beside me, silently, almost
stealthily—for, in the slow and supple grace of her
I seemed to divine something almost menacing to me.

Her account books and rod were in my pack-
basket. She sauntered along the shadow-flecked
path beside me, at first paying me scant attention,
but singing carelessly to herself in a demi-voix
snatches of any vagrant melody that floated through
her mind.

I recognized none of them. One strange little re-
frain seemed to keep on recurring to her at intervals:

> —"And Aphrodite's throat was white
> As lilies opening at night
> In Naxos,
> In Naxos.

And red were Aphrodite's lips—
And blue her eyes and white her hips
As roses, sky, and surf that clips
    The golden shore of Tenedos.

O Tenedos, my Tenedos,
Set in the purple sea!
O Naxos, my Naxos,
I hear you calling me!
    The old gods have gone away;
    I follow them with feet astray,
But in my heart I'll faithful be
    To Tenedos and Naxos!"

She strolled on, singing to herself, an absent look in her starry eyes, switching idly at the leaves with some dead stalk she had picked up. And no matter what other fragments of melody occurred to her she was ever coming back to her odd little song of Naxos and of Tenedos, where flowers and sky and sea matched Aphrodite's charms.

Now and again I was conscious of a leisurely sideways glance from her as though indifferently marking my continued but quite uninteresting existence in the landscape.

When we came to the wooden bridge she rested both hands on the rail and looked down at the limpid greenish pool. But her gaze seemed serious and remote, and I became quite sure she was not thinking about trout.

However, I rigged up her rod for her and was preparing to impale a worm upon her hook when she noticed what I was about and remarked that she preferred an artificial fly.

"*That* one," she added, coming up beside me and looking over my shoulder at the open fly-book in my hand.

So, that matter settled, we took the leafy path which ran through ferns along the northern bank of the stream.

# VII

THUSIS hooked the first trout. It made a prodigious swirl in the pool and rushed to and fro in the shadowy depths—a slim, frantic phantom lacing the crystalline water with flashes of pallid fire.

She drew in the trout splashing and spattering in all its rainbow glory, and I thankfully thumped it into Nirvana and placed it upon a catafalque of wet green moss in my basket. Thusis looked on calmly while I performed the drudgery of the episode, and I heard her singing carelessly to herself:

> "The old gods have gone away;
> I follow them with feet astray,
> But in my heart I'll faithful be
> To Tenedos and Naxos!"

"There seems to be a dryad or two left," said I, looking up over my shoulder where I squatted by the brookside, scrubbing my hands in the under-water gravel.

"You mean me," she nodded absently, loosening and freeing her leader and line.

94

"I sure do, Thusis."

"You're so funny," she said in the same tranquil, detached voice, as though she were some young chatelaine and I her gillie.

We went on to the next pool where the green crystal water gushed in and spread out calmly through the woodland, reflecting every fern and tree.

The silken whistle of her cast made a pretty whispering sound in the mossy silence, and I watched her where she stood slim and straight as a silvery sapling searching the far still reaches of the water with the tiny tuft of tinseled feathers until the surface of the placid pool was shattered into liquid splinters by the splash of a trout, and her line vibrated and hummed like a taut violin string.

Like lightning the convulsive battle was joined there in the woodland depths and the girl, all fire and grace, swayed like a willow under the furious rhythmic rushes of the unseen fish.

Click-click went her reel, and the feathery whirr of the line accented the silence. Then that living opalescent thing sprang quivering out of its element, and fell back, conquered, in a shower of opal rain.

Toward noon we came to a pool into which poured the stream with a golden sound between two boul-

ders mantled thick with moss. And here Thusis
seated herself and laid aside her rod.

"I am hungry," she said, looking over her shoulder at me with the same aloof composure that all
the morning had reversed our rôles as master and
maid.

But even as she spoke she seemed to realize the
actual situation: a delicate color came into her
cheeks and then she laughed.

"Isn't it funny?" she said, springing to her feet.
"Such presumption! Pray condescend to unsling
the basket and I shall give Don Michael his lunch."

"Don Michael," said I, "will continue to do the
dirty work on this expedition. Sit down, Thusis."

"Oh, I couldn't permit——"

"Oh, yes, you could. You've been behaving like a
sporting duchess all this morning. Continue in that
congenial rôle."

"*What* did you say?" she demanded, her gray eyes
frosty and intent on me.

"I said you've been behaving like a duchess."

"Why do you say that?"

"Because it's so."

She sat on her mossy throne, regarding me intently and unsmilingly.

"Don't say that again,—please," she said, coldly.

"I was merely jesting."

"I know. But please don't say it in that way.
Don't use that expression."

"Very well," said I, not relishing the snub. And I laid out the lunch in silence, during which operation I could feel Thusis was watching my sulky features with amusement.

To make sure I looked up at her when I had finished, and caught the little devils laughing at me out of both her eyes.

"Luncheon's ready," said I, infuriated by her mockery.

"Monsieur is served," said Thusis, in a voice so diabolically meek that I burst out laughing; and the girl, as though flinging discretion to the summer breezes, leaped to her feet with a gay little echo of my laughter and dropped down on the moss beside the woodland banquet.

"What do I care after all!" she said. "From the beginning I've been at no pains to deceive you. So in the name of the old gods let us break bread together."

She picked up a bit of bread, sprinkled a pinch of salt on it, broke it, and offered me half with a most adorable air. And we ate together under the inviolate roof of the high blue sky.

"Now," she said, "you'll never betray me."

"You knew that in the beginning."

"Did I? I don't know. I've been perfectly careless concerning you, Don Michael."

"Was it from instinctive confidence, Thusis, or out of disdain?"

The girl laughed, not looking up but continuing to poke for olives with a fork too large for the neck of the flask:

"Disdain *you*, Don Michael? How could I?"

"I sometimes believe you do. You behave very often as though I were a detail of the surrounding landscape and quite as negligible."

"But it's an attractive landscape and not negligible," she insisted, still poking for elusive olives. "Your simile is at fault, Monsieur O'Ryan."

"Thusis," said I, gravely consuming a sandwich, "you have made fun of me ever since I laid eyes on you."

"You began it."

"How?"

"You made fun of my red hair."

"It is beautiful hair."

"Indeed?"

"You know it. You know perfectly well how pretty you are."

"Señor!"

"In fact," said I, offering myself another sandwich, "you are unusually ornamental. I concede it. I even admit that you resemble *The Laughing Girl*."

"The cherished photograph on Monsieur's dresser! Oh, that is too much flattery. What would the Admiral think to hear you say such things to your housekeeper! Don Michael, you are young and you are headed for trouble. I beg of you to remember your ancestors."

"How about yours, Thusis?"

"Mine? Oh, they were poor Venetians. Probably they ran gondolas for the public—the taxis of those days, Don Michael—and lived on the tips they received."

"Thusis?"

"Monsieur?"

"I'd be grateful for a tip—if you don't mind."

"A tip?"

"Yes. Just a little one."

The girl held out her glass and I filled it with cool Moselle.

"You're such a nice boy," she said, and sipped her wine, looking at me all the while. She was so pretty that it hurt.

"A tip," she repeated musingly. "That is the Anglo-Saxon slang for information. Is it then that you request information?"

"If you are willing."

"About what, pray?"

"About yourself, Thusis."

"That is unworthy curiosity."

"No, it isn't curiosity."

She elevated her delicate nose, very slightly. "What, then, do you term it, Don Michael?"

"Sympathy."

"Oh la! Sympathy? Oh, I know *that* kind. It

99

is born out of the idleness of speculation and developed with an admixture of sentimental curiosity always latent in men."

She laughed: "It's nothing but emotion, Monsieur. Men call it budding friendship. But men really care for no women."

"Why do you say that?"

"It's true. Men seek friendship among men. Men like few or no women, but almost any female. That is the real truth. Why dodge it?"

"How old are you, Thusis?"

"Not old—as you mean it."

She had finished her luncheon, and now she leaned over and bathed her lips and fingers in the icy stream. There, like some young woodland thing out of the golden age of vanished gods she hovered, playing at the glimmering water's edge, scooping up handfuls of golden gravel from the bottom and letting them slide back through her dripping fingers.

"I'll tell you this," she said, looking at the water: "I don't like men. I never did. Any I might have been inclined to like I had already been born to hate. . . . You don't understand, do you?"

"No."

She smiled, sat erect, and dried her fingers on her handkerchief.

"Be flattered," she said. "No other man before you has had even a glimpse of my real self. And I really don't know why I've given you that much. I

100

ask myself. I don't know. . . . But,"—and her
sweet, reckless laughter flashed—"the very devil
seemed to possess me when I first saw you, Don
Michael. I was amazingly careless. But you were
so funny! I was indiscreet. But you were so solemn and so typically and guilelessly masculine."

"Was I?" said I, getting redder and redder.

"Oh, yes!" she cried, "and you are still! You are
*all* man—the most comprehensive type of your sex
—the most logical, and the most delightfully transparent! Oh, you *are* funny, Don Michael. You
don't know it; you don't suspect it; but you are!
And that is why I read you to the depths of your
nice boyish mind and heart, and felt that I need be
at no pains to play my little rôle with you."

"Then," said I, "if you consider me harmless, why
not trust me further?"

"I do trust you. You know I'm not born a servant. You know, also, that nevertheless I'm in service. So is my sister. So is my friend, Josephine
Vannis. So is my friend, Raoul Despres. Well,
then! It seems to me that I have trusted you, and
that you know a great deal about us all."

"That is not very much to know," said I, so naïvely that Thusis showered the woods with her delicious
laughter.

"Of course it isn't much, Don Michael. But just
think how you can amuse yourself in dull moments
by trying to guess the rest!"

"I can't imagine," said I, "what your object may be in taking service here in this little lonely valley in the Swiss Alps. If, as seems probable, you all are agents of some power now at war—what on earth is the use of coming here?"

Thusis smiled at me, then, resting on one arm, leaned over the cloth on the moss and made me a little signal to incline one ear toward her. When I did so she placed her lips close to my ear:

"You have promised always to treat us like your servants in the presence of others. Do you remember?"

I nodded.

"Then I ask no more of you than that, Don Michael. . . . *Until your country enters the war.*"

Her breath close to my ear—the girl's nearness, and the sweet, fresh youth of her, all were doing the business for me.

"Thusis?"

"Yes?"

"Lean nearer. I want to whisper to you."

She inclined her dainty head: the fragrance of her hair interfered with my articulation:

"My country," said I, "is not likely to go to war. . . . But I am."

She said, smilingly: "The fine army of Chile is organized and disciplined on the German plan. Doubtless this fact, and the influence of German

102

drill-masters, prejudices many Chileans in favor of
entering this war."

I placed my lips close to her little ear:

"Don't be silly," I whispered.

At that she straightened up with a breathless little laugh and sat looking at me.

"You knew where I stood," said I. "Why practice deception?"

"Yes," said she, "you are practically Yankee."

"So is that Viking, Smith."

"I know. And the Yankees are at war."

"They are, God bless them."

"God bless them," she said; and her face grew
very still and serious.

After a silence: "There is a common ground,"
she said, "on which we both may stand. And that
is no-man's land. To redeem it I am long since enlisted in the crusade. . . . Your heart, Monsieur, is
enlisted too. . . . I knew that. . . . Else I had
never trusted you."

"How did you know?"

She shrugged: "Long ago we had all necessary
information concerning you and your Viking friend.
Yet for all that it was not prudent for me to so
carelessly reveal myself to you. . . . But when I
saw you—" she laughed mischievously—"as I have
admitted, already, you inspired me to indiscreet behavior. And I didn't resist—knowing you to be safe."

"Safe?"

"Certainly. And so I permitted myself to relax
—a little."

"In the cellar?"

"Yes. . . . And I nearly paid for it, didn't I?"

"I ought to have kissed you," said I with sulky
conviction.

"Do you think so?"

"I'm sorry I didn't."

"I'm sorry, too." She sprang to her feet, laughing and scared: "Wait! Listen. I'm sorry only
because it was the only moment that ever could have
happened in my life when I might have submitted
to that simple and bourgeoise experience known as
being kissed. Now it can never happen again, Don
Michael. And I shall journey, unsaluted, to my
virgin tomb."

She lifted her gray eyes sparkling with malice:

"Because a young man was too timid to offer me
the curious and unique experience of being kissed,
I must expire, eventually, in total ignorance of that
interesting process."

Her face changed subtly as I started to my feet,
and something in the beautiful altered features
halted me.

After a moment's silence: "It's perfectly rotten
of me," she said slowly. "But you, also, seem to
realize that it can't happen."

"You mean it can't happen without forfeiting
your friendship, Thusis?"

104

"Without incurring my hatred," she said in a curiously still voice, her eyes as cold as grayest ice. "Do it, if you like," she added. "I deserve it. But I shall hate myself and detest you. . . . Is it worth it? Seriously, Mr. O'Ryan, is your revenge worth my deepest enmity?"

I shrugged. "Thusis," said I pleasantly, "you take yourself very seriously. Don't you?"

"Don't *you!*" she demanded, flushing.

"I'm sorry, but I really can't." And I lighted a cigarette and picked up my fishing-rod.

"You ask me," I continued, switching my flies out over the water, "whether the possibly interesting operation of kissing you would be worth your cataclysmic resentment. How can I guess? It might not even be worth the effort involved—on my part. To be frank, Thusis, I'm not at all convinced that you'd be worth kissing."

"Is that your opinion?" inquired the girl, nibbling at her under lip and regarding me out of eyes that darkled and sparkled with something or other I could not quite define.

"That is my opinion," said I pleasantly. "Besides, I have a photograph on my dresser which if chastely and respectfully saluted, would, no doubt, prove quite as responsive to a casual caress as would you. And without any disagreeable results."

"Do you do *that?*" she asked, coloring brightly to the temples, her teeth still busy with her lip.

"I don't always make a practice of doing it."

"Have you *ever* done it?"

"I haven't happened to."

"Do you intend to?"

"What's the matter with you, Thusis?" I retorted impatiently. "Does it concern you what I do to that picture?"

"Yes, it does," she retorted, turning deeply pink.

"In what way?"

"You say the photograph of the Laughing Girl resembles me. And if you are under that impression I do not wish you to take liberties with it. You have no right to—to kiss a picture because you think it looks like—like somebody you don't dare kiss!"

Her flushed audacity was irritating me.

"Don't dare kiss you?" I repeated, switching my rod about in my increasing exasperation. "You'd better not repeat that, Thusis!"

Her flushed features quivered, then suddenly her eyes were full of little devils all mocking me.

"I do repeat it," she said. "You dare not!"

At the same instant my hook caught in a branch; I gave it a furious jerk; crack!—my rod broke at the second joint. And the clear laughter of Thusis rang out uncontrolled.

"Alas," said she, "this nice young man is violently offended at something or other."

An unfeigned damn escaped me.

"Mea culpa!" she exclaimed, breathless with laughter. "Mea maxima culpa! This exceedingly nice young man is dreadfully offended."

Mad all through, I picked up the wreck of my rod and stood silent, mechanically fitting together the splintered ends of the second joint. Presently I was aware that she had come up behind me.

"I'm a beast," she said in a small, weak voice.

I said nothing.

"Are you *very* angry, Don Michael?"—sorrowful but subtly persuasive.

"I've ruined this rod," said I.

"You may take mine," humbly sweet.

But I feared her gifts and her contrition.

A light breath—a ghost of a sigh escaped her.

"I'm such a beast," she said. . . . "But I've never before taken the trouble to be beastly to a man—if that flatters you at all, Don Michael."

"It does not," said I, coolly.

"It should," she retorted.

"Do you know what I think?" said I, turning, after the manner of other worms.

"What?"

"I think you overestimate your own importance. And that you'd be far more attractive if you were not too bally busy thinking about yourself every minute."

"If that is your opinion," she said, "we had better go home at once."

We went, in solemn silence.

# VIII

THE afternoon was growing very warm. Smith had stretched himself out on his bed to read a novel and combat flies. Occasionally he called out to me demanding to know how soon we were going to have tea by the fountain.

Which incessantly reiterated question put me out of humor—for I was writing another poem—and presently I got up, cursed him out, and slammed the door.

Recently something—whatever it was—had driven me pell-mell toward Parnassus.

As a matter of record, until I had purchased that photograph of The Laughing Girl, I had never before written a poem or attempted to write one, or even considered such an enterprise.

Nor had I most remotely suspected myself capable of producing poetry. Neither had I, hitherto, desired to so express my thoughts and private emotions. Of what serious people call the "Urge" I had, hitherto, been ignorant.

But since the photograph of The Laughing Girl

had come into my possession, hidden springs totally unsuspected had begun to gush and bubble somewhere deep within me. And, to my pleased astonishment, I suddenly found myself not only endowed with the desire but also with the ability to rhyme.

And now on this warm, quiet, flyful afternoon, and still considerably upset over my morning on the trout stream with Thusis, I found myself at my table, abandoning myself to an orgy of self-expression in verse.

Having slammed the door I now returned to my poem; and first I carefully re-read as much of it as I had accomplished:

### To Thusis

#### I

Slender girl with eyes of gray—
Charming mystery called Thusis—
Teach me all your lore, I pray!—
How your loveliness seduces—
How each dimple has its uses
Leading men like me astray!

#### II

You display in gay array
Deadly charms, without excuses;
Are they fashioned to betray
Hearts unwary, naughty Thusis?
Are your russet hairs but nooses
To ensnare some soul distrait?

109

## III

Love's a tyrant, sages say;
What he chains he never looses,
    Making slaves of grave and gay,
Dashing blades and gray recluses,
Snaring with a thousand ruses
    One and all, alackaday!

### Envoi

Cupid's sway the very deuce is!
His caprices and abuses
    All endure and all obey.
Laugh away my pretty Thusis
    He'll get *you* some summer day!

I re-read the Envoi with satisfaction born of the pride of prophecy. Also, no doubt, some slight personal bitterness gave an agreeable tang to the couplets.

"Clever,—very clever," said I, dotting a few i's and crossing several t's. And, feeling better, I laid away the poem and began to walk up and down the room exhilarated by my own genius.

"When a man," said I, "can turn out such verses" —I snapped my fingers—"just like that!—he is in little danger of any sentimental subjugation."

As I turned, my glance chanced to fall on The Laughing Girl, and, for the first time, I thought I noticed a faint and delicate malice in her laughing eyes.

"Good heavens," said I to myself, "how vividly she resembles Thusis!"

Oddly enough as I continued to walk to and fro in my room I began to feel a trifle less gay, less confident regarding my prophetic poem depicting the sentimental fate of Thusis.

"She's really very lovely," thought I, "and three-quarters devil. She'll do mischief to man, yet. Probably she's already done a good deal to some poor young man. . . . Poor simpleton! . . . Unhappy simp!"

I walked over and looked fixedly at The Laughing Girl.

"Poor simp," I murmured mechanically, not meaning anybody in particular. But as I said it I lifted my absent and troubled eyes, and beheld my own reflection in the mirror. It shocked me. Never had I believed myself capable of a simper. And by heaven I wore one now—a moon-eyed sentimental simper upon my virgin features.

"Confound it!" said I furiously, "why should I look like that? What's the matter with my face?"

Very deep somewhere within me, in a still and serene obscurity so far unagitated and un-plumbed, something stirred.

"I—I'm not in d-danger of f-falling in love," said I in a scared voice. "Am I?"

Something was the matter with my heart. It had become irregular and seemed frightened.

111

"If for one moment I supposed," said I, "that I were actually in the slightest danger of—of——"

I looked at the Laughing Girl; looked away. And went to a chair and sat down.

After a long interval I gave tongue to my inmost convictions. "It isn't done," said I. "Fancy! Haha!"

But my laughter was a failure.

I looked up at the Admiral to steady myself. I had never before considered his features sardonic. He seemed to grin.

"W-what the devil's the matter with everything to-day!" I exclaimed, getting up and beginning to pace the room.

But there was no use blustering. I suspected what the matter was. I was falling in love with Thusis.

"Good Lord!" said I in unfeigned distress, "an adventuress camouflaged as a servant! Has an O'Ryan come to this?"

Smith opened the door. He was in his shirt sleeves and had a pipe in one hand, a book in the other.

"Whatthehellsthematter?" he asked. "You're thumping about in here like an epileptic cat."

I told him I was exercising.

"Well, you'd better exercise your legs down the stairs," he remarked; "there's a wagonful of tourists at the front door."

"The deuce there is!"

112

"Look out of the window and then get a wiggle on."

Sure enough! From the window I beheld them. They already were disembarking.

"Where's Thusis!" I exclaimed. "This is the limit. It's—it's a confounded nuisance."

"Better go below, mine host," said Smith, resuming his recumbent attitude on his bed and opening his book. He puffed at his pipe, swatted a fly with a paper-knife, and looked at me.

"Mine host," he said, "you should greet your guests on the doorstep wearing a napkin over one arm."

I turned on my heel and went out, and met Thusis in the hallway.

"What the dickens is all this?" I demanded. "Have those tourists the impudence to come here and ask for accommodations in my house?"

She seemed surprised and also I thought a trifle excited.

"But, Monsieur, was it not understood?"

"Oh, yes, of course it was understood because the idiotic Swiss law must be obeyed," said I, gnawing my lip in vexation. "What do they want—these tourists? Tea?"

"I think," said Thusis, "they intend to stay."

"Over-night?"

"Longer, Monsieur."

113

"Hang it all!" I blurted out. "That spoils our perfectly delightful privacy."

Thusis observed me sideways. She wore the fine chemisette of some sheer stuff and the velvet bodice of the peasantry, both coquettish and cut low. Her straight short wool skirt and buckled slippers set off the fascinating costume of the Canton; but no peasant ever possessed such slender and thoroughbred loveliness.

I glanced down at her slim feet, at her hands so smooth and so prettily fashioned; I looked up into her gray eyes uneasily. And I thought to myself that I'd show the door to any guest who tried any nonsense with Thusis.

"Where are these tourists?" I asked sulkily.

"In the big lounging room."

As I started to descend the stairs Thusis touched me on the arm. A tiny and complex shock went quite through me at the contact.

"Don Michael?"

"Yes."

"Are you still vexed at me?"

"No."

"Because—I *was* rude to you. I did provoke you. I did lay myself open to light treatment from you. But—I do respect you, Don Michael."

"You are always laughing at me."

"I know. It's my way—if I like a person. . . . I plague them a little. . . . *If* I like them."

114

"But you not only plague me, you ridicule me!"

"You don't understand. You couldn't understand. I myself don't understand why I laugh at you and torment you. . . . Because I never before did that to a man. . . . To my sister—to my girl friends, yes. But never before to any man."

She stood near me, smiling, watching my expression.

"I like you, Don Michael," she said.

"And I you, Thusis."

"I know it. It won't do, either. I mean that we may laugh a little together, now and then. But it is safer not to think of each other as—as socially—equal."

I said magnanimously: "I am beginning to think of you in that way already."

"Are you really?" Her smile flashed out, mischievous, almost mocking.

"A servant?" she added. "Possibly even an adventuress? An agent, anyway, in the service of some government not yours? You consider admitting such a woman on terms of social equality? Oh, Don Michael! If you like me as much as that you must care a little more for me than mere liking."

"I do."

She began to laugh—a hushed, delicious sort of laughter, checked suddenly by my quick flush.

"If I take the trouble to be serious with you," said I, "as much is due me from you, I think."

It was, for me, utterly impossible to define the series of complex expressions which succeeded one another in her face.

She seemed inclined to laugh again but bit her lip and looked at me out of brilliant eyes. Mirth, surprise, gay disdain, a fleeting uncertainty, a slight blush,—then the familiar sweet mockery once more —these I read and followed as I watched her.

"Such a strange young man," I heard her murmur to herself.

"And such a strange girl, Thusis."

"I know. And you and I have no business to play together. And we can't unless we're very, very careful. We ought not to. You think so from your standpoint, and I know it from mine. And yet—if you will be very, very careful—I'll risk it—a little while longer. . . . Because I—I don't know why—I like to laugh at you, Don Michael. . . . And I laugh at those only whom I like."

"I think," said I, "that I'm rather near to falling in love with you, Thusis."

"Oh!" she cried with her breathless, bewildering smile, "I couldn't permit you to do that!"

"Permit me?"

"No. You mustn't. That would never do! No —no indeed! Never! Just find me gay and frivolous and rather pretty in my way—just attractive enough to remain good humored when I plague you."

"If I should fall in love with you I couldn't help it."

"But it would be such a mistake. You mustn't do it. I don't wish to think about such things. It wouldn't do for me. Or for you. I mean as far as I am concerned."

"You mean you could not respond, Thusis?"

"Oh, no, I couldn't." In her hurried voice there was a faint hint of alarm, I thought.

I was falling in love. I knew it.

"Unless you take me lightly—unless you are willing that we play together," she said, "I couldn't talk to you, Don Michael. I may not take you seriously; nor you, me. That is essential."

"I may not p-pay court to you, Thusis?"

"Oh, that? Yes—in the nice way you have been doing. At least I thought you had been doing it, haven't you?"

"Yes—not realizing it. Yes—that's what I have really been doing. . . . Am I not to make love to you, Thusis?"

"W-what kind of love?"

"Honest, of course."

"D-demonstrative—love?"

"Yes."

"Oh, no! No, not that sort. No, please." For I had taken her smooth little hand in mine, and she withdrew it swiftly.

"You know," she said, "your guests are waiting."

She laughed. Then she came up to me slowly: "Don Michael, do you really like me?"

"Yes."

"Then—will you do something for me?"

"Yes."

"It is this. In the presence of these tourists remember always that I am your servant and a Swiss peasant. Never by word or glance permit them to believe otherwise. Do you promise?"

"Yes."

She smiled, laid both her hands frankly in mine.

"I'm going to tell you something," she said. "Your guests below are the ex-king Constantine of Greece, his wife, the ex-queen; Ferdinand, King of Bulgaria—or Tzar of all the Bulgars—as he loves to call himself;—and their several assorted shadows."

My eyes were widening at every word.

"Thusis," I said, "what nonsense are you talking?"

"Michael," she said, using my given name for the first time without some absurd prefix, "I am telling you the truth. Those are the people who, dressed like ordinary tourists, are now seated below drinking coffee and cognac and eating nice little cakes prepared by Josephine and served by my sister Clelia."

"Do you mean to say that the ex-king and queen of Greece, and King Ferdinand of Bulgaria are in

118

Switzerland incognito?" I demanded incredulously.

"They are,—that is, Ferdinand is here incognito for the first time. You know, of course, that Constantine and his queen were living in Berne since the Allies kicked them out of Greece?"

"I have heard so."

"Well, then, here they are, incognito, without servants or any outward show, dressed like any tourists, arriving in an ordinary wagon. Yes, here they are, evidently desiring to escape observation, arm in arm with him of Bulgaria. I thought I'd tell you, Michael."

There was an odd little glint in her gray eyes; an odd smile on her lips.

"What the devil are these birds doing here?" I asked, astonished.

"These allies of Germany?"

"Yes," I said, disgusted; "what do you suppose these fancy gentlemen are doing here in a little obscure inn among the Alps while all the world which they have helped to set on fire is in flames around them?"

Her firm hands pressed mine, very slightly.

"Do you feel it so keenly, Michael?"

"Feel what?"

"That these kings below have helped set the world afire?"

"Certainly I do."

She stood looking at me, her hands still resting in mine.

"And now," she mused, "the Americans are in it. But you are not a Yankee. . . . Otherwise—"

"Otherwise what?"

"But you are a Chilean."

"I'm a human being, too. What do you want me to do, Thusis?"

"Permit me to assign them their rooms."

I said: "You are here to watch these kings. You knew they were coming. You are here to watch them in the interest of your government."

"Well, Michael?"

"Is it so?"

"Yes."

I looked at her in wonder, dismay, and deep concern.

This young girl—this fresh, sweet, laughing, slender little thing a spy? And yet I had vaguely supposed her to be some sort of political agent masquerading in my service for purposes occult.

But the sinister agent who lurks at the heels of suspects—the shadow that haunts marked men— the unseen, unheard presence that lingers by doors ajar, by unlighted corridors, in the shade of trees! —I had not thought of Thusis in such a way.

Something of this I think she read in my eyes fixed on her, for she flushed slightly and made as though to withdraw her hands.

But, still looking at her, I lifted her hands tightly imprisoned between my own, and touched them lightly with my lips.

"Oh," she said faintly, and I felt her sudden impulsive clasp.

"You *are* fine, Michael," she whispered. "I ask nothing in the way of help, only that you give me my chance in this affair."

"Take it," said I. "There are those imbecile kings! Raise the devil with them if you like. And if you need help——"

"Michael!"

"——You know where to look for it," I ended. "But for goodness' sake be careful, Thusis. Not that I care about myself. The chances are that I'll enlist anyway. But they'd intern you here in Switzerland if they catch you at anything militant. And that would worry me half to death."

"Would it?"

In her laughing voice there was the vaguest hint of a softness I had never heard there.

"Yes, it would." I drew her a little toward me, but she turned grave, immediately, and we stood so in silence while her gray eyes regarded me.

Then she gently disengaged herself.

"Be nice to me, Michael, even when I don't deserve it," she said; "even when"—she laughed almost maliciously—"even when I seem to court destruction."

"Nevertheless," said I, reddening, "I shall pay court to you."

"Please do."

"And make love to you, Thusis."

"That," she said, "is not even on the knees of the gods: it is impossible."

# IX

A S I descended the stairs to greet my unbidden guests, through my noddle ran the flippant old time sing-song of earliest schooldays—"Rex, Regis, Regi, Regem, Rex, Rege"—an ironic declension of the theoretical in contrast to the actual which I could not very well decline.

Now, as I entered the long lounging room which Smith and I had used as our living-room, I very easily recognized God's anointed, thanks to Thusis. Otherwise it never would have occurred to me that what I now beheld was a bunch of kings in camouflage.

Constantine, the ex-King of Greece, sat near a window drinking a pint of impossible Greek wine and reading one of last month's New York newspapers. The ex-Queen of Greece stood with hands linked behind her well-made back, looking out at the mountains. At another little table the Tzar of all the Bulgars loomed up majestically. He was eating coffee-cakes and drinking coffee. I could hear him.

As I entered the room they all turned their heads

123

to look at me. And I thought I had never gazed upon anything more subtly disturbing than the Hohenzollern visage of the ex-queen. Indeed she seemed to lack only the celebrated imperial mustaches to duplicate the sullen physiognomy of her brother, the Kaiser. That family countenance of a balky horse was unmistakable; so were the coarse features of Constantine, with his face of a typical non-commissioned officer. But of all faces I had ever gazed on the fat, cunning visage of the Bulgarian Bourbon, Ferdinand, was the most false. A long thin nose split its fatness; under a pointed beard a little cruel and greasy mouth hid close, while two stealthy eyes of a wild thing watched over this unpleasant and alarming combination.

Normally these people would not have noticed me; but now, in their rôles of tourists, they recollected themselves.

When I quietly introduced myself Constantine got up, and I went over and welcomed him, bowed to his wife, and, when Ferdinand, also, concluded to get up, I greeted him with the same impeccable formality.

"So you are the fortunate Chilean gentleman who has inherited this valuable property," said the ex-queen, her hard Prussian eyes fixed intently upon me.

"Yes, madam, I am that unfortunate Mr. O'Ryan," said I smilingly. "The duties of an innkeeper are not yet entirely familiar to me but I trust that my servants can make you comfortable."

The queen remarked indifferently that if she were not comfortable ‚enough she'd let me know,—and turned her back, paying me no further attention. Doubtless her scrutiny of me had satisfied her. Possibly the Chilean flag flying from the flag-pole in front of the house also reassured her. She gazed out at the Bec-de l'Empereur, named from the august nose of her brother. Constantine's flickering glance rested on the rigid back of his spouse, shifted toward me uncertainly, but always reverted to that straight, stiff back as though in awe and unwilling fascination.

I went over to the counter and picked up the guest ledger: "May I trouble you to register in order that I may fulfill my obligations toward the Swiss police?" I said pleasantly. For none of them had so far offered me whatever noms-de-guerre had been decided upon.

At this the queen turned and said something to Constantine in a surly voice, and he got up with alacrity and swaggered over to the desk.

"M. Constantine Xenos, wine merchant, Zurich, and Madame Xenos," he wrote, his tongue in his cheek. His shifty eyes flickered toward King Ferdinand who had again become rather noisy over his coffee and cakes. Then, apparently remembering his instructions, he wrote:

"Monsieur Bugloss Itchenuff. Investments and business opportunities. Zurich."

He handed me the pen with a flourish: "There you are, Mr. O'Ryan," he said with a misleading heartiness in his barrack-room voice contradicted always by restless and furtive eyes and remarkable royal fingers which were never still—twitching, wandering, searching, unquiet fingers,—irresolute, uncertain, timid, prying fingers not to be depended upon in emergencies, never to be trusted, even in their own pockets.

"Do you expect to remain over night, Monsieur Xenos?" I inquired, glancing at the wet signatures on the ledger, and blotting them.

"Oh, yes," he said. "This inn looks like a damn fine place to spend a few weeks in—doesn't it, Sophy?" appealing to his wife in the loud, familiar, bluff tone characteristic of him, and which seemed to me neither genuine nor carelessly frank, but an assumed manner covering something less confident and good humored.

The Princess of Prussia, so abruptly addressed, turned slowly from her contemplation of the Bec-de l'Empereur:

"We shall remain as long as it suits us," she said coolly. "And if our suites are ready——"

"Rooms," corrected the King in jocular protest.

"*Suites,*" repeated his wife sharply.

Ferdinand, gobbling his slopping coffee, wiped his wet beard:

"If there are any suites in your chalet," he said to me, "I'll take one—that is, if it isn't too expensive. I can't afford anything very expensive, and I'll trouble you to remember that."

He got up, continuing to wipe his greasy mouth with the back of a fat, soft hand, and came toward us,—a massive man, and bulkily impressive except that his legs were too short for his heavy body, which discrepancy gave to his gait a curious duck-like waddle.

"I like plenty of privacy," he explained, "that's what I like. I want to see my rooms and I want to know in advance exactly how much they are going to cost me and what extras are not included in the——"

"Oh, for God's sake don't begin that hard luck history of yours," interjected Constantine in his best barrack-room manner. "Mr. O'Ryan is a gentleman and he's not going to rob you, Buggy!"

It was instantly evident to me that the Tzar of all the Bulgars did not like to be called Buggy,—the familiar, affectionate and diminutive, no doubt, for his first nom-de-guerre, which was Bugloss, and was, in the Bulgarian language, pronounced Bewgloss, *not* Bugg-loss.

The Queen, paying no attention to her loud-mouthed husband or to King Ferdinand, crossed the

room with a firm, quick step, and examined the
ledger and the indifferent penmanship of her royal
husband. Then, to me:

"Be good enough to show me to my suite," she
said. "My husband will occupy separate but connecting apartments."

I banged on a large, brass bell. The door opened.
Thusis appeared.

Her instant and abrupt appearance had an odd
effect upon these three people. They all started
perceptibly. The Tzar of all the Bulgars even
jumped. Then he stared at her with the intentness of a wild pig in the rutting season. And King
Constantine also regarded her with a stealthy sort
of pleasure discreetly screened by a mask of bluff
and hearty indifference:

"Now, my good girl," he said loudly, "kindly
show us to our quarters and be quick about it. And
maybe you'll find a pretty silver franc in your
apron pocket if you step lively! Such things have
happened—haven't they, Sophy?"

Thusis curtsied, then I saw her beautiful gray
eyes lifted slowly and fix themselves upon the coldly
staring orbs of the Hohenzollern princess.

"Madame will graciously condescend to follow,"
she murmured. "A thousand reverent excuses that
I precede the gracious lady. But it is inevitable
when the humble guide the well born."

The Queen's hard, suspicious face never stirred

a muscle. She leisurely inspected Thusis from head to toe, from toe to head without approval and without mercy.

"Are you the chamber maid?" she demanded coldly.

"My house-keeper and waitress, Madame," I explained. "Her name is Thusis."

The Queen stared intently at Thusis, then very insolently at me:

"Your house-keeper? Really," she said,—"your *house-keeper?* Fancy! One might almost doubt that such a very young girl could possess sufficient domestic experience for such an important position."

I turned red; not Thusis, however; and either the vulgar innuendo had left her quite unconscious, or she coolly scorned the implication. And she merely smiled upon the Hohenzollern and awaited her Prussian pleasure.

"Come on, Sophy," said King Constantine, with a covert leer at Thusis's ankles. And they all started upstairs, King Ferdinand shuffling in the rear with the peculiarly ponderous waddle which characterizes the progress of an elephant's hind quarters.

King Constantine halted on the stairs to turn and call back to me in his noisy, unceremonious, jovial way:

"Wait a bit, O'Ryan! I forgot to say that we're

expecting some friends of ours. So fix 'em up in good shape when they———"

"Go on, Tino!" interrupted the queen impatiently. "Don't you even know enough to keep on going when you start? And God knows," she added in her disagreeable voice, "it's hard enough to start you."

"All right, my dear," he exclaimed with his loud forced laugh. "I only wanted to rest Buggy's legs a bit."

And the anointed of the Lord resumed their shuffling progress upward at the heels of the swift, light feet of Thusis.

As for me I went out to the court where their luggage lay piled. The wagon which had brought them was gone, but Raoul stood there, his hat on one side, hands on hips, chewing a wheat-straw and gazing blandly at the pile of royal luggage.

"These," said I carelessly, "belong upstairs. Thusis will tell you where to carry them, Raoul."

"Bien, Monsieur!"

We both looked gravely at the luggage, then my glance rested on his pleasant, reckless face in which I seemed to notice a gaiety more marked than usual.

For one moment, as he caught my eye, I thought he was going to wink at me, but, even as his eyelid quivered, he seemed to recollect himself. And, with an absolutely indescribable expression, he seized upon the luggage, and, both arms full, strode toward

the back stairs. And, far in the passageway, I
heard him singing under his breath:

> "Crack-brain-cripple-arm,
> You have done a heap of harm——"

until Josephine Vannis came to the pantry door,
her superb arms all over flour, and said in French:
"Hush, Raoul, or I slay thee with my rolling-pin,
thou imbecile, curly, hot-head!"

"My Josephine adored," he retorted, "thou slay-
est me hourly with thy Olympian beauty——"

"Be silent, addlepate, I implore thee! Is the very
devil in thee, Raoul, to endanger everything with
thy empty-headed audacity?"

"Ruler of hearts," he rejoined, "remain tranquil.
*Nous les aurons!*"

I went upstairs, discovered Smith lying on his
bed and reading, and then and there told him
the whole story. He did not appear to be very
much surprised over the royal identity of my
guests.

"That sort of king," he remarked, "is likely to
run about under foot. You'll find them a nuisance."
And he resumed his novel and his pipe.

I went downstairs again. Raoul passed with
more luggage.

I stood motionless listening to the retreating foot-
steps of Raoul through the stone passageway. And,

as I lingered, intensely curious and beginning to feel uneasy, Clelia came out of the kitchen looking like some flushed, excited school-girl, her golden hair in two braids, and her blue eyes very brilliant in the bright sunshine.

# X

## CLELIA

WHEN Clelia saw me a startled expression came into her face, instantly controlled and concealed by the lovely smile so characteristic of her and of Thusis.

"Something," said I, "smells very appetizing in there."

"Tea-cakes," she nodded. "Shall I bring you one from the oven?"

"Bring one for yourself, too, Clelia."

At that she blushed, then with a pretty, abashed smile, went into the pantry and immediately reappeared with two delicious tea-cakes.

"We mustn't be caught here doing this," she whispered, offering me one of the cakes.

"Who'd object? Raoul?"

"Pouf!" she laughed.

"Who then? Josephine? Thusis?"

"Pouf! Pouf!"

"Smith?"

She blushed a deep pink but shrugged her young shoulders.

"Pouf!" she said calmly.

"Well then, who is there to object to our taking tea together?"

"Your guests, Monsieur O'Ryan."

"My guests!" I mimicked her gaily: "Pouf! for my guests, Clelia. Do you think you could find two glasses of fresh milk for yourself and for me?"

"With cream on it?" she inquired naïvely.

"Certainly."

She went back to the pantry. I heard Josephine demurring, then they both laughed, and Clelia reappeared with the milk and two more fresh tea-cakes.

We seated ourselves on the stone milk-bench in the cool, shadowy passageway.

"The way you behave with your servants," she remarked, "seems almost scandalous, doesn't it?"

"Outrageous," said I. "What does Josephine think?"

"Oh, you haven't attempted any familiarities with her."

"No. I'd as soon try to pick up Juno and address that goddess as 'girlie.'"

We both laughed, sitting there side by side absorbing milk and tea-cakes.

"Now," said I, "the illusion would be complete if you wipe your mouth on your apron and I do a like office for myself on my sleeve."

She looked up at me and did it. So did I.

"What else?" she inquired.

"Now we'll kiss each other, Clelia, and then you'll go back to your pots and pans and I'll go out and hoe potatoes."

"Do you think you'd better kiss me?"

"Yes, I do," said I.

"I've never done it."

"What!" I laughed incredulously.

"Why no," she said, surprised.

"Is that true, Clelia?"

"Perfectly."

"And you're willing to begin on *me?*"

"Oh, pour ça—one must *begin*—if only to know how when necessary."

"You think you ought to know how it's done?" I inquired, controlling my gaiety with an effort.

"Well"—she hesitated with adorable indecision—"in an emergency, perhaps, it might be as well that I know how such things are accomplished."

"It's up to you, Clelia."

"Is it?" She thought deeply for a moment. Then: "It's going to be a shock to me, I suppose. But I've made up my mind that it's likely to happen to me some day. And I think I'd better be prepared. . . . Don't you?"

"Yes, I do." . . .

"Besides, I never was afraid of you."

"Of course not. Nobody is!" said I, laughing.

"Oh, yes, they are."

"Who?"

"Well, for one, my sister, Thusis, is."

"Thusis! Afraid of *me!*" I exclaimed.

Clelia nodded: "She's afraid."

"Of me!" I repeated incredulously.

"Well, of herself, too."

"Why?"

"I couldn't tell you why. You know Thusis and I differ in some things. Thusis has her own ideas —about—the world in general. And I'm afraid her ideas are rather old fashioned, and that they are going to make her unhappy."

"Can't you tell me what her ideas are?" I asked.

"No. She may tell you if she chooses. But it isn't likely that she will. Anyway they are not my ideas. My opinion is that the way to be happy is to accept the world as it is, not as it was or should be."

"You are quite wonderful, Clelia."

"Oh, no, I'm not. I'm just a human girl who desires to be happy and who detests gloom of all sorts—gloomy ideals, gloomy pride, gloomy conventions that wrap their shrouds around the living and stifle them in a winding sheet of tradition."

I was astonished to hear this girl so fluently express herself. In her soft, fresh, brilliant beauty she seemed to have stepped but yesterday across the frontiers of adolescence.

"So, if you kiss me," she said, "I don't think the world is going to tumble to pieces. Do you?"

"I do not."

"However," she added, "if Thusis felt the way I do about the world, I wouldn't think of letting you kiss me."

I didn't understand, and I said so. But she laughed and refused to explain.

"Life is short and full of sorrow," she said. "And the world is full of war and we'll all get hurt, sooner or later, I think. What a pity! Because the world really is lovely. And when one is young, and just beginning to fall in love with life, one is naturally inclined to taste what few delights are offered between these storms of death—brief glimpses of sunshine, Monsieur, that gleam for a few moments between the thunderous clouds that darken all the world. . . . So, if you choose to kiss me——"

We sat quite motionless and in silence for a while. Then:

"How about Smith?" I asked tersely.

"Monsieur Smith?" she repeated, flushing. "Why do you ask?"

"I don't know. . . . I wondered—wondered——"

"*What?*"

"How he'd feel about my kissing you. He might not like it, you know."

"You mean to tell him!" she exclaimed in dismay.

"No, of course not! But suppose he sauntered around the corner—during the process——"

Clelia laughed: "It might do him infinite good," she said, "to see that *somebody* is willing to kiss me——"

"What!"

"——Because *he* won't. And he knows, I think, that he could if he asked to."

"Good heavens!" I said, "I thought Smith had become sentimental over you, Clelia!"

"He is a very gloomy young man," said the girl with decision.

"But isn't he very evidently enamored of you?"

"He's too respectful."

I gasped.

"I can't goad him into human behavior," she went on with lively displeasure. "He must see that I am quite willing to be friendly and light-hearted, —that I am always ready to stop dusting and sweeping and making beds to converse with him. But all he does is to follow me about and remind me of the solemnity of life, and tell me that he is deeply concerned about my attitude toward the world. Fancy! It is not very gay, you see, my acquaintance with Monsieur Smith."

I was surprised. What she said presented Smith at a new angle. I had supposed him an idle philanderer.

"What worries him about you?" I demanded.

"He seems to think I'm an idiot. I told him I

meant to take life gaily and happily when opportunity offered, because I, probably, had only a very
short time to live. I told him that I found the
world beautiful and that I had fallen ardently in
love with life. I told him that I didn't want to die
without learning a little something about men, and
that my time was short, and I ought to neglect no
opportunity."

"What on earth did he say?"

"He became angry."

"Didn't he say anything?"

She blushed: "Oh, yes. He said he wouldn't be
used in such a manner. He said that he desired to
be taken seriously or not at all. At which sólemn
statement I laughed, naturally enough. Then he
became furious, demanding to be informed whether
I had the soul of a soubrette or of a modest and
properly brought up young girl.

"And I replied that to be modest did not neces-
sitate deceit and hypocrisy; that I had told him
the truth; that I loved life, adored happiness, was
enamored of the world, knew nothing of men but
wished to; imagined nothing more delightful than
to be made love to, intended to take advantage of
the first opportunity that offered."

"W-what did he say to that, Clelia?" I faltered,
utterly bewildered.

"A lot of nonsense. He tried to make me believe
139

that love is a tragic and solemn business—as though I were not fed up on the solemn and tragic!

"He said I was a fool and didn't know what I was talking about. He said, in substance, that the subject of love was one to be approached on tip-toe, with awe, formality, prayer, and fasting. He said that such a man as he could love only an ideal, not a human and happy thing in love with life and willing to prove it with the first young man that passes. He said that I alarmed and grieved him; that I am unmoral; that my impulses are purely pagan; that the formalism of civilization alone can sanction any impulse attraction between his sex and mine."

"What did you say?" I asked, feebly.

"I said, 'Pouf!' And I meant it."

Her color was high and her eyes very bright.

"I did like him. He was the first man I had ever had a decent chance to talk to alone,—I mean the first young man of education. And, knowing I hadn't much time, I was quite willing to play at being in love with him. I told him so."

"Maybe," said I, in a weak voice, "he wanted to do more than merely play at being in love."

"But my time is too short," she explained. "I haven't time to fall in love. Why doesn't he take what there is to take?"

"Your time is short—what do you mean, Clelia?"

"It is."

"Are you—ill?"

"No," she said impatiently, "I'm in perfect health."

"Then—what makes you suppose you're going to die soon?"

"I can't tell you. Of course I may not die very soon. But it's likely I shall. . . . And if I do I hope it will teach Mr. Smith a good lesson!"

"W-what lesson?"

"To take what offers and thank the gods!"

She looked up at me and laughed: "You'd better kiss me," she said: "you'll never have a chance with Thusis."

I blushed violently.

"Did you think I desired to k-kiss Thusis?"

"I think you are a little in love with Thusis."

"I am."

"How wonderful! And don't you desire to kiss her?"

I was silent.

"Because," said Clelia, laughing, "I think she'd like to have you do it. She'd slay me if she heard me. And she'd slay herself before she'd ever let you. . . . And yet—it *is* odd!—I'm willing to learn how it feels to be kissed, but I am not in love; and Thusis likes you and won't admit it;—you've turned my sister's head and she's horribly afraid of you; and never, never will she let you kiss her. And there you are!"

After a long silence she looked up at me shyly: "Shall we?" she asked naïvely.

"I could show you how it's done," said I.

And then, just at the moment when the deed was about to be accomplished, a shadow fell across the floor. I looked up. Thusis stood there.

Her beautiful face flamed as she met our eyes.

Clelia stood up with a light laugh. "My first lesson!" she exclaimed, "and already ended before I learned a word of it! Take your young man, sister! He's quite as disappointing as his solemn friend!"

And she went into the pantry taking with her our empty glasses.

"So *that* is the sort of man you are," said Thusis calmly.

The utter hopelessness of the situation turned me flippant.

"Yes," said I, "I am a very dangerous, unprincipled man. I'm thoroughly and hopelessly bad, Thusis. What do you think about me now?"

"What I have always thought about your class, —nothing!" she said in an even, smiling voice.

"Class!" I repeated, perplexed by the word, and the faint contempt in her voice.

"Exactly. That is most accurately what I mean —your class in the social scale, Mr. O'Ryan. And you live—down to it."

142

"Will you explain," said I, amazed and angry, "what you mean to infer?"

"I don't infer. I am direct and implicit. You behave as might be expected. Quality demands certain things of itself. Of you, Mr. O'Ryan, nothing is demanded. And nothing involving quality is expected. . . . And I have been a great fool," she added quietly. And walked out the way she entered, leaving me perplexed and thoroughly enraged.

And I would not have it left in any such way; and sprang up and overtook Thusis as she entered the empty living-room.

"What I want to know," said I, "is what you mean by implying that any social inequality exists between you and me?"

"Between you and your servant?" she inquired mockingly. And tried to pass me.

"You didn't mean that! You meant something entirely different. Who are you, Thusis? And I don't care a sou who you are,—*what* you are!— I am in love with you——"

"—And with my sister?"

"I'm in love with *you!* You know it!"

"I do *not!*"

"You *do* know it! And it disturbs you——" My voice shook.

"It leaves me utterly indifferent," she said disdainfully; but her gray eyes were lifted slowly to mine and the color came into her beautiful face.

"What sort of man are you!" she demanded. "You see how young my sister is—how silly and inexperienced! And yet——"

"I'd as soon kiss a healthy kitten," said I. "She's attractive because she is your sister. Anyway Smith is in love with her——"

"I won't permit it!" cried Thusis. "I'll not tolerate such a thing!"

She clenched her hands; there was a glint of something in her eyes—but if it came from angry tears they dried before I was sure.

"I've brought this on myself," she said. "I laid myself open to it—invited familiarity and disrespect from you! The very devil must have been in me to so utterly forget myself! Now I've got to pay for it—pay for it in bitter humiliation—witness such a scene as I have just witnessed—and then stand here and hear you tell me that—that you are in love with me!—endure what you say——"

Suddenly it became clear to me what Clelia had meant when she said that Thusis was afraid of me.

"Thusis," said I, "you won't have to listen to any more of that from me. I shall not tell you again that I care for you. And anyway, in a little while it will no longer be true. Because I shall get over it."

She looked up.

"And I want you to know that I am not angry.

144

And even if I were I want you to understand that you need not be afraid of my resentment."

"I am not!" she flashed out.

"You are! You are afraid that I might be the sort of creature to revenge wounded amour propre by proving faithless to the confidence you gave me. Don't worry," I added angrily, "because I'd cut my tongue out or face a firing squad before I'd utter one word to anybody concerning what you told me about your mission here."

There was a silence. Then Thusis' smile came back, a trifle tremulously:

"You silly boy!" she said. "Did you think I was afraid of *that!*"

"You say that, in my case, noblesse oblige means nothing to me."

She blushed scarlet: "I was angry—hurt. I did not mean that."

"You meant it."

"I did *not!* I tried to believe I meant it. I knew it wasn't true. I knew it would anger you; that is why I said it."

"Then why are you afraid of me?"

"I?"

"Yes, you, Thusis."

"I am not. I am afraid of nobody. . . . Except . . . myself."

She looked up at me again, flushed, lovely, and her gray eyes seemed distressed.

"It's just myself, Don Michael," she said with a forced smile. "I seem changed, different,—and it alarms me—scares me—to find myself capable of behaving so—so imprudently—with you."

"Thusis!"

But she had passed me in a flash and I heard her light feet flying up the stairs. I followed. She was at the top of the staircase, but heard me and turned on the landing to look down.

"My behavior with you mortifies me!" she repeated in a hurried whisper. "Why do you follow me, Michael?"

"Do you have to ask me, Thusis?"

"You mustn't ever again pursue me," she repeated in a low, breathless voice.

"Why do you say that?"

"Because—possibly I couldn't run as fast as you can. Do you think I would endure it to be overtaken? Do you suppose I could tolerate being run down and caught? By *you?* Can't you comprehend that such a thing is unthinkable?"

Again that slightest hint of contempt in her voice, not entirely recognized yet vaguely divined.

I said slowly: "If I really understand, Thusis, then you need not worry. Because I shall never again take a single step in the world to follow you."

She seemed to consider this very deeply, standing on the landing and looking down at me out of her beautiful and serious eyes.

146

"Suppose," she said, "that you do follow me—not very fast—just saunter along—so that I need not run?"

She did not smile; neither did I.

"Would that be agreeable to you, Michael?"

"Would it be agreeable to you, Thusis?"

"Yes, it would. . . . *Please* don't come upstairs! Does it give you any pleasure to scare me and see me run?"

I had one foot on the stairs; and let it remain there.

"When I say saunter, I mean it, Michael. Just stroll around—in my vicinity—describing a few leisurely circles—so that I'll not notice your approach. Couldn't you do that—and keep within sight?"

"I'll try."

Suddenly her eyes grew brilliant and she smothered a laugh with her hands. Then, as both palms clung flat to her laughing lips she deliberately kissed them and, with a pretty gesture, threw the reckless salute at me.

"Your humble servant, Don Michael!" she whispered, "your housekeeper salutes you—and runs!"

Which she did, vanishing like a flash of sunlight in the dusky corridor.

I dropped one hand on the newel-post quite unbalanced by a complexity of emotions which no experience in life had so far taught me to analyze and catalogue.

"It's probably love," said I to myself, calmly enough. "And what the devil am I to do about it?"

There was no answer. Reason, instinct, emotion, appeared to be paralyzed.

So I climbed the stairs in a blind, mechanical sort of way, and went into Smith's room.

"Were you ever in love?" I asked wearily.

He laid aside his novel, unhooked the pipe from his mouth, and considered me very gravely.

"Yes," he said, "I've been in love."

"What did you do about it?"

"The wrong thing, I fancy."

"What was that, Smith?"

"I took the matter too seriously."

"Shouldn't one?"

"Never!"

I nodded, blankly.

"To be too seriously in love, and to show it," said Smith, "is disastrous to a man. It won't do, Michael. Unless our sex takes it gayly and good humoredly we're patronized. Take it from me, the solemn side, the fasting and prayer, must originate in the other sex. It never does if we betray such symptoms. They always wait to see whether we'll break out. And when we do they treat us as though

148

we were sick—kindly but condescendingly. You get me?"

"Vaguely."

"All right. But here's the other aspect: when we fall in love, and say so, and then take the object of our vows gayly, amiably, and with perfect good humor always—no matter how inwardly we doubt and fear and rage—*then*, Michael, the girl we worship becomes very, very serious—even ponderous at times—and if she's got any brain at all it gets busy and remains busy. And what preoccupies her mind are questions concerning whether or not you really do love her seriously enough; and, if not, whether she can make you do it, which state of intellect causes perpetual anxiety and chronic uncertainty. And only when these emotions perpetually preoccupy a girl, can she finally fall in love with you sufficiently to forget what an ass you really are."

"Smith," said I, "are you in love with Clelia?"

"Yes, damn it," he said serenely.

"Then why don't you practice your theory on her?"

"My theory," he replied, "is the result of my experience with Clelia. That is how I came to evolve it. I believe in it, too. But it's too late to try on Clelia. Because already she has my number, Michael, and she knows me for a solemn, single-minded, and serious ass, very, very deeply in love with her. She's on to me, Michael."

I remembered my episode with Clelia and considered it for a while in silence. It was apparent to me that the girl's affections were completely and healthily disengaged. Her desire for happiness, her almost pagan love of gayety, her sheer delight in the mere joy of living, were not unmoral. And if, in her pursuit of pleasure there seemed something feverish, reckless, that was explained by her odd idea that she had but a little while to live.

"No use to argue, explain, reason, or preach to that girl," said I. "The thing to do is to give her a jolt."

"A jolt?" he repeated. "There's nothing left for me to say or do that could disconcert that girl. She knows I'm in love with her; she knows that I have lived a morally decent life, that my high ideals concerning women have never been lowered, that, to me, love is a sacred——"

"You tried to kiss her sister."

"That," he said, reddening painfully, "was my only lapse from the rigid conservatism of a lifetime. And doubtless I am now suffering from that moment of relaxation into folly——"

"Doubtless you are not!" I returned. "I am certain that Thusis never mentioned it to Clelia. And I'm sorry she didn't because it might have furnished the required jolt."     .

Smith became gloomily interested.

"A jolt," I repeated, "is what starts things.

150

Clelia requires one. All you need is nerve to administer it."

"How?"

"Why not frivol with Josephine?"

"Good heavens!" he exclaimed. "A man can't get gay with a girl like that! You might as well try to two-step with the Statue of Liberty! You might as well play the Doxology on a jazz band! You might as well give a burnt-cork show on the Acropolis! You might as——"

"Calm your alarm," said I. "That girl, Josephine Vannis, is rather an overwhelming beauty, I admit. But it's just those big, handsome, impressive, monumentally magnificent girls who fall for some little squirt——"

"Who the devil do you mean!" he demanded, hotly.

"I don't mean you. But you *are* shorter than she is; you don't weigh as much. Get a move on you! Inject pep into yourself. Become witty, gay, dégagé, inconsequential, brilliant, light-hearted, bristling with quips and epigrams——"

"Who? I?"

"Certainly. Pull yourself up short. Eliminate every moral instinct. Drink more Moselle than you ought to. Hook arms with that brace of kings down stairs and pull your hat over one eye! Then, after you've been the life of the dinner-party, drop into the kitchen and bestow a few repartees on Josephine. And if Clelia isn't shocked I'm a boche!"

"I can't do all those things," he said uneasily.

"You can try."

So I left him a prey to conflicting emotions, and entered my own room and sat down on the bed.

"I'm in love," said I to myself, "deeply, inextricably in love! And what on earth am I to do about it!"

## XI

### A PYJAMA PARTY

ABOUT midnight I was awakened from agreeable slumber by somebody knocking at my bedroom door. I leaned out of bed, switched on the electric light, got up and opened the door.

King Ferdinand stood there in night-shirt and bare feet holding a candle that shook like an aspen leaf in the darkness.

"Somebody's been trying to open my d-door," he stammered. "I want you to come in and help me l-look under the b-bed. Not that I'm n-nervous or af-f-fraid, b-b-but I d-d-don't want to be d-disturbed."

"You say you heard somebody trying your door?"

"Yes, I did. I never sleep well and when I sleep at all I sleep lightly. I heard it p-p-plainly, I tell you."

I smiled. "It's a windy night," said I. "Doors and windows rattle."

"Yes, but the wind can't turn the knob on your door!" he insisted, his eyes of a wild pig roving

153

nervously about my room. "I don't like such things, and I want you to come and look under my bed."

"Very well," said I, "let us go and look under your bed, Monsieur Itchenuff."

The Tzar of all the Bulgars was not an agreeable spectacle in his night-shirt and enormous bare feet. His visage was pasty, his eyes had a frightened, stealthy restlessness like a wild thing's that hears and scents an enemy but has not yet perceived him.

So wabbly was the lighted candle in his large fat hand, that I was afraid he'd set fire to his night-shirt, and relieved him of it.

"We have our own dynamo here," said I. "Why didn't you turn on the electric light by your bed?"

"It wouldn't work," he replied. "Do you suppose somebody has c-c-cut the wire?"

"Who?"

"God knows! Everybody has enemies, I suppose. You wouldn't believe it, Monsieur, if you knew me well, but even I am affected by enemies."

"Impossible!" said I, looking at him askance as he waddled along bare-footed beside me.

"Nevertheless, I assure you," he complained in a voice unctuous with virtuous self-pity, "I, who have never harmed a fly, Monsieur, have secret enemies who would d-destroy me."

Again I glanced sideways at this Bulgarian assassin—the murderer of Stambouleff, and of God knows how many others.

We came to the door of his dark bedroom and I went in with the lighted candle. First I examined the electric fixture.

"Nobody's cut your wire," said I. "The globe's burnt out."

"Does that seem at all suspicious to you?" he asked in an agitated voice, coming up behind me.

I smiled. "That happens daily as you must know." I got down on my knees and peered under his bed. Of course there was nobody there. Nevertheless he got down on all fours and took the candle to examine every corner. Then, puffing, he reared up, shuffled to his flat, splay feet, and went about peeping into closets, behind curtains and sofas, moving from room to room in his suite with a stealthy flapping of his bare feet on the parquet.

Meanwhile I went around trying the several electric switches. It *was* odd that all the globes should have been burnt out at once. Evidently some fuse in the cellar had blown out.

There was another candle on his dresser. I lighted it. And, as it flickered into yellow flame, something on the floor of the dressing-room beyond caught the light and sparkled. And I went forward on tip-toe and picked it up.

The Tzar of all the Bulgars was busy searching the sitting-room. Now, satisfied that there was no intruder concealed about the apartment, he waddled massively back to where I stood.

"All the same," he said, "I heard the knob of my door squeak."

"There are no robbers in this region," said I with a shrug.

"Monsieur O'Ryan," he said solemnly, "you may not know it but I am a very important personage —person, I mean—that is," he explained hastily, "I am important in a business sense. And I have many envious business rivals who would not hesitate to follow me secretly from Berne and attempt to possess themselves of any—papers I might carry —in hopes of obtaining business secrets."

I said nothing. He stood on one leg, rubbing one shin with his large, fat toes, and his little mean eyes roaming everywhere.

"You should have brought a servant or two," I suggested.

"No, no, not this time," he said hurriedly. "No, this is just an—an informal little p-pleasure trip with friends—the Xenoses—quite—er—al fresco— sans façon, you see. No, I didn't want servants about." He shot a cunning glance at me and checked himself.

So I shrugged, showed him how to double-lock all his doors, bade him good night, and went back to my own room, trying the corridor lights on my way. None of them worked.

"There's no fuse blown out," thought I to myself, staring at my own bedroom light which burned brightly and which was controlled by the same switch.

Then, locking my door, I took out of my pocket the small bright object which I had picked up in Tzar Ferdinand's dressing-room.

It was a silver filigree button from the peasant costume of Thusis.

Of course she had probably lost it sometime during the day when airing the suite. Untidy little Thusis!

I dropped onto my bed still holding the silver button in my closed hand. Presently I touched it, discreetly, with my lips. And fell asleep after a while—to dream that the Bulgarian and the Hohenzollern had cut off my hands at the wrists and were nailing them to my front door, as happened, I believe, to Major Panitza.

About three o'clock I awoke in pitch darkness, all quivering from my dream, and heard the wind in the fir-trees and the slam of a heavy shutter.

For a while I lay there hoping the shutter would stop banging. But it did not. Then I tried to locate it by the sound. And after a while I decided that it must be some shutter on one of the windows overhead.

The servants' quarters were there. I didn't exactly like to go up and hunt about. But the racket was becoming unbearable; so I rose again, got into slippers, trousers and dressing gown, and went out along the corridor. It was pitch dark, but I decided not to go back and hunt up a candle because I could follow the strip of carpet and feel my way to the service stairs.

And I was doing this in a blind, cautious way, and was just turning the corridor corner with groping arms outstretched, when, with a soft and perfectly silent shock, somebody walked into them.

Such a thing is sufficient to paralyze anybody. My heart missed like a flivver out of gear, then that engine started racing, and my arms mechanically and convulsively closed around that unseen thing that had collided with me.

"W-who the devil is it!" I said shakily, as a shocked gasp escaped it and the thing almost collapsed in my terrified embrace.

Then, as I spoke, my half-stunned wits awoke; a faint fragrance grew on my senses; the yielding ghost in my arms came to warm life, and two hands clutched at my imprisoning arms.

"Michael!" she panted.

"Great heavens! Thusis!" I faltered.

Freed, she leaned against the corridor wall for a few moments in palpitating silence. I also needed that interval to recover.

"What on earth is the matter, Thusis?" I managed to whisper at last.

"N-nothing. There was a shutter blowing——"

"But it's on the floor above! It's on your floor, Thusis."

She was silent for a moment, then: "What are *you* doing—prowling about the house at this hour?" she demanded.

"In my case," said I, "it *was* the shutter."

"Very well. I'll go up and fix it, and you may go back to bed."

But I had begun to feel a little troubled, and I made no motion to depart.

"I'll fix it," she repeated. "Good night."

"Thusis?"

"What?" In her voice I distinguished the slightest tone of impatience, perhaps of defiance. "What is it?" she repeated.

"Tell me the truth. What are you really about in this corridor at three in the morning?"

"I've told you."

"No, you haven't, Thusis."

After a silence I could hear her laughing under her breath.

"Mind your own business, Michael," she whispered; "I'm not going to confide in you."

"I want to know what brought you here," said I.

"What if you do wish to know? I am not obliged to inform you, am I?"

I heard her retreating, and I followed to the service stairs. Here a dim light came through a high

159

window faintly silvering the stairs; and I saw the phantom figure of Thusis standing where she had suddenly arrested her steps on the stair-case, half-seeing, half-divining, my pursuit.

"Is that you, Michael?"

"Yes."

"Why do you follow me?"

"I want to talk to you."

"What nonsense! At three in the morning? Also I am not in conventional attire."

"I'm not, either," said I, "but we'll waive ceremony."

"No, we won't!"

"Yes, we will——"

"No!"

"Why?"

"I've told you why. Do you suppose I wish Clelia or Josephine to find me sitting on the stairs with you under such circumstances?"

She seated herself on the stairs as she spoke and I came up and leaned on the newel-post.

"I'm a perfect fool," she said. But she looked like an angel there in the vague light of the windy sky, her splendid hair about her face and shoulders, and her little naked feet drawn close under the hem of her silvery chamber-robe which she was belting in with rapid fingers.

"Well?" she said, looking up at me.

160

"I found something which belongs to you," said I, quietly.

"What is it?"

"A silver filigree button."

"Oh. Where did you find it, Michael?"

"In the dressing-room of King Ferdinand."

There was a pause—a second's hesitation. "Well," she said, smiling, "you've a clean mind, Michael. Also you have a sense of humor. What do you infer from your very immoral discovery?"

"You might have lost the button this afternoon while airing his apartment."

"Thank you," she whispered laughingly.

"Or," said I, "you may *not* have dropped it then."

"What do you mean?" she said bluntly.

"Thusis," said I, "what do *you* mean by wearing a pistol under your chamber-robe?"

After a long silence she looked up at me.

"A guess?"

"No. I felt it when you ran into me in the dark."

She hesitated, then:

"If I should say that I am timid you wouldn't believe me. Would you, Michael?"

"No."

"Then—what do you wish me to tell you?"

"Tell me, for example, why no lights work in King Ferdinand's suite."

Again there was an interval during which I rather

felt than saw her gray eyes fixed intently on my shadowy face.  Then:

"Has a fuse blown out?"

"No, Thusis."

"Then no doubt the globes are burnt out."

"Do you think it likely that they all burnt out at the same time?"

"It is possible, isn't it?"

I did not reply.

She waited, then asked me in a mocking voice whether there was anything further that worried me.

"I was merely wondering," said I, "who it was that awoke King Ferdinand to-night by trying the knob on his bedroom door."

"Michael!"

"Well?"

"Do you mean to be insulting?"

I went over to her and coolly seated myself on the stair upon which her feet rested.

"Thusis," said I, "I'm just worried about you. That's all."

"Will you give me a single sensible reason, Michael, why you should be worried about me?"

"Yes.  That fat Bulgarian keeps two big automatic guns under his pillow.  And he's a physical poltroon.  And you can never tell what a coward may do in a panic."

Her eyes were fastened on me all the while I was speaking but her expression remained inscrutable.

162

As I ended, however, it changed subtly.

"And—*that* is what worries you," she said in an altered voice,—a voice so winningly sweet that I scarcely recognized it for the gay, engaging, bantering voice I knew so well.

Then Thusis rose, and I stood up on the step below her.

"You funny boy," she said, "you mustn't worry about me."

"Does it surprise you?"

She laughed under her breath.

"Nothing surprises me any more, Michael. I am past being astonished at anything—at my own behavior, at yours. You wouldn't understand me if I say that, ordinarily, this rather improper costume of mine wouldn't embarrass me."

"You mean," said I, "that the social difference between us leaves you indifferent to me as a man?"

She bit her lip, looked at me with a flushed, distressed little smile.

"Yes, I meant that."

I nodded: "The indifference of a bathing princess to the slaves who stand beside her litter."

"It was—that way with me—once," she said, wincing, but still smiling through the color that surged in her face. "You would wish me to be honest with you, wouldn't you, Michael?"

"Certainly. And tell me, Thusis, who are you who condescend to converse with a plain republican?

163

And what democratic whim has possessed you to so unbend?"

"Michael!"

"Yes?"

"You are mocking me!"

"But at least," said I, "you are a princess in camouflage—I don't mean a Russian one——"

She turned scarlet with anger and I saw her teeth busy at her under lip again.

"Piffle," said I. "You take yourself too seriously, Thusis. Whatever else you are you're the young girl with whom I'm in love—deeply in love. And I'm going to tell you so, and love you with all my might, and worry over you, and pursue you with advice and devotion until you make yourself too impossible."

"And—then?" she demanded in a voice strangled with rage.

"Then," said I, "if you really prove to be too idiotic and impossible, I shall stroll on until I encounter the next."

"Next—what?" The fury in her voice scared me, but I pulled myself together.

"Next girl," said I flippantly. "You know, Thusis, there *are* others."

She stood like a statue for a moment. Then:

"This," she whispered, "is what I ought to have expected for lowering myself! . . . I invited it— this affront——"

164

"Piffle," said I, "you know in your heart I'd sooner blow my bally brains out than affront you. Why say such things? Why pretend to yourself? You know well enough that I'm so head over heels in love with you that I don't know what I say——"

"*I* do!" she retorted in a white heat. "And I've got to listen to it—I'm obliged to listen to—to an insolent inferior——"

"I'm not your inferior."

"You are!"

"Why, you silly, unhappy little thing," said I, "what if you are some funny sort of princess—some pretty highness of the Balkans? Literature is full of them, and if you'd read a little fiction you'd learn that they all marry ordinary, untitled young men like me."

"Must I listen to such outrageous insults?" she demanded, standing up very straight and slender in her offended pride, and forgetting that her bare feet under her nightie became the more visible the straighter she drew herself—lovely, snowy little naked feet as slim and delicate as the pedal extremities of a perfectly moral and early Victorian Bacchante.

"Am I to stand here and endure this insolence from you?" she repeated, her gray eyes ablaze.

"Not at all," said I. "You can always go upstairs to bed, Thusis."

Angry tears glittered in her eyes, not quenching

their dangerous brightness, however. But I was now as mad as she was.

"Do you suppose," said I, "that this world war, this overwhelming disaster that is razing hill and city to one horrible and bloody level—this cataclysm which is obliterating the very contours of the world God made—is not also going to level such flimsy structures as the social structure?—such artificial protuberances as elevation of rank? I tell you, Thusis, that mankind will emerge naked and equal from this blood-deluge. You and I, too, are going to come out of it—if we do come out—not what our ancestors thought they were, but what we actually are! Very possibly, in generations gone with buried years, some doddering potentate may have managed to beget some ancestor of yours.

"What of it? Who cares to-day?—outside of the Huns and their barbarian allies? Who cares what you call yourself, I say? Who in God's name will care to-morrow? Do you imagine that the peoples who, like Christ, have descended into hell, can come out of those flames without the tinsel of rank being burned off? Do you suppose anything can remain except pure metal?"

I had let myself loose; and I fairly took away her breath.

She put out one hand and rested it on the bannisters in a dazed sort of way, still looking at me with a kind of fixed fascination.

"Have you any answer to what I have said?" I added after the silence had been sufficiently impressive.

She said faintly: "How about the Admiral, Don Michael?" And, as I choked and turned crimson, the girl turned, dropped onto the stairs, and rocked there convulsively, stifling her helpless, hysterical laughter with both hands over her lips.

I waited, hot with exasperation. There was nothing else for me to do.

Thusis struggled fiercely with her uncontrollable mirth, evidently terrified lest the indiscretion of her laughter awake the sleepers in the house.

"Thusis——"

"Wait! If you speak I shall expire. Because you never will know how funny you are, Michael! Oh——"

I waited until she was able to control herself.

"Thusis," I began, stiffly——

"Oh, don't! Please don't! I'm too weak. I'll go to bed—really I will, Michael. And leave you to wrap yourself in your nightie and stalk back to the Admiral——"

"Damn it all!" I broke out. She rocked, helplessly, her face buried in her hands.

After a while she got up, supporting herself by one hand on the stair-rail. The other hand pressed her heart.

"Michael dear," she said, "you are perfectly right. We are what we are. Nothing alters that. We are born what we are; we die what we are. No cataclysm can change what we really are. . . . As for distinction of rank, don't you know, Michael, that social inequality always has existed and always will?"

"Not artificial social inequality. Minds alone will dominate. Personality only will count. Inheritance and tradition will play no part in the world's future after this war ends."

"You seem to be quite sure, Michael."

"Perfectly."

"But you are so young to be a prophet and a seer!"

"Good heavens, Thusis, is there nothing serious in you!" I exclaimed wrathfully.

"Not just at the moment," she retorted, controlling her laughter. "And I'd better go to bed or I'll be suggesting that we start that music-box down stairs and try a two-step."

I took a step toward her: "It amuses you to be funny," said I, "but before we take leave of each other suppose you hand me that pistol."

"Indeed I shall not!"

"If you don't hand it over," said I, "I shall be obliged to catch you and take it away from you." And I started toward her.

"Go to the devil!" she whispered softly

At that she flew up the stairs, turned on the land-ing and leaned down toward me with an adorable gesture.

"Go to the devil!" she whispered softly. And van-ished in the dusk above.

# XII

THE Queen demanded her breakfast in bed. Clelia came to the breakfast room to tell me so.

I had heard the furious ringing of her bell and I said to Smith that something of that sort was likely to happen.

"You tell her," said I to Clelia, "that no meals are served in rooms. What does she expect with only one waitress?"

Clelia went away and Smith and I resumed coffee, toast, and a poached egg apiece. Presently Clelia returned, her eyes and cheeks brilliant with suppressed emotion.

"Well," said I, "what's the matter now?"

"Madame Xenos is very, very angry, and she demands to see the landlord."

"Did she employ that word?"

"Yes, she did."

"You say she wants to see me?" I asked.

"She insists."

"But you tell me she's in bed, Clelia. How can I go up?"

Clelia shrugged her pretty shoulders! "Queens

170

don't care. A landlord of an inn has no masculine meaning to a queen."

"Is that so!" I said. "Very well"—I finished my
coffee at a gulp—"I'll go and see Madame Hohenzollern."

"You'd better be careful," said Clelia, smiling.
"She really is a vixen."

I recollected the story of Constantine, and that it
was commonly believed she had once stuck a knife
into Tino when annoyed about something or other.

But I rose from the table determined to settle her
status in my house once for all.

"And, Clelia," I said, "I've heard other bells
tinkling. Those kings upstairs are no good, and I
wouldn't put it past either of them to demand that
you serve them breakfast in their rooms."

"They have demanded it."

Smith turned an angry red and made as though
to rise, but sat down again.

For a moment I was too mad to speak. Finally
I said: "Of course you ignored their bells."

"No, I answered them."

"You didn't go into their rooms!"

"No. I knocked politely. Monsieur Xenos
flirted with me——"

"What!"

"In a whisper through the keyhole. So I went
away to see what Monsieur Itchenuff desired." She
laughed and, lifting the coffee-pot, filled Smith's

171

cup. "Monsieur Itchenuff wanted me to bring him breakfast. He also said he always breakfasted in bed——"

"Keep away from that pair!" said Smith violently.

But Clelia's eyebrows went up and so did her nose, mutely signaling Smith to mind his own affairs.

"Clelia," said he, "I want to talk to you——"

"I'm here to wait on you, not to talk to you!" she retorted.

"Then at least you must listen——"

"Must? *Must?* Monsieur Smith, your bullying tone does not please me!"

Here was the beginning of a pretty row. But I had another on my own hands so I left them and went upstairs to interview the Queen.

"Come in!" she snapped when I knocked. Her voice chilled my courage and I sidled in batting my eyes ingratiatingly.

The Queen was in bed. Her hair was done up like a lady Hottentot's, all screwed into tight little kinks. Over her sharp, discontented features cold cream glistened like oleomargarine on a bun.

"I've ordered breakfast in bed," she said sharply. "Why am I kept waiting?"

I explained that there was only one waitress.

"But what of that?" she asked in astonishment. "The other guests can wait."

"Why should they wait?" I inquired, annoyed.

She shot an arrogant glance at me and started

to say something but, evidently recollecting her incognito as Madame Xenos, merely choked and finally swallowed her wrath.

"Madame," said I soothingly, for I was really afraid of her, "I am extremely sorry to inconvenience you, but the rules of the chalet must be observed by everybody, otherwise confusion in the service is certain to result——"

"I am not interested in your domestic problems," she said, and turned over in bed.

"Madame," said I, "let me trouble you to remember that I am not an innkeeper whom you can bully. I am the grandson of an Admiral!"

At that the Queen sat up and stared at me like a maverick.

"That's true," she said. "I had forgotten that distinction. I am sorry if I spoke too severely. Nevertheless it's very annoying."

I said I regretted the necessity of making rules; she yawned and fiddled with her corkscrew kinks, but nodded acknowledgment to my perfectly correct bow. And so I left the Queen, yawning, stretching, and rubbing her neck and ears with the sleepy satisfaction of an awakened cat.

The bell of King Constantine was still ringing at intervals. So I continued along the corridor and knocked very lightly at his door. Listening, I heard a shuffle of unshod feet within, a rustle, then through the key-hole a persuasive voice thick with suppressed affection:

"Why so cruel, little one? Bring me my breakfast on a pretty tray—there's a good little girl. And maybe there'll be a big, shiny gold-piece for you if you're very amiable."

I hesitated, listening to his heavy, irregular breathing, then opened the door.

The King looked intensely foolish for a moment, then seized me by the shoulder, drew me into the room, and shut the door.

"We're a pack of sad dogs, we men!" he said jovially, smiting me familiarly on the shoulder again. "We're all up to our little tricks—every one of us, eh, O'Ryan? No—no! Don't pull a smug face with me—a good looking young fellow like you! No, no! it won't do, O'Ryan. We men ought to be frank with one another. And that's me—bluff, rough, frank to a fault!—just a soldier, O'Ryan——"

"I thought you were a wine-merchant, Monsieur Xenos."

"Oh, certainly. But I've been a soldier. I'm more at home in barracks than I am anywhere else." He chuckled, dug me in the ribs with his thumb:

"Be a good sport, O'Ryan. You don't want both of them, do you? My God, man, you're no Turk, I hope. Why can't that very young one—I mean

174

the yellow haired one—bring me my breakfast and——"

Probably my features were not under perfect control for the King stopped short and took an instinctive step backward.

"Where do you think you are, Monsieur Xenos?" I asked, striving to keep my voice steady. "Did you think you are in a cabaret, or a mastroquet or a zenana?"

"Oh, come," he began, losing countenance, "you shouldn't take a bluff old soldier too precisely——"

"You listen to *me!* Mind your damned business while you're under my roof or I'll knock your silly head off!"

I looked him over deliberately, insultingly, from the tasseled toe of his Algerian bed-room slippers to his purple pyjamas clasped with a magnificent ruby at the throat.

"Behave yourself decently," said I slowly, "or I'll take you out to the barnyard and rub your nose in it."

And I went out, leaving Tino stupefied in the center of his bedroom.

The Tzar's bell was ringing again, but I made no ceremony in his case, merely jerking open his door and telling him curtly to come down to breakfast if he wanted any. Then I closed his door to cut off argument and continued on.

I met Thusis in apron and dust-cloth, sweeping the stairs.

She looked up almost shyly as I passed her with a polite bow.

"Good morning," she said. "Did you sleep well, Monsieur?"

"The wind kept me awake," said I drily.

"And me, also." She glanced out of the stair window, leaning on her broom. "It is raining very hard," she observed. "The mountains will not be safe to-day."

"How do you mean?" I inquired coolly, but willing to linger, heaven help me!

"Avalanches," she explained.

"I see."

We remained silent. Thusis inspected her broomhandle, tucked a curl up under her white head-cloth.

I said: "You and Clelia seem to exchange jobs rather frequently."

"It mitigates the monotony," she remarked, resting her rounded cheek against the broom-handle.

"Where did you leave that gun?" I demanded in a low voice.

"Do you remember my reply to you on the stairs last night, Don Michael?"

"You bade me go to the devil."

"That *was* rude of me, wasn't it? And so frightfully vulgar! Oh, dear me! I really don't know what I am coming to."

176

She smiled very gaily, however.

"Thusis," said I, "you wouldn't shoot up any of these kings and queens, would you?"

At that she laughed outright: "Not if they behave themselves!"

"Seriously——"

"I am quite serious, Don Michael."

"You're bent on searching their luggage," said I. "And Ferdinand has two big automatic pistols."

"You're such a funny boy," said Thusis with her adorable smile. "But now you must run away and let me do my dusting."

Her sleeves were rolled to her shoulders. I had never seen such perfect arms except in Greek sculpture. I said so, impulsively. And Thusis blushed.

"That is the sort of thing I had rather you did not say," she remarked.

"But if it's quite true, Thusis——"

"Does one blurt out anything merely because one believes it to be true? Besides, ill-made or agreeable, my arms do not concern you, Monsieur O'Ryan."

"Everything that you are concerns me very deeply, Thusis——"

"I will not have it so!"

"But you said I might pay my court to you——"

"But you don't pay court! You make love to me!"

"What is the essential difference?"

177

"To court a woman is to be polite, empressé, always ready to serve her, always quick with some stately compliment, some pretty conceit, some bon-mot to please her, some trifle of wit, of gossip." She cast a deliciously wicked look at me. "I have no doubt, Michael, that you could, without effort, measure up to the standard of a faultless courtier. . . . If you'd be content to do so."

That was too much for me. I stepped toward her and slipped my arm around her pliant waist. She laughed, resisted, flushed, then lost her color and clutched my hand at her waist with her own, striving to unloosen it.

"Don't do that, Michael," she said, breathing unevenly.

"I love you, Thusis———"

"I don't wish to listen———"

"I'm madly in love with you———"

"Michael!"

"What?"

"*Are* you trying to kiss me?"

That is what I was trying to do. She twisted herself free and stepped aside; and I saw the rapid pulse in her white throat and the irregular flutter of her bosom.

For a moment the old blaze flamed once more in her gray eyes and I expected a most terrifying wigging, but all she said was: "You are very rough with me," in a small and breathless voice; and, sud-

178

denly, to my astonishment, turned her back and laid her head on the handle of her broom.

"Thusis——"

"Please d-don't speak to me."

"I only——"

"I ask you to go."

So I went, leaving her standing there with her clasped hands on the broom supporting her bowed head.

Smith was sulkily smoking his pipe. Clelia, beautiful and indifferent, leaned against the sideboard, awaiting the advent of royalty in the breakfast-room.

I went on out. Raoul, standing under the dripping eaves, was just hoisting an umbrella, and I took advantage of it and went over to the bottling works.

"We're making quite a lot of money," said I, looking over the order book and ledger.

Raoul smiled and ran his well shaped fingers through his curly hair.

"It's good spring-water," he said, "and God permits you an innocent income not wrung out of the poor, not cheated out of the less fortunate, not gouged out of business rivals whose loss is your gain."

I also smiled: "It is quite true, Raoul, that I do harm to nobody by bottling and selling the water which God has seen fit to send out gushing from these deep rocks."

"*You'd* never harm anybody anyway!" he said coolly. "One knows a gentleman."

And he went about his work, singing the song he seemed always to prefer——

> "Crack-brain-cripple-arm,
> You have done a heap of harm——"

And I began to wonder how the Queen would like that song if he came carelessly caroling it in her vicinity.

However, it was not my business to direct the musical inclinations of my household. I took the umbrella and, stepping to the door, spread it.

"It's quite a storm," I remarked.

"There'll be avalanches," said Raoul. I thought he spoke uneasily and that there was a hint of apprehension in the glance he cast up at the Bec de l'Empereur.

"Of course," said I, "we are safe enough in this valley."

"Yes, but a bad slide might choke the pass."

"What would that do to us, Raoul?"

"Cut us off from the rest of the world," he said simply.

"For how long?"

"Days, weeks—longer perhaps. Who knows what

180

might happen if a big snow broke loose from the Bec-de l'Empereur?"

"Anyway," said I, "we have sufficient provisions."

"Plenty, Monsieur."

"Then it would mean only a rather dull and exasperating imprisonment."

He looked at me with an odd smile: "It might mean the salvation of the world—or its damnation," he said.

I was silent but curious. He smiled again and shrugged. "For me," he said, "I pray that no avalanche falls to block this valley within the week." He looked upward into the heavily falling rain, standing there bare-headed.

"I ask," he said in a low, serious voice, "that God should be graciously pleased to hold His hand for one week longer before He lets loose His eternal snows upon this valley."

When I returned to the breakfast-room royalty was feeding. All acknowledged my greeting with civility, even Tino who, however, also turned red and nervously pasted his roll with marmalade.

"For diversion," inquired the Queen, "what does one do here?"

I enumerated the out-door sports. Nobody cared to fish except with a net. Tino expressed himself vaguely as in favor of a chamois hunt when he felt up to it. The Queen wished to climb the Bec-de

181

l'Empereur, but when I told her there were no guides nearer than Berne and also that this rain made the mountains very dangerous, she decided to postpone the ascent.

As for the Tzar of all the Bulgars he paid strict attention to his plate and betrayed no inclination for anything more strenuous than the facial exercise of chewing.

While the Queen was there neither King ventured to annoy Clelia, but after her majesty had left the table they both evinced symptoms of pinching, furtive leers and smirks.

However, there was a stoniness about my expression which served to discourage them. Ferdinand scrubbed his beard in his finger-bowl with a wallowing sound, dried it noisily on his napkin, rose, bowed to me, and waddled back upstairs.

Tino seemed very uncomfortable to find himself alone with me. But I conversed with him as good humoredly as though I had never told him what I should do to him in the event of his misbehavior under my roof. And we got on well enough.

He had mean eyes, however, and a fussy, jerky, nervous manner, yet furtive for all that. An odd monarch with the most false face, except for Ferdinand's, that I had ever beheld, though at first encounter one might easily be deceived and take him for what he pretended to be—a bluff, noisy, unceremonious, and somewhat coarse soldier with his tête-

`de-militaire and his allure and vocabulary of the *Caserne*.

"We've some friends arriving to-day," he said. "Did my wife tell you?"

"Somebody mentioned it yesterday, I believe."

"Well, they'll be here to-day, so fix them up snugly, O'Ryan."

"The rain may prevent them from starting," I suggested.

"Rain or no rain they'll be here," he repeated, lighting a strong cigarette.

He went away presently upstairs. And I did not doubt they would all have their noses together in a few moments discussing whatever crisis had brought them to this lonely little valley without escort or servants and carefully camouflaged.

I went into the living-room where Smith sat reading.

"What the devil," said I, "has brought these Kings here, Smith? Can you guess?"

"I don't know. I might," he replied, looking over his book at me.

"Well, what is your guess?"

"Why, I suppose they're worried. Things are going very rottenly for the hun. British, French and Yank are kicking them about most brutally from Arras to the Vosges. That pasty-faced pervert, the Crown Prince, has had the very pants kicked off him. The U-boats are a fizzle. The Bolsheviki are running into cracks like vermin to escape fumigation. Austria is sick from Italy's kick delivered into the pit of her stomach. Enver Pasha, who was promised the Khediviate of Egypt when the boche started to carve up the world, is turning ugly and demanding why the banquet isn't ready."

He made a weary gesture toward the ceiling.

"Up there," he said, "sits the most cowardly, murderous, and despicable ruler in the world—Ferdinand of Bulgaria—scared stiff because he's beginning to believe he's bet on the wrong horse.

"With him sit a King and Queen recently kicked headlong out of Greece. They also are becoming intensely nervous about that promise made by the hun Kaiser—an oath thundered from Berlin that the boche sword should restore them to their thrones.

"You see, Michael, they're worried. They've sneaked away from Berne incognito to meet here and lay all their cards on the common table. They're here to consult, bargain, cheat if they can, but anyway they're here to come to some understanding and arrive at some agreement as to the best means to avert utter disaster. That's why they're here.

"They couldn't feel safe in spy-ridden Berne; they evidently dare not trust their own servants. It is plain to me that Switzerland, which is mostly proboche, engineered the affair, willingly or reluctantly, because the Kaiser's sister is involved and the Federal Government is horribly afraid of the boche.

"You see how it came about, don't you? This bunch of royal crooks desired a safe place for a get-together party. Long ago they had planned it. Then you appeared to take possession of your inheritance.

"What could be safer for them than this lonely valley and a neutral gentleman from Chili to make 'em comfortable?"

"And a Norse Viking," said I.

"Be careful," he said gravely.

"Of course. But they believe you are what you pretend to be, don't they?"

"Absolutely. . . . And how do you know I am not?" he inquired smilingly.

We exchanged gay but significant glances. He went on speaking:

"That's all there is to it," he said, "a bunch of dips trying it on each other and still held together by the 'cohesive power of plunder'—the Prussian hun, the Austrian hun, the unspeakable Turk, the bloody Bulgar, the besotted Bolshevik!—a fine mess, Michael!—and here, under your roof, are three who have long ago been mugged, and who are known to the police of civilization everywhere."

"They've got their nerve," said I angrily, "to come here and discuss their dirty schemes! I've a damned good mind to ask them for their rooms. I've got enough of them already, Smith. I'm hanged if I stand for this another day——"

185

His hand closed on my arm in a leisurely grip of steel, and I winced and looked up at him in surprise and protest.

"*Don't—spoil—things,*" he said quietly. His level glance met mine with a metallic glint, and I saw in his features something terrible—a fleeting gleam like the far reflection of lightning across a thunder cloud.

"Smith!" I exclaimed.

"Don't raise your voice, old chap."

"N-no. But—can't you tell me just what you really are?"

"I'm really quite all right," he assured me, laughingly.

"I assumed that. But—are you here, also, to keep an eye on these kings?"

"Well, you know one can't help noticing them——"

"Damn! Answer me."

"I admit," he said, "that they interest me."

So *that* was what brought Smith here, too! He must have known they were coming. He must have deliberately scraped acquaintance with me for this purpose.

"I thought," said I bitterly, "that you really liked me, Smith."

"I do, confound you!" he said. "If I didn't both like and trust you, do you think I'd have been so careless in concealing my identity?"

186

Both Thusis and Clelia had said the same thing to me.

"Smith?"

"What?"

"Did you know Thusis and Clelia before you met them here?"

"No."

"Do you know why they're here?"

"I can guess."

"Do you know who they really are?"

"No," he said honestly, "I don't. And I can not seem to find out. All I know is that their purpose in coming here does conflict with mine——"

The pretty fanfare of a postilion's horn cut him short.

"There," said I, "comes the rest of the precious bunch!"

" 'Hail, hail,' " said he gravely, " 'the gang's all here!' "

And we got up and went to the window to inspect the arriving diligence.

# XIII

THAT afternoon I fled the house. This new invasion of my privacy had quite upset me. Bulgarian and Greek royalty had been difficult enough to endure, but this new wagon-load of huns and near-huns proved too much for me.

If there were any privacy at all to be had it seemed that I must seek it in the woods. And thither I fled under an umbrella, a book under one arm, a fishing rod under the other, and my pockets full of smoking material.

For I preferred to sit on the wet moss in the rain, and read and smoke and fish under my ancient green gamp—even if the seat of my trousers did become soaking wet—rather than listen to the gobbling gabble of those Teutons and witness their bad manners and their unpleasant personal habits.

So, as I say, as soon as the new arrivals had registered and had been assigned to rooms I made up my mind to inhabit the woods during their occupation of my property, and invited Smith to share my indignant seclusion.

He declined, probably because, whoever he really was and whatever might be his job, the one and the

188

other very evidently had to do with this bunch of assorted boches.

He said very politely that he didn't enjoy privacy when it was sopping wet. He smiled when he said it. We were standing at the desk in the big living-room: the huns, both royalty and new arrivals, had gone to their rooms, and Smith was carelessly examining the register where my guests' signatures had been inscribed in the pale and watery ink of the country.

"A pretty kettle of fish," I commented, looking over his shoulder. "But this new consignment of boches doesn't seem to be camouflaged. These are their real names, I fancy."

"I happen to know that they are," said Smith.

He began to read the names aloud just as they were written; and I noticed the lazy amusement in his pleasant, even voice as he commented upon each signature:

" *'General Count von Dungheim'!* Oh, yes; he belonged to Tino's suite when he was kicked out of Athens. They call him 'Droly.' He did some dirty work there—instigated the murder of the allied detachments. He's a big, thin Prussian with a capacity for gluttony equal only to the Bulgarian King's. He enjoys only one eye.

" *'Baron von Bummelzug'!* Oh, certainly. He's a Bavarian civilian. He engineered the treacherous surrender of that Greek army corps. He also was in Tino's suite, and still is.

" '*Admiral Lauterlaus*'! Tino's ex-naval aide. Tried dirty work on the Allied fleet off Samos. A Prussian,—mostly belly and head.

" '*Princess Pudelstoff*'! She was that enormously fat woman, Michael, who kissed King Ferdinand on both cheeks and left two wet spots. She's one of those German-Russians from Courland attached to the Bulgarian court, and related to Ferdinand in some degree or other,—irregularly.

" '*Countess Manntrapp*'! The pretty girl. You remember her honeyed, cooing voice when you were presented to her?—and her ecstatic baby stare, as though acquaintance with a Chilean gentleman had been the secret ambition of her life, and the realization overwhelmed her? Well, old top, there you have Lila Shezawitch, Countess Manntrapp—the widow of that brainless old reprobate, the cavalryman, who disappeared in some Russian swamp-hole when Hindenburg made his mark among the lakes.

" '*Adolf Gizzler*'! Look out for that rat, Michael. He's a bum school-teacher, Bummelzug's secretary.

" '*Leo Puppsky*'! What do you know about that Bolshevik being here in Switzerland? And

" '*Isidore Wildkatz*,' too! Here they are with the huns, this pair of Judases! Oh, you're quite right, Michael. It's a pretty kettle of fish. I don't blame

190

you for taking to the woods, rain or no rain."

"You won't come, too?" I asked. He smiled, and I understood.

He was *such* a decent sort. I had become very fond of him.

"All right," said I; "don't get yourself into trouble. That's certainly a sinister bunch of boches as well as an unpleasant one."

"Good old Michael," he said, patting my shoulder.

So I took to the woods with rod and book, and a camp-stool I picked up on the veranda.

Heavéns, how it rained! But I stopped at the barn-yard, found a manure-fork, and disinterred a tin canful of angle-worns. Then I marched on in the teeth of the storm, umbrella over my head, and entered that pretty woodland path which Thusis and I had once trodden together on our food-conservation quest.

The memory inclined me to sentimental reverie, and, with my dripping gamp over my head, I slopped along in a sort of trance, my brain a maze of vague enchantment as images of Thusis or of my photograph of The Laughing Girl alternately occupied my thoughts.

For, when alone, these two lovely phantoms always became inextricably mixed. I could not seem to differentiate between them in memory. And which was the loveliest I could not decide because the resemblance was too confusing.

191

And so, in a sort of delicious daze, I arrived at the foot-bridge.

Here I spread my camp-stool by the green pool's edge. It was a torrent, now, but still as brilliant and clear as a beryl, and that it lacked its natural and emerald clarity did not deter me from baiting my hook with several expostulating worms, and hurling it forth into the foaming basin.

To hold a fishing rod in one fixed position bores me, and always did. So I laid the rod on the bank, placed a flat stone on the butt, and, sheltered under my umbrella, lighted a pipe and opened my book.

But the book soon bored me, too. It was a novel by one of the myriads of half-educated American "authors" who resemble a countryman I once knew who called himself a "natural bone-setter" and enjoyed a large and furtive practice among neighboring clodhoppers to the indignation of all the local physicians.

There are thousands of "authors" in the United States. But there are very few writers.

And this novel was by an author, and my attention wandered.

Through an opening in the forest on a clear day one might look out upon a world of mountains eastward. I realized there could be no view through the thickly falling rain, but I turned around. And, to my surprise, I beheld a cloaked figure poised upon the chasm's distant edge, peering out into the storm through a pair of field-glasses.

I knew that figure in spite of the cloak. Nor could the thickly slanting rain quench the glorious color of that burnished hair.

"Thusis!" I shouted.

Slowly the figure turned, glasses still poised; and I saw her looking in my direction.

"I'm fishing!" I called out joyously. "Come under my umbrella!"

She cast a glance behind her toward the blank void where, on clear days, the bulk of the Bec-de l'Empereur towered aloft in its mantle of dazzling snow. Then she slowly walked toward me through the rain.

When she came near to where I sat, she began to laugh; and I never saw such an exquisite sight as Thusis, bare-headed in the rain, laughing.

"What on earth are you up to, Michael?" she said.

"Fishing. That herd of huns will eat us out of house and garden if we don't catch something. Sit beside me under the umbrella, Thusis. There's room if we're careful and don't let the camp-stool collapse."

She gave me an inscrutable glance, stood motionless for a few moments, then slowly came over.

"Careful now," I cautioned her, rising. "We must both seat ourselves at the same instant or this camp-stool will close up like a jack-knife. Are you ready?"

She laughed and inclined her pretty head.

"Then—one! two! three! Sit!"

We managed to accomplish it without an accident.

"We're too close together," she protested.

"Don't stir," said I. "Do you feel how it wabbles?"

She tested the camp-stool cautiously, and nodded.

"What an absurd situation," she remarked, glancing up at the gamp which I held over us.

"I think it's very jolly." She didn't look at me; we were too close—so close that we might possibly have rubbed noses if either turned. But in her sidelong glance I noted both amusement and irony.

"Have you caught anything, Don Michael?"

"Not a bally thing."

"What are you reading?"

"A book of sorts—a novel by an 'author' who lacks education, cultivation, experience, vocabulary, and a working knowledge of English grammar. In other words, Thusis, a typical American 'author,' —one of the Bolsheviki of literature whose unlettered Bolshevik readers are recruited from the same audience that understands and roars with laughter at the German and Jewish jokes which compose the librettos of our New York musical comedies."

Thusis turned up her pretty nose and shrugged
—or tried to,—but nearly upset me, and desisted.

"It's silly to sit here like two hens on a roost,"
she said.

"It's cozy," said I with a blissful smile that perhaps approached the idiotic.

"Cozy or not," she insisted, "we resemble a pair
of absurd birds."

"Then," said I, "one of us ought to twitter and
begin to sing."

We both laughed. "The last time we were here
together," I reminded her, "you were singing all the
while."

"Was I?"

"Yes, and I liked it—although your detachment
was not flattering to me."

"Poor Michael. Did you feel abused?"

"It's no novel feeling," said I.

"You ungrateful young man! Do you mean to
insinuate that *I* abuse you? I—who go fishing with
you, stop my house-work to gossip with you, sit on
the stairs with you at three in the morning—and in
my nightie, too——"

"What an incident for a best-seller!" said I.
"Fancy the fury of the female critic! Imagine the
rage of the 'good woman'!"

"You are satirical, Don Michael."

"Doesn't satire amuse you?"

"I adore it."

"Nothing," said I, "so angers ignorance as satire, because it is not understood, and ignorance becomes suspicious when it does not understand anything. Ignorance mistakes dullness for depth. That is why dull books are so widely read.

"There is, in America, Thusis, a vast desert inhabited by 'authors' who produce illiterature.

"Similar deserts, though less in area, exist in other sections of America. By its ear-marks, however, I guess that this book was 'authorized' somewhere west of Chicago. Don't read it. Only 'a good woman' could enjoy it."

Thusis laughed. "Don't you admire good women and critics?"

"The American critic," said I, "is usually female but not necessarily feminine in sex. It is what is reverently known as 'a good woman'—and like a truffle-hound its nose for immorality is so keen that it can discover a bad smell where there isn't any."

Thusis threw back her head and yielded to laughter unrestrained.

"So you think there was nothing immoral in sitting on the stairs with you in my nightie?"

"Was there?"

"Of course not. Clean minds are independent of clothes. As for clothing, I often wish these were Greek times and I were rid of all my duds except sandals and a scarf."

"It's all very well for you to wish that, Thusis, but consider the spectacle of the Princess Pudelstoff, for example, in Olympian attire——"

And Thusis went off into a gale of laughter, endangering our mutual stability on the camp-stool. Which scared her,—an unpremeditated bath in the pool having been narrowly averted—and she said again that it was silly of us to sit there like a pair of imbecile dicky-birds.

"Then tune up, Thusis. You seem to know a lot of songs. I liked that odd, weird, sweet little song you kept singing about Naxos and Tenedos."

"I didn't suppose you noticed it, Michael."

"I notice everything concerning you."

Looking at her sideways I saw the charming color deepen in her cheeks.

"Is that paying court to you or making love to you?" I added.

"I don't know. Somehow, when you pay court to me, you make it sound like—the other thing."

"But I *am* in love——"

"Wait," she said hastily. "I'll sing another funny song—the same sort of song you found so amusing—about Naxos and Tenedos. It is called 'Invocations.'"

As a little bird looks up to heaven after every sip of water, so Thusis looked up after inspiration had sufficiently saturated her. She lifted her pretty

197

voice as clearly and sweetly as a linnet sings in the
falling rain:

"Wine poured out to Aphrodite,
On thy sacred sands,
In libations to the mighty
Blue-eyed goddess Aphrodite
Perfumes all thy strands,
Scents the meadows and thy woodlands,
Tenedos, my Tenedos!
Every maiden understands
Why each flowering orchard close
Swims with fragrance of the rose.

Votive wine that long ago
Set thy sacred soil aglow
Sweetens still each Grecian nose
In Tenedos, my Tenedos!

## II

God-like Bacchus with his flighty
Band of laughing jades,
Drank and sang and every night he
Got so classically tight he
Sought thy sylvan glades,
Snoring where he gaily reveled,
Tenedos, my Tenedos!
Mid his pretty nymphs disheveled
Sleeping off the over-dose,
Waking late to vinous woes!

Votive wine that long ago
Set thy sacred groves aglow,
Still exhilarates each nose
In Tenedos, my Tenedos!"

198

"Oh, the cunning little song!" I exclaimed enchanted. "But what is Tenedos, anyway? It's an island, isn't it?"

"It is," said Thusis solemnly.

"Certainly. I remember. And so is Naxos—Greek islands in the Ægean."

"I shall mark you perfect," said Thusis gravely. And she wrote "perfect" in the air with one slim forefinger.

"Why," said I curiously, "do you sing songs about Naxos and Tenedos?"

"Perhaps because I have lived in Naxos and Tenedos."

"I see."

"No, you don't," said Thusis, smiling.

We sat for a while in silence watching the foaming current swerving my line. But no fish moved it.

"They must be pretty—those Greek islands," said I vaguely.

"Do you know their history?"

"No."

"Would you like to hear it?"

"Whatever you say I like to hear," I replied, beginning to ooze sentiment as well as rain.

"You annoy me," said Thusis. "Listen sensibly, if you wish me to tell you about those islands."

Snubbed, I sat silent with an injured expression that afforded her lively satisfaction, judging from her vivacious voice and manner:

199

"You are to know, Michael," she began, "that Naxos is one of the Cyclades, and from the day of the old gods it has been famous for its wine.

"In the thirteenth century it was conquered by Venice. It was made into a duchy. So was Tenedos.

"But these two Venetian Duchies were conquered and annexed by the unspeakable Turk in the sixteenth century. Then Greece recovered Naxos."

She looked down pensively at her folded hands. Presently they became interlocked and I saw the fingers twisting nervously.

"There are," she said, "some people—descendants of the old Venetians in Naxos, who believe that the island ought to belong to Italy . . . and that the duchy ought to be revived and reconstituted."

"Are you one of these people, Thusis?"

"Yes. I am descended from those Venetians. I was born in Naxos."

She remained absorbed in her own reflections for a few moments, then:

"Tenedos, also, ought to become a duchy again. The Turk rules it. He calls it Bogdsha-Adassi. But it was allied with Greece before Christ lived. It should be either Grecian or Italian. . . . And Clelia and I believe that it rightly belongs to Italy."

"How big an island is it?"

"About seven miles long."

We both laughed.

"Are seven miles worth fighting for?" I asked, amused.

"One's back-yard is worth fighting for, isn't it?" she asked calmly.

"Of course. But not for the purpose of establishing a duchy in it."

Thusis didn't seem to consider that remark very funny.

"I'll freely give anything I have," she said hotly, "but I'll fight like a wild-cat to resist the robbery of a single button!"

"I *didn't* steal that button," said I. "I brought it back to you—from Ferdie's dressing-room."

"I wish you wouldn't be so flippant, Michael!"

"Am I?"

"Very."

She really seemed vexed and I asked her pardon.

"But you oughtn't to mention theft to a thief," I added. "I'm trying to steal your heart, you know——"

"Michael, you are insufferable!" she exclaimed with a movement of impatience that almost sent us into the pool. In fact she clutched me and held fast while I struggled to recover our balance. And after I had reëstablished our equilibrium I was low enough, mean enough, to pretend we were still in danger, so heavenly sweet it was to me to feel her little hands close clinging.

Whether or not she discovered my perfidy I was

not certain, for presently she released her grasp and sat very still and flushed beside me, her eyes fixed on the frivolous brook.

Which drove me uneasily toward conversation—the first refuge of the guilty.

"And so," said I, in a casual and pleasant voice, "you are really a descendant of those ancient Venetians who once occupied Naxos."

"I don't wish to continue the subject," she said.

Snubbed again I relapsed into mournful inertia. Which presently she inspected sideways. And after a while she laughed.

"You *are* so ridiculous," she said. "No girl, I fancy, can remain angry with you very long."

"Thusis?"

"What?"

"I want to court you. May I?"

"Yes—if you don't make it resemble the other thing."

"I'll be careful."

"Very well."

And, as I remained buried in reflection: "You may fire when ready, Michael."

"Have you ever lived in the United States?" I asked, astonished.

"I was educated there," she replied demurely.

"Oh, Lord!" said I, "that accounts for a lot of things! Why on earth I didn't suspect it I can't imagine——"

· "Oh, I'm not typical; I'm international, Michael
—cosmopolitan, inter-urban, anti-insular, so to
speak——"

"You're inter-stellar, you beautiful bright
star!——"

"Michael!"

"What?"

"Is that courtship? Or the other?" she inquired.

"Courtship. It's a perfectly proper flight of as-
tronomical fancy. It's a scientific metaphor, Thusis
dear. I'll tell you another:

> "Some lovers woo the Pleiades
> Who shyly flirt from midnight skies,
> But all my vows and all my sighs
>    Are centered in the Cyclades
> Where she I love first saw the light
> —Thusis divine so slim and white—"

"Michael!"

> "I love her noble mind serene,
> I love her ruddy tresses bright,
> I love her slender neck so white,
> I love her heart so young and clean,
> In fact I love her, if she please,
> My goddess of the Cyclades—"

"*Michael!!!*"

"What?" said I, annoyed at being checked in
my fine frenzy.

"Is—is *that* courtship?"

"Certainly! Did you never hear of a troubadour? I'm improvising and for God's sake don't interrupt me."

At that she relapsed into meek silence. But I had lost my momentum. It was all off; she had ruined that totally unexpected burst of inspired fluency which had astonished and intoxicated me, whatever it had done to her.

' "Damnation," I said.

"Forgive me, Michael. I'm so truly repentant.
. . . And it was very, very beautiful."

"It wasn't so bad," I admitted, mollified. "I had no idea I could do it, Thusis."

"It was—agreeable. I liked it. Will you forgive me? Because when I interrupted I punished myself most of all."

"You sweet little thing!——"

"I did. I was worse than Psyche," she went on, "who blew out the candle—too late—the torch of inspiration—Oh, dear, that metaphor is very sadly mixed, Michael, but you understand what I mean. Do you pardon me?"

To reassure her I touched her hands which lay clasped in her lap. She gave a slight start, but as my hand settled and rested there upon both of hers she seemed to become unconscious of the contact.

"I had no idea that you could improvise so cleverly," she said.

"Nor I," said I, frankly. "It's true, however, that I've had some little practice in writing verses —er—recently."

"Have you been writing verses, Michael?"

"Yes."

"About what?"

"About you."

She became interested in my fishing line, and watched it intently. But it was only the current moving it.

"Thusis dear——"

She said hastily: "Remember the difference between courtship and the other!"

"Won't you let me make love to you?"

"I can't, Michael!"

After a pause: "Would you let me if you could?"

"Yes," she said under her breath.

"Dear——"

"Please don't say that!"

"I want to ask you one thing."

"What?"

"You're not married, are you?"

"No."

"Then——"

"It's a more hopeless barrier than that!" she interrupted with a sudden catch in her breath. "I can't let you make love to me. I can't let you love me! I c-can't love you—let myself—do it——"

Her voice was drowned in a terrific roar. All the

thunders of the skies seemed to unite in one tremendous outburst.

Deafened, almost stunned, we sat there partly stupefied by the mighty concussion which lengthened into bellowing thunder until the bank of the stream trembled under our feet, and the umbrella wiggled in my hand.

"Good Lord!" I whispered; but Thusis sprang up with a little cry of dismay.

"Don't be afraid, darling!" I cried, preparing to gather her to my breast. But she was excitedly adjusting her field-glasses and focussing them on the Bec-de l'Empereur.

And then I perceived that the rain had ceased; that the sun was already blazing through the pass below.

"The devil!" cried Thusis, stamping her pretty foot. Then, in a fury of despair, she turned to me and stretched out one arm, pointing toward the valley pass.

And I saw that it had been utterly obliterated by the mighty avalanche, the earth-shaking thunder of which had petrified us.

Suddenly the gray eyes of Thusis filled with tears of fury and disappointment.

"Oh, Michael! Michael!" she faltered, "what shall we do now! We had them all in the trap! We were ready to spring it to-night! Oh, Michael! Michael! M-my heart is b-broken——"

She walked blindly into my arms—she didn't know what she was about, I suppose. I petted and soothed her; she hid her face on my breast.

"Darling," I said, "I can't bear to see you suffer. I suppose that you and Clelia and Josephine and Raoul had some scheme cooked up to kidnap that bunch of huns at the house and get them over the frontier into France. Didn't you, dear?"

"Y-yes. And just l-look what's happened! Look at this act of God! Why has God let it rain? Why has He let loose this avalanche at such a moment!— at such an agonizing moment when we had all the rats trapped! And our own agents on the frontier to let us through! . . . Doesn't God realize that all civilization—all Christendom is tottering? Doesn't He know what hell threatens it? Why has He done this thing to us! Can He not see France bled white! —England reeling!—Italy agasp!—America only half ready!—Naxos prostrate under the Greek tyrant's usurping heel!—Tenedos thrown to the Turk! I—I have begun to lose my faith in God!" she cried violently; "the old gods were less cruel—less indifferent. And at least they displayed enough interest to take sides!"

I continued to pet and comfort and soothe her as I would a half hysterical child.

"God is on duty," I said. "Who are we to divine His strategy? Why take even General Foch. His own officers can't penetrate his purpose; much less

207

can the huns. But he drives the spirits of evil before him; he hustles the hellish legions toward destruction in his own way. The maddened swine are stampeding, Thusis! God's ocean waits."

"Y-yes. I—shall pull myself together. . . . I'm ashamed."

"No, you're all right, Thusis. Take heart. And, if there's any comfort in knowing I'm with you, always, loyally, through life to death——"

I thought, against my breast, there was the slightest pressure in response, but concluded that Thusis had merely braced herself to get away and stand on her own legs. Which she now did, resolutely, but keeping her face averted.

We stood so, gazing down in silence at the snow-choked pass which now cut us off from the world entire.

"After all," said I, "it pens in the huns as well as it cages us. We may get them yet."

The girl straightened up and turned toward me. Her features were radiant, transfigured.

"Nous les aurons!" she cried, throwing her arm out toward the valley with the superb gesture of some young goddess launching thunderbolts.

## XIV

THE distinguished company at the chalet had already gathered on the veranda apparently to contemplate the flaming sunset when, separating from Thusis in the woods behind the barn, I sauntered into view with rod and creel.

Instantly I became a target for Teutonic eyes of the several sorts peculiar to the hunnish race,—cold disapproving eyes, narrow bad-tempered eyes, squinting eyes, gimlet eyes, pale pig-eyes,—all intent on my approach.

"Hello!" cried King Constantine in his loud, bluff way, "have you had any luck, O'Ryan?"

The fat Princess Pudelstoff began to pant cheerfully in anticipation of finny food:

"I hope you've caught some trout," she said in a thick, good-natured voice which the rolls of fat on her neck rendered husky and indistinct. "I like to eat mine *Meunière* and *Blaue-gesotten*. I like 'em breaded and fried in butter. I like plenty of melted butter." She pried open the creel cover as I passed. "Where are the fish?" she asked with a gulp of disappointment.

"I'm sorry, Princess——"

"Droly!" she exclaimed in English, turning to General Count von Dungheim, "he ain't caught a fish! And me smackin' my lips like I was eatin' onto a fat filet! Oh my God!"

Astonished to hear such east-side accents spurting from the lips of the Princess Pudelstoff, I politely explained that the stream was in flood, and that trout wouldn't take hold in high water. In the midst of my apology Baron von Bummelzug uttered a disagreeable laugh and said something rude to Admiral Lauterlaus who stared at me insultingly as he replied: "Skill is not to be expected in a Yankee. Instead of a rod he should have used a net. That's the way *our* peasants fish for trout."

I turned red and looked hard at the Admiral. "There's a net in the barn," said I, "if you want to try your skill!" which infuriated that formidable sea-warrior whose ancestry was purely peasant. He glared at me angrily and his bushy eyebrows worked up and down like the features of a mechanical toy.

"I said our *peasants* fish with a net!" he began, a far, hollow roar audible in his voice like the sound of the sea in a big shell.

"I heard you," said I. "You're welcome to use the net in your own fashion. Gentlemen fish otherwise."

I think everybody was astounded. Only the pretty Countess Manntrapp shot an amused glance at me.

The others were dreadfully shocked. As for the Admiral he got to his feet almost dazed with rage; but before he could expel the bellowing fury which was congesting his features I lost my own temper and walked over to him.

"Behave yourself!" I said sharply. "I tolerate no bad manners under my roof. And if you show me any further disrespect you'll have to leave my house!"

I think he was too amazed to roar. King Ferdinand waddled over to him and plucked him by the arm, restraining him. King Constantine burst into a heavy laugh:

"Here, gentlemen! This will never do! It's all a misunderstanding. No offense was intended, Mr. O'Ryan——"

"Monsieur Xenos," said I, "it is difficult, I fancy, for a Prussian Admiral to avoid taking the offensive—except at sea."

And I walked into the house amid the most profound and paralyzed silence that ever assailed my ears.

Smith, in the living-room, having heard it all, was doubled up with laughter, but I was in no mood for mirth.

"Did you hear what Admiral Lauterlaus said to me!" I demanded, still hot. "Did you hear what that Prussian had the impudence to say to me under my own roof?"

"Yes, and I heard what you said to him, Michael!" And off he went into another fit of laughter.

"You don't know how funny it is," he said. "They've all been conspiring and perspiring all day long shut up in Tino's apartment with those two smelly Bolsheviks. And just when they'd come to some agreement about slicing up the world and ruling it among themselves, along you come and take all the joy out of life by sitting on a Prussian admiral!"

"I certainly shall put him out of the house if he's impudent to me again," said I, wrathfully. "And it will be tough on him if I do, because an avalanche has blocked the pass and we're all sewed up here together!"

"What!" exclaimed Smith with lively interest.

"It's a fact, Smith. The entire snow-field on the south shoulder of the Bec de l'Empereur let go about an hour since. Didn't you hear it?"

"I heard what I took to be thunder. Do you mean we're blocked from the outside world?"

"Completely."

"We can't dig out?"

"Who's to dig?"

"Good business!" he said, plainly delighted by the news. "How long will it last?"

"Thusis says they'll start digging from the other side, but that it may take weeks."

"Thusis knows about this?"

"She was with me at the time," said I, blushing.

He looked at me absently: "I wonder," he mused, "what Thusis thinks about the situation now."

"Our sudden isolation here?"

"Exactly."

"She doesn't seem to like it. . . . Tell me something, Smith?"

"What?"

"Do you know why Thusis and Clelia and Josephine Vannis and Raoul Despres are here?"

"I can guess," he replied, coolly.

"They came here," said I, "to nab Tino and that murderous ass, Ferdinand, and spirit them across the frontier into France."

"I believe so," he said in a serene but preoccupied voice.

"Now they can't do it," I added, "because the only way out of this valley is blocked."

"Quite so."

"Smith?"

"Yes."

"What do *you* think of their doing such a thing?"

"It's all right but they can't get away with it."

"Would you—help them?"

"They haven't asked me."

"*Would* you?" I persisted.

"Would. *you*, Michael?"

"Well, if I do, the Swiss Government would confiscate my property. If Thusis and I succeeded in kidnapping this bunch of Kings, I'd lose this place."

"And if you failed to bag your Kings," remarked Smith, "the Swiss Government would still confiscate your estate and lock you up besides."

"And if *you* went into this affair," said I, "the Swiss would cancel your forestry contract."

"That," said he with a grin, "would be ruinous, wouldn't it?"

"What are you, anyway, Smith?" I demanded bluntly.

"A Viking. What do you think I am?"

"An agent," I replied darkly.

"Timber agent," he nodded.

"Timber nothing. Much less a Viking. I'm on to you, Smith."

"Do you think you are?"

"Well, do you wish to know what I believe you to be?"

"You probably have guessed. So don't say it too loud, Michael. Besides, I have taken no pains to conceal my business from you."

"I think you are an agent of the United States Secret Service," said I. "And I think you learned, somehow or other, that this bunch of Kings was coming here to conspire. And I think you very cleverly picked me up in Berne with a view to being invited here so that you could watch their activities and keep your government informed. How near right am I?"

"You ought to know," he retorted, laughing.

"Well then—if I do know—what are you going to do about this enterprise of Clelia and Thusis? Help them collar this royal gang and smuggle them across the frontier into France?"

He shook his head: "No, I can't do that."

"Your duties do not permit such amusements?"

"No. I am engaged to fulfill a definite duty. In fact I'm pledged to carry out a certain mission. It's a matter of honor. I'm sorry."

"It limits you?"

"It does."

"Checks any adventurous or romantic inclination toward aiding Thusis and Clelia to nab Tino & Co.?"

"I'm afraid it does."

"So you can't do any kidnaping, Smith?"

He laughed. "Oh, as far as that goes, I may have to do some."

"Kidnaping?"

"Possibly."

"You're a strange creature, Smith. And, speaking of strange creatures, who the devil is that Princess Pudelstoff? She talks English like an east-side Jewess."

"She is."

"W-what!!!"

"Certainly."

"The Princess Pudelstoff!"

"Her name was Leah Puppsky. She's the sister

of Leo Puppsky, the Bolshevik envoy sent here with his confrere Isidore Wildkatz by Trotzky and Lenine to confer with Tino and Ferdie. She was once pretty—and she acted in an east-side theatre with Nazimova. Prince Pudelstoff was an attaché of the Russian Embassy at the time. He saw her act, fell in love, and married her,—of course with the Czar's knowledge and consent. But why the Czar let him do it is one of those diplomatic mysteries which remain unfathomed. Some believe that Rasputin had a reason for approving such an alliance." He shrugged.

"What a strange, fat, vulgar, good-natured woman," said I. "And what a grotesque company! Can you beat it?—Bulgar and Bolsheviki, King, Queen, Countess, Baron, Admiral, all jumbled up in this little rest-house where I am trying to live in peace and privacy. And now comes an act of God called an avalanche!—and we're all trapped together—you and I, Thusis and Clelia, and this beastly Bulgarian with his beak of a bird of prey; and that vulgar Greek King and his vixen of a wife, —Oh, Lord!"

"I'm glad God acted," he said cheerfully.

"You're glad that avalanche fell?"

"Yes; I'm very much relieved."

"Why, in the name of Heaven?"

"It simplifies my duties," he said, smiling. And that's all I got out of him except that he advised me to have nothing to do with this enterprise of Thusis and her sister.

"They'll only get you into mischief," he said. "It's a perfectly crazy scheme. Anyway I think it's nipped in the bud, now."

"If the avalanche hadn't fallen——"

"That makes a difference. But it couldn't have been done anyway. So you'd better not encourage Thusis by enlisting with her as a recruit, Michael. Avalanche or no avalanche it can't be done."

"Smith," said I, "if Thusis needs me I am going to help her bag this brace of kings."

"You are?"

"I am."

"You'll lose your property."

"I can't help that."

Smith glanced up at me curiously: "You are in love, Michael.

"I think I am."

"Don't be."

"What!"

"Don't be in love," he repeated gently. "It isn't any use. It's no good, Michael."

What he said annoyed me and he perceived it.

"Oh Lord," he said wearily, "this *is* a mess all around. You don't know what a mess it is, Michael. But all I can tell you is, *don't fall in love with Thusis!* Because it won't do you any good."

"What do you mean? Do you know who Thusis really is?"

"No, I don't. But I do know that it will do you no good to fall in love with her."

"Has it done *you* any good to fall in love with her sister Clelia?" I retorted sharply.

"Not a particle."

"Then why have you done it?"

He winced but said pleasantly: "I fell in love with her before I realized it. Now I'm falling *out* of love with her. I'm curing myself. . . . Besides, she cares nothing about me. . . . It will be easier for me to cure myself than for you to recover if you fall in love."

"Thusis will not listen to a serious word from me," said I with sudden bitterness. "I ought to try to cure myself *now!* . . . But I don't want to."

"Michael," he said, "the pretty Thusis, also, had better be very careful, because she already is as close to caring for you seriously as it is safe for any young girl to care for a man whom she knows she never is going to marry."

"Why do you say that?"

"Because, although I do not know who Thusis really is, I do know that she is not going to marry you. And I do not believe you will ever see Thusis again after this herd of conspirators leaves Swiss soil."

I thought very hard for a while. Then: "Smith,

I have become firmly convinced that Thusis *is* the original of *The Laughing Girl!* Find out who *she* was and you will learn who Thusis is. I'm certain of this. Now who was this Laughing Girl?"

"Nobody knows."

"Have you tried to find out?"

"Yes."

"Did you learn anything at all?"

"Not much."

"What did you learn?"

"That the photographs of The Laughing Girl are not permitted to be sold in Italy."

I looked at him, perplexed. He shrugged his shoulders: "Photographs for sale in European cities," he said, "are usually portraits of celebrities— actresses, demi-mondaines, royalties. Do you suppose Thusis to be one of these?"

"Good heavens!"

"One of the three alternatives is, of course, unthinkable. Your choice would seem to lie, then, between royalty and the drama. *But*—the photographs of the Italian Royal family are sold everywhere in Italy. So are photographs of pretty actresses. Why is the sale of The Laughing Girl forbidden in Italy?"

"*Forbidden?* You didn't say that."

"Forbidden," he repeated calmly.

"That's very strange," said I. "What does it signify, Smith?"

"Well, of course, I have my own theory, as to that."

"You don't care to discuss it?"

He shook his head.

"No, Michael. But it seems to fit in with my general idea concerning the identity of Thusis."

"And do you, too, believe that Thusis is the original of The Laughing Girl?" I asked.

"I have come to believe so."

"Then," said I, "I shall marry her! I've been in love with that photograph ever since I laid eyes on it, and now, when I've found the original, do you suppose I shall let it go at that? You don't know the O'Ryans!"

He began to laugh, but my excitement was rising.

"I'm going to make love to her," said I. "I'm going to help her bag these kings if she wants them. And when we tie them neck and heels and smuggle them into France and turn them over to a pair of strapping gendarmes I shall enlist with the American forces in France, whether Thusis accepts me for her husband or not. That, Smith, is my unalterable decision and my inflexible programme! And my property in Switzerland can go to the devil!"

"There are," said Smith with a peculiar smile, "two reasons why you should not remain in love with Thusis. One is that she won't marry you."

"What's the other?"

"The other is that she couldn't marry you if she wished to."

There was a short silence, then he went on: "Also there are two reasons why you should not help Thusis to kidnap Tino and Ferdie. One is that she isn't able to."

"What's the other?"

"The other is that—*I won't let her.*"

I felt myself growing red and angry.

"That sounds almost pro-hun," said I.

"It does sound so," he admitted.

"Of course you're not pro-German," I added incredulously.

"Of course not," he rejoined calmly.

"Then——"

"I can't explain. I'm merely warning you not to aid her in this affair."

"Does Thusis know your attitude?"

"No, but she will."

"You are going to tell her?"

"No; but *you* are."

"I certainly shall," said I, warmly. "And I'd like to know why you are interfering with what she desires to do."

"I can't tell you why, Michael; but I'll tell *her* why—if she asks me."

"You may be very sure that Thusis will ask you, Smith," said I, perplexed to the verge of exasperation by his amazing attitude.

"Suppose *you* tell her," he said, amused. "All you need do is to repeat this couplet to her:

*"Grecian gift and Spanish fig
Help the fool his grave to dig!"*

"What idiot's jargon is that!" I demanded.

"A jargon that is likely to hold our pretty Thusis for a while. It is a word of warning—a signal of danger used by members of a secret society known as the Ægean League. Also it is likely to start her looking for me. And when she finds me I think she'll listen to reason and renounce this silly and useless attempt to trap royalty wholesale for export purposes. Not," he added gaily, "that I shouldn't expire with laughter to see Raoul and you, for example, take that pair of kings by the slack of the pants and run them Spanish into France. I'd applaud it, old top. I'd give frequent cheers during the process. But Thusis and Clelia mustn't start any such shindy. No! And if they inquire why, just repeat that verse to them and refer them to me."

"Then you are *not* here to watch these hun conspirators?" I asked in astonishment.

"Only incidentally."

"Do you mean to say that you are here, primarily, to watch Thusis and Clelia?"

"That is exactly why I am here, Michael. And I don't mind your telling them so. I myself was going to tell them. I had intended to break the news to them to-night. But the avalanche makes it unnecessary; they can't get out of this valley with their cartload of kings, now. However, let me suggest that you repeat that couplet to Thusis."

"This," said I, "is a most astounding and disagreeable series of complications. I don't understand them. I don't understand Thusis or you or that bagful of boches downstairs."

"Don't try to, old chap," he said in his friendly way. "And above all, don't break your heart over Thusis. For when the snow that blocks the pass melts, or when somebody digs through, I don't believe you are ever likely to see Thusis again."

His kindly sincerity scared and angered me.

"Watch me!" said I. "An O'Ryan never loves but once. But when he does love——"

"All right, old fellow. Go to it and God help you. They say He has a warm spot in His heart for the Irish."

I nodded, looking at him very seriously: "It's quite impossible," said I, "that she's royal. And if she's an actress I don't care, because I'm so deeply in love with her that I don't know whether I'm afoot or on horseback. And when an O'Ryan feels that way the world is his or he continues on to Heaven."

"Does it really mean Life or Death to you already, Michael?" he asked gravely.

"Life or death, sink or swim, survive or perish,—as some Yankee orator said once. Nothing matters now except Thusis. That's my only reason for living. Yesterday I wanted wealth, to-day my estate can go to the deuce. Yesterday I was a rather sober, decent citizen, perpetrating interior decoration in New York, to-day I figuratively kick the varnish off period furniture, tear down tapestries, smash Chinese pottery, and wipe my feet on the rags of Renaissance! Art is nothing! Thusis is everything. If she wants a few kings to play with, she shall have them. I'll bag them for her. I'll do anything in the world for her. And if that's not enough I'll step off this damned old planet and pull wires aloft for the honor and glory and happiness of the noblest, sweetest, loveliest, most beauti——"

A slight exclamation behind me checked my excited confession.

Slowly turning in my tracks I beheld Thusis at the door in cap and apron.

There was a terrific silence.

Then Thusis, her fair face deeply flushed, dropped us a curtsey.

"Dinner is served, sir," she said faintly. And was gone like a shadow.

# XV

## A TRAVELING CIRCUS

THE royal traveling circus was already seated and whetting its appetite with hors d'œuvres, when I arrived in the dining-room and, saluting my guests, took my place as host at the head of the long table.

Heaven! What a collection! Being incognito, I was not supposed to be aware of the identity of royalty; but Thusis had seated the ex-queen of Greece on my right and Tino on my left, and, beyond Queen Sophia, she had put the Tsar of all the Bulgars,— with a clean napkin where he had soiled the cover.

The new accessions to this traveling show had, very evidently, decided among themselves the places at table to which they were entitled by precedence of rank. And these they now occupied.

The two Bolsheviki, Leo Puppsky and Isidore Wildkatz, had been relegated to the foot of the table where they sat hunched up and scowling about them until noodle soup presently preoccupied them.

I do not know which one of my guests was the noisiest: the Tsar of all the Bulgars sucked up his soup with the distressingly acute sound of a sick

horse drinking; the Princess Pudelstoff lapped and
slobbered and wheezed in her slopping plate; but the
technique of the Bolsheviki was simple and more ef-
fective, being reduced to a primitive, incessant gobbling noise, followed by patient and persistent scraping.

Behind my chair stood Raoul as extemporary but-
ler; Thusis and Clelia in spotless caps and aprons
sped lightly hither and thither; while from the
depths of the kitchen, Josephine Vannis fed us all
with the most delectable dinner which I think I ever
tasted.

Ordinary wine being included on my bill of fare,
the Tsar guzzled it while his sly eye of a wild pig
roved about reading labels on the various bottles
of more expensive wine ordered by the others.

The Bolsheviki, having plenty of the Russian people's money, demanded "bowcoo tchimpagne"; King
Tino drank goblets of a rather heavy claret; his
wife sipped only bottled water, while her cold, steely
eyes glittered from guest to guest.

I conversed politely when spoken to; otherwise I
made no effort. The Prussian admiral worked his
bushy eyebrows and his coarse, fan-shaped beard
while munching, but whether in hostility to me or because he was built that way, I did not know, and
did not care.

He and Baron von Bummelzug sat all hunched up
side by side, gobbling in their whiskers and exchang-

ing Teutonic grunts which seemed to be their sub-
stitute for human conversation. Herr Secretary
Gizzler, factotum to the Baron, and seated with the
Bolsheviki, devastated his plate and seized ravenously
upon anything eatable in his vicinity, which presently elicited a chattering protest from Puppsky; and
a quarrel rapidly developed until squelched by General Count von Dungheim.

"Silence!" he said angrily: "you make so much
noise that it is impossible to hear oneself eat!"

The Princess Pudelstoff nodded violently, balanc-
ing a knifeful of mashed potato before committing
it to its dreadful destiny:

"They act," she said in English, "like they was
never to a high-toned dinner. It's them two Bolsheviks that ain't had a square meal since Hindy
licked the Rooshians at the Missouri Lakes."

Leo Puppsky made a violent gesture at her with
the leg of a chicken:

"Is that the way to speak of us?" he said to his
sister. "And you a Russian and my own sister!"

"Ain't it true?" she asked with a loud laugh.
"Get sense, Leo. There won't be nothing to eat in
Rooshia so long as you act ugly to Germany——"

"Princess!" interrupted the queen of Greece,
sharply.

"That's right," said Tino in a loud, good humored voice; "one doesn't discuss politics while din-

ing. No! One pays strict attention to what one eats and drinks; eh, Sophy?"

The queen ignored him, and he slyly batted one eye at the pretty Countess Manntrapp, his neighbor, and tossed off a brimming goblet of deep red claret.

"Aha!" he said, smacking his lips, "that beats even the wine of Naxos. Did you ever drink Naxos wine, Countess?"

"No," said she; "is it very excellent?"

"Heady, Countess, heady! After you crack one bottle you begin to see the old gods of Greece sitting beside you on pink clouds in their underclothes——"

"Tino!" snapped the Queen.

The Countess laughed. "I'd like to see them." She looked across at me with her fascinating, audacious smile: "Wouldn't you like to drink Naxos wine with me, Mr. O'Ryan, and see the old time gods come down out of the blue sky and sit at table all about you?"

"It seems to me," said I, bowing, "that Aphrodite has already arrived among us mortals."

She laughed, acknowledging the raw compliment, then pursing up her red mouth but uttering no sound she nevertheless formed her question so that I read every word on her mobile lips:

"Do — you — know — anybody — who — would — play — Adonis — to — my — Venus?"

And she laughed her daring little laugh and made

me a pretty gesture, intercepted by Ferdinand of
Bulgaria who took it for himself and continued to
ogle her out of passionate, pig-like eyes until further engrossed in a new relay of food.

It was a dreadful dinner party. Both the kings
made life wretched for Clelia and Thusis as they
waited on table, slyly pinching them when unob-
served until, from Thusis' burning cheeks and trem-
bling hands as she served me, I almost feared she
would launch a plate at the royal libertines.

It was a weird company. The Bolsheviki chattered and grabbed at food; all the Germans ate
noisily—excepting only the pretty Countess Manntrapp, who had been Lila Shezawitch, and not a Teuton by birth.

Constantine had had more claret than was good
for him and now he was pouring into himself count-
less little glasses of brandy, and was becoming
loudly and somewhat coarsely talkative, retailing bits
of barrack-room gossip to General Count von Dungheim and cracking dubious jokes with Baron von
Bummelzug until his wife spoke to him with such
cutting contempt that he winced and relapsed into
a half hazy and giggling exchange of whispers with
the Countess Manntrapp. As for the Princess
Pudelstoff, she had never for one moment ceased
stuffing herself. Sweat stood in oily beads on her
forehead and cheeks; her fat hands plied knife and
fork and spoon without interruption save when

she grasped her beer mug in both jeweled hands and drew mighty and noisy draughts from the heavy quart receptacle.

The whole performance at my table was becoming a horrid nightmare to me; I could not see any signs of satiation among these dreadful people—any desire to call it off and quit and retire to their respective sties.

Smith caught my eye and I saw him suppress the smile that twitched his features.

Then it suddenly occurred to me that I had news for the traveling circus that might modify their appetites; and I said, distinctly, and raising my voice sufficiently to command attention from everybody:

"There is some very serious information which I regret that it is necessary to share with everybody here. I did not wish to spoil your appetites. But dinner is over, and I had better speak."

All feeding ceased; everybody stared at me.

"I regret that I am obliged to inform you," I continued, "that the snow field on the south flank of the Bec de l'Empereur, loosened by the warm deluge of rain, has fallen, completely choking the pass which is our only entrance to and exit from this valley."

"An avalanche!" exclaimed the Queen of Greece sharply.

"Yes, madame, a very bad one."

"We are blocked in," she gasped.

"Absolutely."

At that the Princess Pudelstoff uttered a squeak of fright: "We're all going to starve!" she squealed in alarm; "that's what he means! There isn't enough food for us and we'll all die the way they are dying in Rooshia——"

"There's plenty of food," I interrupted.

"Ach, Gott sei dank! Gott sei dank!" she shouted, clapping her pudgy hands and seizing knife and fork again.

But the others were now rising from their seats, exchanging glances full of anxiety and perplexity; and, as I left the room with Smith, I saw them all gathering around the Ex-Queen of Greece as though general consternation had seized them. Only the Princess Pudelstoff remained in her chair, devouring tartlets, her triple chin agitated by a series of convulsive shudders as she bolted sections of pastry too large for her.

Coffee was to be served *al fresco;* Raoul had set a number of green iron tables and chairs out by the fountain.

"My heavens, Smith," said I, "we should serve them coffee in a common trough. Did you ever before endure such misery at any table?"

"Oh, yes," he said, "I've lived in Germany."

"Well I haven't, and I'm going to skip the demitasse," I rejoined. And I walked around the house and entered the back door where two latticed arbors flanked the stone walk.

Here I seated myself and lighted a cigarette, still unnerved by the martyrdom of that dinner table.

It was quiet and peaceful in the sunset light under my roof of curly grape leaves where sun spots glowed amid the tender green and two little active birds climbed busily and silently about the foliage in search of aphids.

I had been sitting there for ten minutes, perhaps, when the door opened behind me and Thusis appeared with coffee. Her lovely features still were tinged with the rosy glow of recent wrath; her gray eyes were still brilliant with the same emotion.

"Coffee, if you please, sir?" she said crisply.

I had risen, smiling.

"You need not have taken so much trouble, Thusis——"

"Pardon. It is what servants are hired for."

"Why do you keep up this masquerade with me?" I asked, laughingly, taking the cup from the tray.

But Thusis seemed to be in no pleasant humor, and she turned to go without answering.

"Thusis!"

She halted.

"I'm sorry those beastly kings annoyed you at table——"

"They're men," she retorted angrily. "What can a woman expect?"

"Do you think that is fair to me, Thusis, to lump me with men in general?"

"I don't know what's fair to you. And I'm really not very particular about it. Little chance that men ever suffer too much from being misunderstood in this world."

"You are amazingly unjust, do you realize it?"

"I'm not sure that I am," she said sullenly. "You made your début by trying to kiss your own cook. Tino is coarser, he pinches; Ferdie the furtive, pushes one with his knees and rolls wild eyes at one. There are three masculine examples. Take your choice, Monsieur," she added, going.

"Wait!"

She turned haughtily, her gray eyes suddenly insolent.

"Because you are hurt and offended and humiliated by a pair of scoundrels," said I, "is no reason why you should visit your displeasure on me."

"I make no difference in men."

"Not even in the man who is in love with you?"

"Love? *Love!*" She laughed, not agreeably. "I am not flattered, Monsieur, to have offered to me the same adoration which you were quite willing to bestow upon your cook. I tell you all men *are* alike! —including the Pharisee."

"Do you mean me?"

"Haven't you practically just thanked God you are not like other men?"

"What have I done to deserve this, Thusis? I'm trying to be patient——"

"You don't need to be. Heaven deliver me from a patient man!"

Then I blew up: "You listen to me, you little idiot," I said in a low, enraged tone; "I'm in love with you and you can't help it whatever you choose to do about it. You came here as a servant and I fell in love with you as a servant. You are probably something else—God knows what—and I'm more in love than ever with God-knows-what! I don't care what you are, servant, bourgeoise, actress, princess, or demi-mondaine——"

"*What!*"

"I tell you I wouldn't care. I love you. I want to marry you——"

"Marry me if I were—a demi——"

"Yes!" I said violently; "yes! yes! yes! It's too late to have whatever you are make any difference to me. I'm an O'Ryan and I love only once."

"Do you suppose I'm flattered by what you've just shouted at me? You'd marry me—or you'd do the same for a demi——"

"Confound it!" I exclaimed, "it's *you*, whatever you are! Can't you understand——"

"Certainly I can. All men are men first, last, all the time. That Serbian married Draga; any man will do as much for any drab if he can't have her otherwise. I've seen enough of men, I tell you. Royal, noble, landed gentry, bourgeoisie, peasantry

234

—all are men first, last, all the time; and all are exactly alike!"

She clenched her hand and confronted me with scornful eyes:

"And why any honest woman should ever fall in love with one of them is one of those ignoble mysteries which I have never cared to fathom!"

Her contempt and my own fury almost paralyzed me.

I said, finally, in a very quiet voice, not my own:

"Very well, Thusis, expect nothing more of me than you expect of any man—including those royal gentlemen out yonder. And I'll not disappoint you."

I stepped nearer, forcing a smile:

"You've succeeded in slaying any consideration I entertained for your sex. You've enlightened me. In future I'll take them as I find them, easily, lightly, good-humoredly, with gaiety, with gratitude to the old time gods when they send a pretty one my way."

And I smiled at Thusis who looked darkly back at me with the faintest hint of uncertainty in her eyes.

"It is wonderful," said I, "how a word or two from a woman sometimes clears up the most serious situations. Your revelations concerning my sex in general have opened my eyes. I take your word for it that man is always man, as you explain so convincingly, and that he is, first, last, and all the time, merely a jackass endowed with speech."

I emptied my coffee cup and set it upon the tray which she held in her left hand.

"I had," said I, "something else to tell you—and which had nothing whatever to do with love. But, on second thoughts, I am so certain that a self-sufficient girl like yourself is amply able to look out for herself, that I shall not bother to say what I had intended saying."

Her gray eyes became intently fixed on mine while her color came and went under the sting of irony.

But I made up my mind to let matters take their course. If she tried to body-snatch this Greek and Bulgarian carrion, let her! If Smith interfered, let him! What was it to me after all? I was becoming fed up on love and feminine caprice—on kings and queens and shocking manners,—on intrigue and treachery and counter plot.

Suddenly, as I stood there, a wave of disgust swept over me. I was sick of Switzerland; sick of the ridiculous property which was causing me all this trouble and discomfort; sick of the grotesque whim of Fate which had yanked me out of an orderly, unaccented life and a peaceful profession in Manhattan and had slammed me down here in the midst of love and Alps and kings!

"I'll chuck the estate and go home!" I exclaimed. "I'll go now, to-night!" And then I remembered the accursed avalanche.

She was watching me intently, curiously, and I noticed she had lost some of her colour.

"Do you suppose," said I, "that there is any way of climbing over that mass of snow?—any way of my getting out of this valley to-night?"

"Would you go if you could?" she asked in a rather colorless voice.

"Yes, I would," said I savagely. "I've had enough."

"I'm sorry."

"Sorry that I've had enough?" I sneered.

"Sorry you cannot leave the valley to-night," she said quietly.

"Then it is not possible?"

"I'm afraid not. . . . If it were, I also would leave this valley to-night."

"With a bagful of kings," I added.

"Yes," she said simply.

"Oh, no, you wouldn't," said I with unworthy satisfaction in my knowledge of Smith's mission. "And let me tell you a thing or two, Thusis. You seem to resemble, more or less, a very naughty little girl, spoiled but precocious, who has run away from school and is raising the devil out of bounds, throwing stones and ringing door-bells and defying policemen with derisive tongue. Pretty soon you'll be caught and led home and soundly spanked. And," I added fervently, "I'd like to be in the vicinity of that wood-shed when discipline begins."

My laughter was fairly genuine. I lighted a cigarette and, gazing at this girl who had so outra-
geously maligned me, felt so much better that a ma-
cabre sort of gaiety verging upon frivolity invaded
me.

"All women," said I, "are women, first, last, and
all the time."

Thusis flushed.

"I am wondering," said I airily, "whether the rôle
of Adonis might suit me."

"What!" she exclaimed.

"Adonis," I repeated. "He was that poor fish
of an amateur who played opposite Aphrodite. And
got the hook. But the rôle is all right and it's a
no-character part if you play it straight. . . . I'm
wondering——" And I smiled at my own thoughts and
blew three rings of smoke up at the sun-lit grape
leaves overhead.

Suddenly Thusis unclosed her soft, fresh lips,
which seemed a trifle tremulous:

"That woman," she said breathlessly, "is notorious in Vienna! And if you are—sufficiently aban-
doned—to d-degrade yourself by—an affair—with
her——"

"But what do you care, Thusis?"

Her face flamed. "I care—*that!*" she said, snap-
ping her white fingers. And turned swiftly on her
heel.

# XVI

I WAS very unhappy. I was not only madly in love with Thusis but also mad enough to spank her. And I sat down in the arbor once more a prey to mixed emotions.

The two silent little birds had gone to bed. Soft mauve shadows lay across the scrubby foreland; snow peaks assumed the hue of pink pearls; a wavering light played through the valley so that the world seemed to quiver in primrose tints.

Then, through the pale yellow glory, a girl came drifting as though part of the delicate beauty of it all,—her frail, primrose evening gown and scarf scarcely outlined—scarcely detached from the golden clarity about her. It was as though she were lost in the monotone of living light—the only accent the dusky symmetry of her head.

I had not realized that the Countess Manntrapp was so pretty.

I was not sure that she had discovered me at all until she turned her head *en passant* and sent me one of those vague smiles calculated to stir the dead bones of saints.

"I suppose," she said, "you only look lonely, but really you are not."

I *was* lonely and sore at heart. Possibly she read in my forced smile something of my state of mind, for she paused leisurely by the arbor and glanced about her at the grape leaves.

"Evidently," she said, "this spot is sacred to Bacchus. But I was not looking for gods or half-gods. . . . Do you prefer your own company, Mr. O'Ryan?"

"No, I don't," said I. So she entered the arbor and seated herself. There was only that one seat. With strictest economy it could accommodate two; but I had not thought of attempting it until she carelessly suggested it.

"How heavenly still it is," she murmured, an absent expression in her dark eyes. "Are you fond of stillness and solitude?"

"Not very," said I. "Are you, Countess?"

She said, dreamily, that she was, but her side glance belied her. Never did the goddess of mischief look at me out of two human eyes as audaciously as she was doing now. And it was so transparent a challenge, so utterly without disguise, that we both laughed.

I don't know why I laughed unless the soreness in mind and heart had provoked their natural reaction. A listless endurance of suffering is the first symptom of indifference—that blessed anodyne with which instinct inoculates unhappy hearts when the bitterness which was sorrow wears away and leaves only dull resignation.

"At dinner," she said, "I made up my mind that you are an interesting man. I am wondering."

"I came to a similar conclusion concerning you," said I. "But I'm no longer wondering how near right I am."

"Such a pretty compliment! Also it dissipates any doubts regarding you."

"Did you have any, Countess?"

"Well, you know what I asked you at dinner. You understood? You read lips, don't you?"

"I read yours."

"I wasn't sure. You gave me no answer."

We laughed lightly. "What answer can a mortal make when Aphrodite commands?" said I.

"Then you are willing to play Adonis?"

"Quite as willing—as was that young gentleman."

"That isn't kind of you, Mr. O'Ryan. He wasn't very willing, was he?"

"Not very. But possibly he had a premonition of the tragic consequences," said I, laughing. "One doesn't frivol with a goddess with impunity."

"Are you afraid?"

She turned in the narrow seat. She was altogether too near, but I couldn't help it. And I was much disturbed to find our fingers had become very lightly intertwined.

She was smiling when I kissed her. But after I had done it her smile faded, and the gay confidence in her expression altered.

I had never expected to see in her eyes any hint of confusion, but it was there, and a sort of shamed surprise, too—odd emotions for a hardened coquette with the reputation she enjoyed.

"You proceed too rapidly," she said, the bright but subtly changed smile still stamped on her lips. "There seems to be no finesse about Americans— no leisurely technique that masters the intricacies of the ante-climax. Did you not know that hesitation is an art; that the only perfect happiness is in suspense?"

"Didn't you want to be kissed?" I asked bluntly. "I had perhaps surmised that it might not be a disagreeable sensation. Was it?"

She seemed to have recovered her careless audacity, and now she laughed.

"At all events," she said, "I shall not repeat the experiment . . . this evening." She laid one soft hand in mine with a gay little smile: "Let us enjoy our new friendship serenely and without undue emotion," she said. "And let me tell you how you have made me laugh at what you said to those absurd Prussians!"

We both laughed, but I was now on my guard with this girl who had come here in such company.

"No Prussian ever born ever knew how to make a friend," she said. "To-day they have the whole world against them—even your country——"

"I am Chilean," said I pleasantly.

"Are you *really?*"

"I think you and your friends are quite sure of that," said I drily.

"Suppose," she said in a lower voice, "I tell you that they are not my friends?"

I smiled.

"You wouldn't believe me?" she asked.

"What I believe and do not believe, dear Countess, should not disturb you in the slightest."

"I thought we were friends."

"Do you *really* think so?"

"I hope so. I wish it—if you do. And friendship does not fear confidences."

"Neutrals have no confidences to make. My country is not at war."

"Is not your heart enlisted?" she asked, smilingly.

"Is yours?"

"Yes, it is! See how my friendship refuses no confidence when you ask? *I* do not hesitate."

"On which side," said I, warily, "is your heart enlisted?"

"Shall I tell you?"

"If you care to."

She sat looking at me intently, her soft hand in mine. Then, with a pretty gesture, she placed the other hand over it, and her shoulder came into contact with mine.

"I am Russian," she said. "Is that not an answer?"

"So is Puppsky," I remarked.

For a second an odd expression came over her face and it turned quite white. Then she laughed.

"I'll tell you something," she said. "I have a girl friend. I love her dearly. I have a country. I love it still more dearly. The girl I love is Adelaide, Grand Duchess of Luxemburg. Prussia has practically annexed it. The country I love is Russia. Prussia holds it. . . . Do you still doubt me?"

"Good Lord," thought I, "how this girl can lie!" But I said: "Tell me about Luxemburg, Countess. Is it true that Prince Ruprecht of Bavaria means to marry the seventeen-year-old sister of the Grand Duchess Adelaide?"

"Yes," she said. And I distinctly heard her teeth snap.

"What sort of man is Ruprecht?" I inquired, to steer the conversation toward easier ground.

"Ruprecht! Did you ever see him?"

"No."

"Well, he has the manners of the barn-yard and the distinction of a scullion! Picture to yourself a man of fifty-seven with a head as square as a battered bullet and the bodily grace of a new-born camel. He is the stupidest, coarsest, commonest vulgarian in Europe.

"Why, the man is ridiculous! He once set all Munich laughing by appearing in the English Garden on skates wearing his spurs and saber. And all his military suite had to do likewise. Picture the result—and Ruprecht scarcely knew how to stand on the ice! Why their swords got between their legs and their spurs did the rest, and the entire lake resounded with the incessant crash of falling warriors."

She threw back her head and laughed; and I laughed too.

"Such a brute," she said. "His first wife, daughter of that kindly and philanthropic oculist, Karl Theodore of Tegernsee, died of his neglect and ill treatment. And now, at fifty-seven, he rolls his hog's eyes in his freckled face and smirks at a seventeen-year-old child—God help her!"

I gazed in amazement at the Countess Manntrapp. This was acting with a vengeance. Such perfection, such flawless interpretation of the rôle she was playing for my benefit, I had never dreamed possible. No emotion could appear more genuine, no sincerity more perfectly mimicked. Here was an actress without equal in my entire experience.

Suddenly I caught her eye, and turned very red.

"You don't believe me," she said calmly, and dropped her head.

There was a painful silence between us. Presently she looked up at me, flushed, curious, amused:

"You take me for a Hun, don't you?"

"If you are not pro-German," said I, much embarrassed, "what are you doing with those people?"

"Watching them. And you don't believe that, either?"

"I'm sorry, Countess."

"Why do you doubt me?"

"Because only a pro-German would confide to a stranger that she is not one. Were you really in the Allied service you'd keep your own council. Secret agents don't betray themselves to strangers. You have no means of knowing where my sympathies lie. How do you know I am not pro-German?"

"By your letters."

"My letters?"

"I opened several," she said naïvely.

"Where!"

"In Berne."

"You stole my letters?"

"Yes, I had to."

"How did you do it?"

"The postman is in my pay."

"That," said I angrily, "is a most outrageous confession, Countess."

"But I had to know what your politics are," she explained gently. "Besides, if I had not stolen all your letters the Swiss authorities would have opened

them and found out that you are pro-Ally in sentiment. And then you would not have been permitted
to come here and live in this house. And all these
people would not have come here either. And I
should have had nobody to help me while keeping
these people under surveillance."

"You count on me to help you?" I demanded, too
astonished to remain angry.

"May I not?" she asked sweetly.

"So that's the reason," said I, "that you let me
kiss you."

"I must be honest, it is."

With every atom of conceit knocked out of me,
wincing, chagrined, I found nothing to say to this
pretty woman who sat so close beside me and looked
at me with a half smile hovering on her lips and out
of sweet, dark eyes that seemed utterly honest—
God help her.

"It is only your vanity that is smarting a little,"
she said, smiling, "not your heart. I haven't touched
that at all."

"How do you know?" I retorted.

"Because you are in love with somebody else, Mr.
O'Ryan."

"With whom?" I demanded defiantly.

"I don't know. But you are in love. A woman
can tell."

"I am *not* in love," said I with angry emphasis,
recollecting the treatment meted out to me by

Thusis. "I'm not in love with anybody." I caught her doubting but interested eyes fixed intently on me —"unless," I added recklessly, "I'm in love with you."

"But you're not."

We looked at each other curiously, almost searchingly, not inclined to laugh yet ready, perhaps, for further mischief. Why not preoccupy my mind with this amusing and pretty woman, and slay in my heart all regard for Thusis?

So I kissed her with that object in view. She said nothing—scarcely defended herself—sitting with pretty head lowered and white jeweled hands tightly folded in her lap.

"I'll take you trout-fishing," said I, determined to exterminate and root out all tender memories of Thusis.

She looked up: "May I ask you a question?"

"What is it?" I returned, suspiciously, instantly on my guard again.

"Who is Mr. Smith?"

"A Norwegian." And I explained Smith's business with the Swiss government.

She nodded absently. Probably she did not believe this. As far as that was concerned, neither did I.

"Answer me a question, will you, Countess?" said I in my turn. She smiled: "What is it?"

"Is your kiss really worth the information you extract from me?"

In spite of her light laughter she turned quite pink, and when I bent toward her again, she laid her arm across her lips, defending them.

Then, as I was preparing for further indiscretion, the door behind us opened and was closed again instantly. I knew it was Thusis. The certainty chilled my very bones.

"Who was it?" I asked carelessly.

"Only the waitress," said she.

"The red-haired one?"

"I believe so. Is she Swiss?"

I did not answer.

The Countess looked up and repeated the question. "Where did you find her?" she added.

There was a short silence. An almost imperceptible change came over her features. Then, daintily, and by degrees, she inclined her head a little nearer.

But it was not in me to betray Thusis for a kiss. Slowly, however, I became aware that I was betraying myself.

Presently the Countess rose in the gathering dusk, and I stood up immediately.

She inspected me steadily for a full minute, then that almost imperceptible smile edged her lips again and she gave me my *congé* with a gentle nod.

# XVII

I DISCOVERED Smith sitting on the rim of the fountain all alone in the dusk.

"Good heavens!" I blurted out, "was any man ever so completely entangled in the web of intrigue as I am? Plot, counterplot, camouflage, mystery—I'm in the very middle of the whole mess!

"I don't know who anybody is or what they're up to! Who is Thusis? Who is Clelia? Who is Josephine Vannis? Raoul? The Countess Manntrapp? And who are *you*, for that matter? I don't know! I don't pretend to guess."

"What's the trouble?" he asked, amused.

"Trouble! I don't know. There's all kinds of trouble lying around. I'm in several varieties of it. Where is the traveling circus?"

"In Tsar Ferdie's apartments."

"Probably conspiring," I added.

"Probably."

"What are you doing out here?"

"Oh, I'm not conspiring," he said, laughing, "I'm no saint to converse with the fishes in your fountain."

"Where is Clelia?"

He said he didn't know but somehow I gathered the impression that she was somewhere behind the lighted kitchen windows and that Smith was hanging around in hopes she mi it come out to take the air by starlight.

"Have you seen Thusis?" I asked guiltily. And felt my ears burning in the dark.

"Why, yes," he said. "She walked down the road a few moments ago."

"Alone?"

"Yes."

"Probably she went to take a look at the snow blockade," said I.

He nodded.

"Perhaps," I added carelessly, "I had better saunter down that way."

"No," he said, "you'd better not."

"Why?" I asked sharply.

"Starlight and Thusis might go to a young man's head."

"I'm no longer in love," said I in the most solemn tones I had ever used. "I am now able to contemplate Thusis without the stormy emotions which once assailed me, Smith. All that is over. To me she is merely an interesting and rather pathetic woman. I feel kindly toward Thusis. I wish her well. I would willingly do anything I could to——"

"Piffle."

251

"What the devil do you mean by that?" I demanded.

"What the devil do you mean by kidding yourself?"

"Haven't I just explained?"

"You've given yourself away. A man doesn't utter pious sentiments about a girl he no longer cares for. He doesn't bother to explain his regenerated attitude toward her. He doesn't trouble himself to talk about her at all. Nor does he go roaming after her by starlight. If you really care for her no longer, let her alone. If you do care you'll get mad at what I say—as you're doing—and start off to find her in the starlight—*as* you're doing——"

But I was too exasperated to listen to such stuff.

I discovered her, finally, in the starlight just ahead of me,—a slim shadow on the high-road, outlined against a stupendous mass of snow which choked the valley like a glacier.

She heard my steps on the hard stone road, looked over her shoulder, then turned sharply, paying me no further attention, even when I came up beside her.

"Gracious!" said I, attempting an easy tone and manner; "what a tremendous fall was here!"

"I have known greater falls," she said very quietly.

"Really?"

"Yes; I once had a friend whose fall was greater."

"Poor fellow! He fell off a precipice, I presume."

"He fell from his high estate, Mr. O'Ryan."

"Oh. Did he also have an estate in the Alps?"

She said scornfully: "He fell in my esteem— deep, Mr. O'Ryan—into depths so terrible that, even if I leaned over to look, I could never again perceive him."

"Poor fellow," I muttered, chilled to the bone again.

"Yes," she said calmly, "it was tragic."

"D-did you care for him, Thusis?" I ventured, scared half to death.

"I trusted him."

"D-don't you trust him any more?"

"He is dead—to me," she said coldly.

There ensued a silence which presently I became unable to endure.

"You know, Thusis, that man isn't dead——"

"He might better be!"

"You don't understand him!"

"I no longer wish to."

"He loves you!"

"He does *not!*" she cried in tones so fierce that I almost jumped.

"Thusis," said I in a miserable voice, "you hurt and wounded that man until he was almost out of his senses——"

"And he lost no time in consoling himself with another woman!"

"He didn't know what he was doing——"

"He seemed to! . . . So did *she!*"

"Thusis——"

"*Did* you kiss her?"

"I——"

"Did you?"

"Yes."

I was so scared that my teeth chattered when Thusis turned on me in the starlight.

Her gray eyes were aflame; her little hands were tightly clenched. I hoped she would upper-cut me and mercifully put me to sleep, for this scene was like a nightmare to me.

Then, of a sudden, the slender figure seemed to wilt before my eyes,—shrink, bend, stand swaying with desperate hands covering the face.

"Michael," she whispered. "Michael!"—and her voice ended in a sigh.

Scared as I was I took her in my arms. She rested her face against my shoulder.

"You—you don't really care," I stammered, "do you, Thusis? *Do* you, my darling——"

"Oh, I don't know—I don't know. You've hurt me, Michael; I'm all hurt and—and quivering with your wound. I don't know!—I don't understand myself. My heart is sore—all raw and sore. So is

254

my mind—i..e blow you dealt hurts me there,
too——"

"But, Thusis dear!  *You* wounded me, too——"

"Oh, I know. . . . I scarcely knew what I said.  I
don't know now what I'm saying—what I'm doing—
here in your arms——"  She tried to release herself, and, failing, buried her face against my shoulder with a convulsive little shudder.

"You *must* love me," I whispered unsteadily.  "I
can't live without you, Thusis."

"But I *can't* love you, Michael."

"Can't you find it in your heart to care for me?"

"In my heart, perhaps. . . . But not in my
mind."

"What do you mean?"

"I mean exactly that. . . . I can't consult my—
my heart alone. . . . I must not.  I dare not.  I am
obliged to consult my senses, too.  And—dear
Michael—my senses tell me that I may not care for
you—must not fall in love—with you——"

"Why?"

After a silence she lifted her lovely head and
looked up at me out of beautiful, distressed eyes
that dumbly asked indulgence.

"Well, then, you need not tell me, Thusis."

"You'll know, some day."

"I'll know, some day, why I won you in spite of
everything."

She gently shook her head.

"Yes," said I, "I shall win you, Thusis."

"My heart—perhaps."

"Your mind, too."

We remained so, for a while, not speaking lest the spell be broken. And at last she slowly disengaged herself from my arms, then, confronting me, placed both her hands in mine with a sudden impulse that thrilled me.

"Let it remain this way, then," she said. "Win my heart, if you care to. I don't mind going through life with my heart in your kind keeping, Michael. I had rather it were so. I should be less unhappy."

"Unhappy?"

"Yes—because I am going to be unhappy anyway. And if I knew that you once cared, it would be easier for me—in after years. . . . Michael——"

"Yes?"

"Would you care for that much of me?"

I drew her nearer.

"You must not kiss me," she whispered.

"I——"

"Please. . . . It is a sign of troth plighted. . . . And is desecration else. . . . Troth plighted is a holy thing. And that cannot be between us, Michael. That cannot happen. . . . And so, you must not touch my lips with yours—dear Michael. . . . Only my hand—if you do care for me——"

I kissed her hand—then, slowly, each finger and

the fragrant palm, until it seemed to disconcert her and she withdrew it.

"Now take me back," she said in an uncertain voice that trembled slightly, "and remain my dear, frank, boyish friend. . . . And let me plague you a little, Michael. Won't you? And not be angry?" She asked so sweetly that I began to laugh—covered her hand with kisses—and laughed again.

"You little girl," I exclaimed—"oddly mature in some ways—a child in others—you may torment me and laugh at me now to your heart's content. Isn't laughter, after all, your heaven born privilege?"

"Why do you say that?"

"Oh, Thusis! Thusis! I am more convinced than ever of what I have half believed. Before I ever set eyes on you I had begun to care for you. Before I ever heard your voice I had begun to fall in love with you. Thusis—my Thusis—loveliest—most wonderful of God's miracles since Eden bloomed—*you* are The Laughing Girl!"

"Michael——"

"You *are!*"

Suddenly, as she walked lightly beside me, resting on my arm, she flung up her head with a reckless, delicious little laugh: "I *am* The Laughing Girl!"

A slight yet exquisite shock went clean through me as I realized that even to the instant of her avowal I had not been absolutely convinced of her identity with the picture.

"And I wish to tell you," she went on, her smile changing, "that when the photograph—which unhappily has become so notorious—was taken, I never dreamed that it would be stolen, reproduced in thousands, and sold in every city of Europe!"

"Stolen!"

"Certainly! Do you imagine that I would have permitted its publicity and sale? Never has such an exasperating incident occurred in my life! And I am helpless. I can't prevent it."

"Who stole it?"

"I haven't the slightest idea. It was this way, Michael; it happened in my own home on the island of Naxos, and my sister Clelia and I were amusing ourselves with our cameras, dressing each other up and posing each other.

"And she dressed me—or rather almost *un*-dressed me—that way—isn't it enough to make a saint swear —for when I had developed the plate and had started to print, somebody stole the plate from the sill of the open window. And the next thing we knew about it was when all Europe was flooded with my picture under which was printed that dubious caption—'The Laughing Girl.' Can you imagine my astonishment and rage? Could anything more utterly horrid happen to a girl? Had I at least been fully dressed—but no: there I was in every shop window among actresses, queens, demi-mondaines, and dissipated dukes just as Clelia had posed me in the intimacy of our own rooms, all over jewels, some of me mercifully veiled in a silk scarf, audaciously at ease in my apparent effrontery—oh, Michael, it nearly killed me!"

"Didn't you do anything about it?"

"Indeed I did! But where these photographs were being printed we never could find out. All we were able to do was to forbid their importation into Italy."

"How did you manage that?" I asked curiously.

She hesitated, then carelessly: "We had some slight influence at court——"

"*Influence?*"

"Possibly it amounted to that," she said indifferently.

"You are known at court, Thusis?"

She shrugged: "We are not, I believe, completely unknown." She walked on beside me in silence for a few moments, then:

"I do not wish to convey to you that I am *persona grata* in Italian court circles."

"But if you are known at court, dear Thusis, how can you be otherwise than welcome there?"

"I am *not* welcome there."

"That is impossible."

"You adorable boy," she laughed, "I must beg of you to occupy yourself with your own affairs and not continue to occupy yourself with mine."

"That's a heartless snub, Thusis."

"I don't mean it so," she said, her hand tightening impulsively on my arm. "But, Michael dear, I don't wish you to speculate about my affairs. It does no good. Besides, the situation in which I find myself is fearfully complex, and you couldn't help me out of it."

"Perhaps I can, Thusis."

She laughed: "You are delightfully romantic. You almost resemble one of the old time cloak-and-sword lovers of that dear Romance which died so long ago on the printed page as well as in human hearts."

"It is not dead in my breast, Thusis."

"It is dead in every breast. Only its frail ghost haunts our hearts at moments."

"When I offered you my heart, Thusis, did you suppose it empty save for a trace of selfish passion?"

"Men are men. . . . I do not understand their hearts."

"Take mine; tear it apart, look into it,—even if I die of it. Will you?"

Her laugh became less genuine and there was no gaiety in it.

"Tell me what I should find in your heart if I dissected it?"

"Love—and a sword!"

"You—you offer me your life, Michael?"

"This life—and the next."

She made no answer, walking slowly on beside

260

me, her arm linked in mine, the starlight glimmering on her bent head. Down the road beyond us the illuminated windows of my house glimmered. As we moved toward them along the stony highroad, I said:

"Thusis dear, I know nothing about you or about your affairs. I do not even guess your identity. But that you and your sister are here for the purpose of taking these miserable kings across the frontier into France, by violence, I do know.

"And this, also, I have learned, that, if you attempt to execute this *coup-de-main*, my friend Shandon Smith will do all he can to prevent it."

The girl stopped as though I had struck her and stared at me in the silvery lustre of the stars.

"What?" she said slowly.

"I have told you what Smith told me. He said that he didn't care whether or not I informed you. He added that, in case I chose to inform you, I should also repeat to you the following couplet:

'Grecian gift and Spanish fig
Help the Fool his grave to dig.' "

A bright flush stained her face yet she seemed to be more astounded than angry.

"Is it possible," she said, "that your friend Mr. Smith—this Norwegian promoter—repeated that couplet to you?"

"He certainly did repeat it to me, Thusis."

"Did he—did he tell you what it meant? Did he tell you anything more?"

He mentioned a secret society called the Ægean League.

"This is amazing," she murmured, looking up the road at the lights of the house.

"Of all people," she added, "that man Smith, the last person on earth we could suspect." She passed her hand across her eyes—a gesture of perplexity and consternation:

"I wish to find Mr. Smith, Michael. I desire to see him immediately. Please let us walk faster."

We fell into a quick pace and she released my arm as the light from the windows fell on us.

"He was sitting by the fountain," I began.

"He is there now, with Clelia," she exclaimed, and walked directly toward him where he was seated near Clelia on the stone rim of the pool.

They looked up as we approached, and Smith rose.

"Mr. Smith," said Thusis with a trace of excitement in her voice, "have you any knowledge concerning my identity?"

If the blunt question were a shock to him he did not show it. He answered in his pleasant, even voice:

"I don't know who you are, Thusis."

"Have you any idea?"

"None."

"How can that be," she asked, flushing, "when you send me such a couplet?"

"I've told you the truth," he said simply; "I don't know who you are, Thusis. I don't even suspect." He turned and looked at Clelia who had risen from her seat on the fountain's edge.

"You do not like me, Clelia, and now you are going to like me less. You resented it when I preached at you concerning proper behavior for a young girl. And now that you learn I am going to interfere in your political and military maneuvers, I suppose you hate me."

Nobody moved or spoke for a moment. Then Clelia took a step toward Smith, and I saw her face had become deadly pale.

"No," she said, "I don't hate you. On the contrary I am beginning to like you. Because it takes a real man to tell the woman he loves that he means to ruin her."

"Clelia, you and Thusis are ruined only if I hold my hand."

"We are done for *unless* you hold your hand!" she said. She stepped nearer.

"Mr. Smith?" she said sweetly, "you think you are on your honor. You are not. He who has sent you here to thwart us is deceiving you."

"He who sent *you* here, Clelia,—and *you*, Thusis, is deceiving you," he rejoined very quietly.

263

Thusis said: "You know who sent us, and yet you don't know who we are! How can this be, Monsieur?"

"It's true. I *do* know who sent you here. But you *don't!*"

Clelia, still very pale, bent her gaze on him. "Mr. Smith?"

"Yes, I hear you, Clelia."

"Suppose—suppose—I prove kinder to you."

"No," he said, grim and flushed.

Thusis turned sharply on her sister: "Have you given him your heart?"

Clelia answered, her eyes still fixed on Smith:

"I gave it to him from the first—even when I thought him a pious dolt. And was ashamed. And now that I know him for a man I'm not ashamed. Let him know it. I do care for him."

Smith stood rigid. Thusis, looking intently at Clelia, went to her and passed one arm around her waist.

"This can't be," she said. Clelia laughed. "But it *is*, sister. It isn't orthodox, it isn't credible, it is quite unthinkable that I should care for him. But I do; and I've told him so. Now he can ruin us if he wishes." And she flung a sweet, fearless glance at Smith which made him tremble very slightly.

Thusis turned to me an almost frightened face as though in appeal, then she caught her sister's hands.

"Listen!" she cried, "I also gave my heart as

you gave yours, sister! I couldn't help it. I found myself in love—" She looked at me—"I was doomed to love him.

"But for God's sake listen, sister. It is my *heart* I give. My mind and my destiny remain my own."

"My destiny is in God's hands," said Clelia simply. "My mind and heart I give—" She looked at Smith—"and all else that is myself . . . if you want me, Shan."

"You cannot do it!" exclaimed Thusis in a voice strangled with emotion. "You can do it no more than can I! You have no more right than have I to give yourself merely because you care! Your heart —yes! There is no choice when love comes; you can not avoid it. But you can proudly choose what to do about it!"

"I have chosen," said Clelia, "if he wants me."

Thusis clenched her hands and stood there twisting them, dumb, excited, laboring evidently under the most intense emotion.

And what all this business was about I had not the remotest notion.

Suddenly Thusis turned fiercely on her sister with a gesture that left her outflung arm rigid.

"Do you wish to find the irresponsible political level of those two Bolsheviki in there?" she said with breathless passion. "Are you really the iconoclast you say you are? I did not believe it! I can't. The world moves only through decent procedure, or it disintegrates. Where is your reason, your logic, your pride?"

"Pride?" Clelia smiled and looked at Smith: "In him, I think. . . . Since he has become my master."

"He is not our master!" retorted Thusis. "If what we came here to do is now impossible—thanks to a meddling and misled gentleman in Rome—is there not a sharper blow to strike at this treacherous Greek King and his Prussian wife and that vile, Imperial Hun who pulls the strings that move them?"

Clelia looked at Smith: "Do you know what my sister means?"

"Yes."

"Will you stop us even there?"

"I must."

Thusis, white with passion, confronted him:

"It is not you who are bound in honor to check and thwart us," she said unsteadily, "but your duped block-head of a master who exasperates me! Does he know from whom I take my orders?"

"Yes."

"I take them from the greatest, wisest, most fearless, most generous patriot in the world. I take my orders from Monsieur Venizelos!"

I started, but Smith said coolly: "Is that what you suppose, Thusis?"

"Suppose? What do you mean?" she demanded haughtily.

"I mean that you are mistaken if you and Clelia believe that your orders come from Monsieur Venizelos."

"From whom, then, do you imagine they come?" retorted Thusis.

"From Tino!"

"You dare——"

"Yes, I dare tell you, Thusis, how you have been deceived. Tino himself plotted this. Your orders are forgeries. Monsieur Venizelos never dreamed of inciting you to the activities in which you are now concerned——"

"That is incredible," said Thusis hotly. "I know who sent you here to check us and spoil it all—as though we were two silly, headstrong children! Tell me honestly, now; did not that—that gentleman in Rome give you some such impression of us?—that we were two turbulent and mischievous children?"

"I was not told who you were."

"But you were told that we are irresponsible and headstrong? Is it not true?"

"Yes."

"And you were sent here to see that we didn't get into mischief. Is it true?"

"Yes."

Thusis made a gesture of anger and despair:

"For lack of courage," she said tremulously, "a timid King refuses the service we try to render! We offer to stake our lives cheerfully; it frightens him. We escape his well meant authority and supervision and make our way into Switzerland to do him and Italy a service in spite of his timorous fears and objections. He has us followed by—*who* are you anyway, Mr. Smith?"

"I happen to be," he said pleasantly, "an officer in a certain branch of the Italian Army."

"Military Intelligence!" exclaimed Clelia. "And we were warned by Monsieur Venizelos!"

Thusis flung out her arms in a passionate gesture: "We offer the King of Italy two royal scoundrels! And he refuses. We offer the King of Italy two islands? And you tell us he refuses. When we were in Rome he laughed at us, teased us as though we had been two school-girls bringing him some crazy plan to end the war. And now when we are practically ready to prove our plan possible—ready to consummate the affair and give him the two most dangerous royal rascals in Europe—restore to Italy two islands stolen from her centuries ago—the King of Italy turns timid and sends a gentleman to ruin everything!"

"Because," said Smith pleasantly, "although King Constantine and Queen Sophia have been deposed, yet, were you to seize them and carry them across this frontier into France, Greece would resent it. So also would Switzerland. And the Allies would merely make two enemies out of an Allied country

and a neutral one for the sake of a few odd kings
and queens.

"And, moreover, if you should proceed, as you had
planned, to the Cyclades; and if you succeed in
fomenting a revolution in Naxos and Tenedos, and
induce these two islands to declare themselves part
of Italy, because seven hundred years ago a Venetian conquered them, then you turn Greece into a
bitter enemy of Italy and of the Allies. And that
is what you accomplish in exchange for a couple of
little islands in the Ægean which Italy does not
want."

"Then," retorted Thusis violently, "why did Monsieur Venizelos suggest that we attempt these things?
Is the greatest patriot on earth a traitor or a fool?"

"No, but Constantine of Greece is. And the
boche is his tutor. Oh, Thusis—Thusis! Can't you
see you have been tricked? Can't you understand
that Venizelos had no knowledge of these things you
are attempting in all sincerity?—that you have been
deluded by the treachery of the hun—that those
who counseled you to this came secretly from Tino
and the Kaiser, not from Venizelos?"

Thusis gazed at him bewildered. Clelia, too,
seemed almost stunned.

"Do—do you mean to tell me," stammered Thusis,
"that these kings know that Clelia and I are here to
try to kidnap them?"

"No," said Smith coolly, "because I censored their

mail in Berne. Their agents in Rome had warned them, in detail, by letter."

"Had those agents penetrated our identity?"

"They seemed to have no notion of it. But they described you both minutely."

Clelia seemed to come out of her trance. She turned to Thusis and said in a naïve, bewildered way:

"It's rather extraordinary, Thusis, that nobody seems to have found out who we really are. . . . It's almost as though we are not of as much importance as we have been brought up to suppose."

Thusis blushed hotly: "Because," she said, "nobody has discovered our incognito, is no reason for us to underrate our positions in Europe."

"Still—it is extraordinary that nobody recognizes us. And we use our own names, too. I can't account for it," she added honestly, "unless we are of much less importance than we have been accustomed to consider ourselves——"

Her voice was lost in a fearful scream from the house.

"Good Heavens!" said I, "what has happened?"

At that moment the door flew open and King Ferdinand waddled out in his wrapper and slippers.

"Help!" he shouted, "help! Is there a physician in the Alps?"

"I'm one," said Smith, coolly, "among other things."

And we all started hastily for the house.

# XVIII

THE Tsar of all the Bulgars, wearing a green and yellow wrapper, and bright blue slippers over his enormous flat feet, exhibited considerable nervousness as we entered the house.

"I wasn't doing anything," he said; "I trust that nobody will misunderstand me. Heaven is my witness——"

"What's the matter?" asked Smith tersely.

"The Princess Pudelstoff is screaming. I don't know why; I didn't go near her——"

We hurried up stairs. The door of the Princess' room was open, the light burning. The Princess sat up in bed, tears rolling down her gross, fat face, screaming at the top of her voice; while beside her, in Phrygian night-cap and pajamas, stood King Constantine.

He had her by the elbow and was jerking her arm and shouting at her: "Shut your fool head! Stop it! There's nothing the matter with, you. You've been dreaming!"

Smith went straight to the bed, shoved Constan-

271

tine aside, and laid a soothing hand on the Princess' shoulder.

"I'm a physician," he said in his pleasant, reassuring voice. "What is the trouble, Princess?"

"There's turrible doin's in this here house!" she bawled. "I peeked through the key-hole! Them there Bolsheviki next door is fixin' to blow us all up. I seen the bomb a-sizzlin' and a-fizzlin' on the floor like it was just ready to bust! And then I run and got into bed and I let out a screech——"

"It's all right," said Smith kindly. "It was just a bad dream. There isn't any bomb. Nobody is going to harm you——"

"I didn't dream it! I——"

"Yes, you did. Calm yourself, Princess. You have eaten something which has disagreed with you."

She ceased her screaming at that suggestion and considered it, the tears still streaming over her features. Then she began to blubber again and shook her head.

"I ain't et hoggish," she insisted. "If I had et hoggish I'd think I drempt it. But I ain't et hoggish. That wasn't no dream. No, sir! I had went to bed, but I was fidgety, like I had a load of coal onto my stummick. And by and by I heard them Bolsheviki next door whisperin'. And by and by I heard a fizzlin' noise like they was makin' highballs in there.

"Thinks I to myself that sounds good if true. So

"I seen the bomb a-sizzlin' and a-fizzlin' on the floor."

I gets up and I lights up and I peeks through the key hole. And I seen King—I mean Monsieur Xenos, and Monsieur Itchenuff, and Puppsky and Wildkatz and a long, black box on the floor in the room next door, and somethin' sticking out of it which fizzled without smokin'——"

"It was all a dream, madame," interposed Smith soothingly. And to my surprise, he took from his inner breast-pocket a small, flat medicine case.

"A glass of water and two spoons, please," he said to Clelia. And she went away to fetch them.

There was another glass on the wash-stand. In this he rinsed a clinical thermometer and inserted it under the tongue of the sobbing Princess.

Thusis and I stood near him, silent. King Constantine and the Bulgarian Tsar appeared to be unsympathetic and at the same time slightly nervous.

"If she'd stop gorging herself," remarked Tino, "she'd have no nightmares."

"I seen *you* in there! Yes I did!" retorted the Princess in another access of wrath and fright, the thermometer wagging wildly between her lips. "And I seen you too!" she went on, pointing at King Ferdinand, who stared wildly back at her out of his eyes of an alarmed pig and wrinkled his enormous nose at her.

"Don't tell me I was dreamin'," she added scornfully, "nothing like that."

Clelia came with the two spoons and glass of water; Smith selected a phial, mixed the dose, withdrew the thermometer, shook it, examined it, washed it at the basin, and, returning to his patient, administered a teaspoonful of medicine.

Then, in the other glass, he dissolved a powder, gave her three teaspoonfuls of that, and placed the two glasses on the night table beside her bed.

"If you happen to awake," he said gently, "take a teaspoonful of each. But I think you'll sleep, madame. And in the morning you'll be all right."

He turned on King Constantine and the Tsar so suddenly that they both took impulsive steps backward as though apprehensive of being kicked.

"The Princess needs quiet and rest, gentlemen," said Smith. "Kindly retire."

"Perhaps I'd better sit beside her for a while," began Constantine, but Smith interrupted him:

"I'll call you into consultation if I want you, Monsieur Xenos." His voice had a very slight ring to it; the ex-King of Greece looked at him for a moment, then winced and backed out of the room, followed by King Ferdinand who seemed to be in a hurry and crowded on his heels like an agitated pachyderm.

Clelia, who had remained mute and motionless, looking at Smith all the while, now came toward him. And in the girl's altered face I saw, reflected, deeper

274

emotions than I had supposed her youthful heart could harbor.

"Do you need me?" she asked. "I am at your service."

"Thank you, there is nothing more," said Smith pleasantly. He turned to include Thusis in kindly but unmistakable dismissal.

Clelia gave him a long, slow look of exquisite submission; Thusis sent an odd, irresolute glance at me. As she passed me, following her sister, her lips formed the message: "I wish to see you to-night."

When they had gone Smith shut and locked the door, and with a slight motion to me to accompany him, walked over to the bed, seated himself beside it, and took the fat hand of the Princess Pudelstoff in his as though to test her pulse.

The lady rolled her eyes at us but lay still, her mottled cheeks still glistening with partly dried tears.

"What's on your mind, Princess?" inquired Smith in a soft, caressing voice.

"Hey?" she exclaimed in visible alarm, and evidently preparing to scream again.

"Hush. Don't excite yourself, madame," he said in his pleasant, reassuring way. "There is no occasion for alarm at all."

"Am I a sick woman?" she demanded anxiously. "Is that what you're a-goin' to hand me? *Is* it?"

"No, you're not physically ill. You have no

275

temperature except as much as might be due to sudden shock."

"I got the scare of my young life all right," she muttered. "Say, Doc, *was* it a dream? On the level now, was it?"

"Probably——"

"Honest to God?" she insisted.

"Why do you think it was not a dream, Princess?" he asked gently.

"Why? Well, I've run with Rooshians enough to know a infernal machine when I see one. And I never dream plain, that way. I can see that darn thing yet—and hear it! And I can see them men in there all a settin' onto chairs in a circle like, and a-watching that there bomb sizzling. It made a blue light 'but no smoke and no smell. How could I have drempt all that so plain, Doc?"

"Princess! You're not afraid of me, are you?"

She looked up into his clean-cut, pleasant American face.

"No, I ain't," she said. "You come from God's country"—she suddenly began to beat her pudgy fists on the sheets—"and whyinhell I ever was crazy enough to leave little old Noo York I don't know excep' I was damfoolenough to do it!"

Smith smiled at her: "You sure were some peach," he said, dropping gracefully into the vernacular, "when you played with Nazimova in that Eastside theater."

The Princess flushed all over, and the radiance of her smile transfigured her amazingly.

"Did *you* see me in them days, Doc?"

"You betcha!"

"Well-f'r-God's-sake!" she gasped in wonder and delight. "Say, you had me fooled, Doc. I understood you was a Norsky—a sort of tree-peddlin' guy. But, thinks I to myself, he looks like a Yank. I says so to my brother, Leo Puppsky——"

"Don't say it to him again, Princess. Or to anybody."

At that the Princess fixed her shrewd little eyes on Smith, shifted them for an instant to me, then resumed her scrutiny of his serene and smiling features.

"What's the idea?" she asked at last.

"I'm going to lay all my cards down for you, Princess,—faces up. I am an American serving in the Italian army."

"The-hell-you-say!" There was a silence that lasted a full minute. Then, suddenly, the Princess began to laugh. Soft, fat chuckles agitated her tremendous bosom; a seismic disturbance seemed to shake her ample bulk beneath the bed-clothes.

"Tabs!" she exclaimed. "You're keepin' tabs on these here down-and-outers! That's what you're a doin' of! Am I right?"

"And what are *you* doing here in Switzerland, Princess?" he inquired smilingly.

"Say! I'm their goat! Now, do you get me?"

"Not exactly——"

"Well listen. Puppsky's my brother. He was in the suit and cloak business in Noo York before the Rooshian revolution. Then he beat it for Petrograd—workin' for his own pocket same's you and me, Doc; and seein' pickin's—Trotzky bein' a friend of ours, and Lenine a relation. I was in Stockholm fixin' to go to Noo York, when that poor fish, Wildkatz, comes in and talks me into this game. And look at me now, Doc! Here I am financin' this here bunch o' homeless kings, sittin' into a con game, holdin' all the dirty cards they deal me—busted flushes, nigger straights, and all like that! And what," she demanded passion-ately, "is there in it for me? Tino, he says I'll be a Greek duchess an' rule a island called Naxos!— And, Gawd help me, I fell fur it. And wherethehell is Naxos? And is it as big as Coney Island? Wasn't I the big dill-pickle to stake 'em to a Greek revolution? And me a princess! Sure, I know a Rooshian princess ain't much of a swell, and the Duchy of Naxos looked good to me.

"But the more I mix in with these here kings the wiser I get. Four-flushers is four-flushers wherever you find 'em. And these guys is all alike— old Admiral bushy-whiskers, Bummelzug, General Droly, and that sore-eyed little Gizzler!—all want to sell me gold bricks for real money!"

She waved her short, fat arms in furious recollection of her wrongs.

"Say, even the Greek Queen ain't too particular about chousing the long-green outer me! She wants to hand me the order of the Red Chicken!—costs ten thousand plunks! What do you know about that, Doc?"

I don't know whether Smith was as amazed as was I by these revelations in argot. He smiled his kindly, undisturbed smile and patted her hand encouragingly; while from depths long plugged burst the excited recital of the woes of the Pudelstoffs.

"I'm through," she said. "I got enough. And I told 'em so at the meeting after dinner to-night. They talked rough to me, they did. Puppsky, he got riled and tells me I'm no sister of his. And the Greek Queen she was crazy and called me a kike in German. Which upset my dinner.

"Say, Doc, the Gophers and Gas-house gangs ain't one-two-three with this bunch. I'm scared stiff they'll get me—that Ferdie has croaked more guys 'n people know. I'm scared Sophy sticks me. They say she stuck a hat-pin into Tino. You bet she knows how to make that big stiff behave! And she's got a way of lookin' at you!—Me, I quit 'em cold to-night. 'Nothing like that,' says I; 'no revolution in Greece at $250,000 a revolute! No Naxos! No Red Chicken! Me, I'm on my way via Berne, Berlin, Christiania. and Noo York!'"

"You've quarreled with them, Princess?" asked Smith.

"I sure did. Say, I don't have to stand for no rough stuff from Wildkatz neither. We ain't in Petrograd. But, mind you, I don't put it past him to try his dirty tricks on me with bombs!"

"But why——"

"They're like all gun-men! Once in you can't get out, or they'll try to get you. If you've got enough and try to quit peaceable they think you've been bought out. You're a squealer to them."

"You believe they might offer you violence?" I asked, incredulously.

"How do I know? What was they doin' with that bomb? They're sore on me. They know they're gettin' no more dough outen me. They know I've quit and I'm goin' back to God's country."

"But Leo Puppsky is your own brother!" I exclaimed, horrified.

The Princess shrugged her fat shoulders.

"He's a Red, too. Bolsheviks is Bolsheviks. You don't know 'em. You don't know what they done in Rooshia. No boche is bloodier. Call 'em what you like—call 'em all sons of boches—and you won't be wrong."

Her flabby features had grown somber; suddenly a shudder possessed her, and she opened her mouth to scream; but Smith instantly filled the gaping orifice with medicine, and only a coughing fit followed.

To me he said: "Please leave me alone with her now. It will be all right, Michael."

And he turned tenderly to the convulsed Princess and patted her vast back.

# XIX

A S I walked through the corridor considerably concerned over the statements made to us by this east-side Princess and seriously disturbed by finding myself in the very vortex of this whirlpool of intrigue which every moment seemed to spew up from its dizzying depths new plots and counter-plots, I almost ran into the ex-Queen of Greece.

She was in curl-papers and negligee, standing just outside her door, an electric torch in one hand, a pistol in the other.

"Madame!" I exclaimed, "what in the world is the matter?"

"I don't like this inn," she said. "I consider it a suspicious place."

"Madame!"

"What do I know about your inn?" she demanded insolently, "or about you, either?"

"*Madame!*"

"You *say* you are a Chilean. You don't look it. Neither does your friend resemble a Norwegian. If you desire to know my opinion you both look like Yankees!"

"Madame, this is intolerable——"

"Possibly," she interrupted, staring at me out of chilly eyes that fairly glittered. "Possibly, too, I am mistaken. Perhaps your servants, also, unduly arouse suspicion—your pretty housekeeper may really be your housekeeper. The waitress, too, may be a real waitress. This is all quite possible, Monsieur. But I prefer to be prepared for any eventuality in this tavern!"

And she went into her room and shut the door.

The ex-queen's insolence upset me. I was possessed by a furious desire to turn them all out of doors. The prospect of living in the same house with these people for days—perhaps for weeks, seemed unbearable. Surely there must be some way out of the valley!

Down stairs I saw Raoul coming from the front courtyard leading two strange horses attached to a sort of carryall.

"Where on earth did you discover that rig?" I called out to him in the starlight.

"Two guests have just arrived," he replied, laughing.

I hurried out to where he stood.

"Guests!" I repeated. "Where did they come from? Isn't the pass closed?"

"Sealed tight, Monsieur O'Ryan. But when the avalanche fell this vehicle and its passengers were just far enough inside the pass to be caught.

"I understand they've been digging themselves out of the snow all this time. They've just arrived and are in the long hall asking for accommodations."

"Who are they?" I demanded in utter disgust; "more huns?"

"One is a Turkish gentleman," he said. "The other is the driver. I will take care of him. The Turkish traveler's name is Eddin Bey, and he says he's a friend of Admiral Lauterlaus."

I went into the house and discovered Eddin Bey entering his signature on the ledger while Clelia with keys and candle waited beside him to show him to his quarters.

"Ah!" he exclaimed cordially when I named myself, offering his dark, nervous hand, "I am inexpressibly happy to have the privilege, Monsieur O'Ryan! A narrow escape for us, I assure you!—that mountain of snow roaring down on us and our horses whipped to a gallop! Not gay—eh? No, sir! And I thought we'd never dig out the horses and our wagon and luggage!"

I replied politely and suitably, and Clelia presently piloted this dark, lean, vivacious young man to his quarters across the corridor from General von Dungheim.

When she returned her flushed, set features arrested my attention. "Did that Turk annoy you, Clelia?" I asked sharply.

She shrugged: "Tavern gallantry," she replied briefly: "men of that sort are prone to it."

I said: "If any of these people annoy you and Thusis come to me at once."

She laughed: "Dear Monsieur O'Ryan," she said, "Thusis and I know how to take care of ourselves." She came nearer, looking up at me out of her lovely, friendly eyes:

"Thusis is in her room. It isn't very proper, of course, but she is waiting for you. Will you go?"

"Yes."

Clelia laid one hand lightly on my arm, and her smile became wistful and troubled:

"You do care for my sister, don't you?"

"I am deeply in love with her."

"I was afraid so."

"Afraid?"

"Oh, I don't know how Thusis is going to behave, —how she is going to take it!" said Clelia in frank anxiety. "Never before has she cared for any man; and I don't know what she's going to do about you —indeed I don't, Mr. O'Ryan!"

"Could you tell me," said I bluntly, "what obstacles stand in the way of my marrying your sister?"

"Thusis should tell you."

"She isn't already married?"

"Good Heavens, no!"

"Is it a matter of religion?"

"Thusis must tell you. I could not speak for her,
—interfere with her. My sister will act for herself
—assume all responsibility for whatever she chooses
to do. . . . As I do."

I took Clelia's soft hands in mine and looked earnestly into her face:

"You, also, care for a man; don't you?"

She bent her head in wordless assent.

"What are *you* going to do about it, Clelia?"

"Whatever *he* wishes."

"Marry him?"

"If he wishes."

"You are an astounding girl!"

"I am an astounded girl. I never supposed I
should take such a view of life, of its obligations,
of my own position in the world. . . . Lately, in the
probable imminence of sudden death, I became a
little reckless—perhaps excited—willing to learn in
these brief hours the more innocent elements of love
—curious to experience even the least real of its
mysteries—to play coquette in the pretty comedy—
even with you——"

She gave me a vague smile and slowly shook her
head.

"All the while," she said, "I was in love with *him*.
I didn't know it because I didn't know him. When I
felt frivolous and wished to laugh he was serious.
His solemnity stirred me to audacity; and when I
said a lot of silly things I didn't mean he preached

at me; and I bullied him and was impudent and showed my contempt for a man who would endure such tyranny. . . . That is how it began. . . . And all the while, not knowing it, I was falling more completely in love. Isn't it odd?"

She smiled, pressed my hands, shook her head as though at a loss to account for her behavior.

"The first hint of it I had," she said, "was when he coolly warned me that he would thwart me. And I looked into his eyes and knew him for the first time—knew him to be the stronger, the wiser, the more capable,—and the more powerful.

"And I realized, all in a moment, that he had endured my contempt and tyranny merely because he chose to; that he was a real man, in cool possession of his own destiny; that, if he chose, he could clear his mind of me, and presently his heart; that I was not essential to him, not necessary; that, indeed, unless I instantly took myself in hand and made an effort to measure up to him, he'd turn from me,— quite courteously—and go his own way with a kindly indifference which suddenly seemed terrifying to me. . . . And I loved him. . . . And let him know. . . . And that is how it happened with me."

After a long pause: "What would happen," I inquired, "if I tried that sort of thing on Thusis?"

Clelia shook her head: "Thusis and I are different. I don't wish to be a martyr."

"Does Thusis?"

287

"I'm rather afraid she is inclined that way. Of course we both were quite willing to suffer physical martyrdom if we failed to carry off these wretched kings. That is a different kind of martyrdom—a shot in the brain, a knife thrust—perhaps a brutish supplice from the boche——" She shrugged her shoulders. "We were not afraid," she added. "But when another sort of death suddenly confronted me —the death of love in him I loved—I had no courage—none at all. You see I am not the stuff of which martyrs are fashioned, Mr. O'Ryan."

"Is Thusis?"

"Alas!"

"She prefers to suffer?"

"I am afraid she will become a martyr to a pride which interprets for her the old, outworn doggerel of ages dead. . . . I can't repeat it to you."

"Noblesse oblige?"

"That phrase occurs in it."

"Oh. . . . So Thusis, caring for me, will send me away," I said.

"I cannot answer you."

"Can you advise me, Clelia?"

She looked up at me; tears sprang to her eyes; she pressed my hands, but shook her head.

## XX

I KNOCKED very gently at Thusis's door and she opened it, signed for me to enter, then closed it cautiously.

"Do you know," said I, "that it is after midnight?"

"I know it is. But as long as others don't know you are here, what does it matter, Michael?"

"Of course," I muttered, "you and I know there's no cause for scandal."

Her delightful laughter welled up from the whitest throat I have ever seen, but she instantly suppressed it.

"We're very indiscreet," she said mockingly; "we've exchanged hearts and we're here in my bedroom at midnight. Can you imagine what that queen downstairs would say?"

"Had you meant to kidnap her, also?" I inquired.

"No," she said scornfully. "The Allies can take care of the Hohenzollern litter after they take the sty."

"Berlin," I nodded.

"Berlin. Hercules had no such task in his Augean stable. It *was* Hercules, wasn't it, Michael? I always get him and his labors mixed up with Theseus. But the Prince of Argolis used address, not bull force. . . . His mother's name was Æthra. . . . My mother's name was Æthra, too."

"That is Greek."

"Very. And the name of the ancient pal—I mean the name of our old house on the island of Naxos was Thalassa!—You remember the Ten Thousand?"

"Yes. Your house overlooked the sea?"

"The Ægean! You enter from the landward lawn, advance toward the portico—and suddenly, through the marble corridor, a sheet of azure! Thalassa!"

I said slowly: "Little white goddess of Naxos with hair like the sun and eyes of Ægean blue, why have you sent for me to come to your chamber at midnight?"

Thusis looked at me and her happy smile faded.

"To ask one question," she said very gravely, "and to answer one—if you ask it."

"Ask yours, first."

"What did that dreadful Princess say to you and to Mr. Smith after I left the room?"

I told her what had passed.

"What!" she cried fiercely, clenching her hands. "Tino had the impudence to offer her Naxos as a bribe!"

"The Duchy of Naxos," I repeated.

I have never seen an angrier or more excited girl.

She sprang to her feet and began to pace the bedroom, her hands doubled in fury, her face tense
and white.

"Naxos!" she kept repeating in a voice strangled
by emotion. "That treacherous Tino offers Naxos
to a miserable, fat Russian Princess! Oh! Was
ever such an insult offered to any girl! Naxos! My
Naxos! Could the civilized world believe it! Can
the outrage on Belgium equal such an infamy! Even
with the spectacle of martyred France, of Roumania
in Teuton chains, of Russia floundering in blood—
could the world believe its senses if Naxos is betrayed!"

Her emotion was tragic, yet it seemed to me that
the lovely Thusis took Naxos a trifle too seriously.
Because I was not at all certain that this same civilized and horrified world was unanimously aware of
the existence of Naxos. But I didn't say this to
Thusis.

As she paced the room she wrung her hands once
or twice naïvely deploring the avalanche.

"Because," she said, halting in front of me, "Smith
or no Smith, I should certainly attempt to seize this
treacherous, beastly Constantine, and smuggle him
over the frontier. The traitor! The double traitor! For Naxos is *not* his! No! It is a Venetian
Duchy. What if Turkey did steal it! What if
Greece stole it in turn? It is Venetian. It is Italian. It is my home and I love it! It is my birth-

place and I worship it! It is my native land and I adore it!"

"The King of Italy," I reminded her, "does not seem to desire that Naxos be included in his domain."

"But *I* do!" she said passionately. "I am a Venetian of Naxos. Have I not the right to decide where my island belongs? For six hundred years my family has owed allegiance to Venice—and naturally, therefore, to Italy. Have I not every right to raise the banner of revolt in Naxos and defy this ruffianly ex-king who comes sneaking stealthily into Switzerland to plot for his own restoration?—who comes here secretly to offer Naxos to a vulgar Russian as a bribe for financial aid?—offers to sell my home for a few millions cash and buy cannon and men and send them into Greece to fight for him and his rotten throne?"

"Thusis——"

"No!" she said violently, "there is no argument possible. And God never sent His avalanche to ruin my hopes and destroy all chance of freedom for Naxos! It was the bestial Gott of the boche who loosed the snow up yonder—the filthy fetish of the hun who did that!" She flung out her white arms and looked upward. And "oh!" she cried, "for one hour of the old Greek gods to call on! Oh for the thunderbolts of Zeus!—the spear of Athene!—the tender grace and mercy of Aphrodite, and her swift

and flaming vengeance when her temples were pro-
faned!—when her children were betrayed and dis-
inherited!—Naxos—my Naxos——"

All Greek now, pagan, beautiful, the girl's whole
body was quivering with rage and grief. And I
knew enough to hold my tongue.

While the fierce storm swept her, bending her like
a sapling with gusts of passion, I stood silent, awaiting the rain of tears to end it.

None came to break the tension, though the gray
eyes harbored lightning and her brow remained dark.

"As Naxos falls, so falls the world," she said.
"The eyes of civilization are on her; the fateful writing runs like fire across God's heaven! Let the world
heed what passes! The doom of Naxos is the doom
of freedom and of man!"

I, personally, had scarcely looked at it in that
light. It did not strike me that the hub of civilization rested on Naxos. Nor do I believe the world
was under that impression. But I was not going to
say so to this excited young Naxosienne—or Nax-
osoise—or Naxosette,—whichever may be the respectful and properly descriptive nomenclature.

And so, standing near the window, I watched the
tempest wax, wane, and gradually pass, leaving her
at last silent, seated on her couch, with one arm
across her knee and her head bent like the "Resting
Hermes."

When I walked over and stood looking down at

her she reached out and, without looking, took my hand.

"It is your turn now, Michael; and I already know what question you mean to ask."

"Shall I ask it, Thusis?" After a silence her hand closed convulsively in mine.

"I *do* love you. . . . I am not—free—to marry you."

"Could you tell me why?"

She slowly shook her head: "You will learn why, some day."

"Is there no chance, Thusis?"

Again she shook her head. Presently her hand slipped out of mine and she rested both elbows on her knees, covering her face.

I dropped onto the couch near her, framing my own head in both hands.

The world had become sunless and quite empty except for human pain. . . . And so, thought I in a dull sort of way, this ends my romance with The Laughing Girl. . . . The Laughing Girl of Naxos. . . . Not laughing now, but very much subdued, brooding beside me with both hands covering her face, and the splendid masses of her hair now loosened to her shoulders like a hood hiding the bowed features.

"Don't grieve, Thusis," I whispered, forgetting my own pain; but she suddenly huddled up and doubled over, crying:

"If you speak to me that way I—can't—endure it——" Her voice broke childishly for the first time, and I saw her shoulders quiver.

We had a rotten time of it—self-restraint on my side, and on hers—a hard, sharp shower of tears—terrifying to me because of her silence; not a sigh, not a sob, not even one of those undignified gulps which authors never mention—but which nevertheless usually characterize all lachrymose feminine procedure, and punctuate its more attractive silences.

It resembled a natural rainstorm in April—abrupt, thorough; and then the sun. For after considerable blind fumbling, she suddenly leaned forward and dried her eyes with the edge of the bed-sheet.

"There," she said, "is an intimate act which ought to breed mutual contempt!"

We both laughed. She found a fresh section of the sheet and used it.

"You are an adorable boy," she said, keeping her face turned away but busy, now, with her sagging hair.

"It's got to come right some day," I said with the fatuous stupidity characteristic of the stymied swain.

"It won't," she remarked, "but let's pretend it will. . . . Is my nose red, Michael?"

"I can't see it when you turn your face away."

"I don't wish you to see it if it's red."

"But how can I judge——"

We burst into that freer laughter which welcomes the absurd when hearts are heavy laden.

Her dresser was within reach. I gazed at her back while she powdered her nose.

"My eyes are red," she observed calmly.

"No, they're gray; it's your hair that is red, Thusis."

It was silly enough to invoke the blessed relief of further laughter. But when Thusis finally turned toward me there was a new shyness about her, exquisite, captivating, that held me quiet and very serious.

"What a dreadfully sober gentleman," she said. "The storm's all over, and it isn't going to rain again."

I quoted: "It rains—in my heart——" And she laid a quick, impulsive hand on my arm:

"Have I not confessed that I love you?"

"Yes——"

"Very well. Is it a reason for rain—in your heart or anywhere else?"

"No——"

"Well then! . . . You may touch my hand with your lips."

Only her lips could be sweeter than the soft hand
I kissed, long and closely, until she withdrew it with
a tremulous little laugh of protest.

"We're becoming infamous; we're a scandal, Michael. Have you anything further to say to me? If
not, please go home to bed."

Casting about in my mind for an excuse to linger
I recollected the advent of Eddin Bey; and I told
her about it.

"What a barnyard full!" she said scornfully, "all
the creatures, now,—Turk, Bulgarian, Bolshevik,
and boche! . . . To see them here—and the two
principal scoundrels almost within my grasp! I
don't believe I can stand it," she added breathlessly.
"Smith or no Smith, and his exasperating majesty
the King of Italy to the contrary, I think something is going to happen to Tino and Ferdie as soon
as the pass is cleared."

"One thing more," I said; "do you believe there
really was a bomb in the room next to the Princess
Pudelstoff's?"

"Do you mean, Michael, that those murderous
Russians might possibly suspect Clelia, Josephine,
Raoul, and me?"

"Oh no, I don't think that. But possibly they
had other assassinations in mind and were trying out
a new species of bomb—experimenting with some un-
tried fuse. That's what occurred to me—unless the
fat Princess really did dream it all."

"When I make the beds to-morrow," remarked Thusis, "I shall search very carefully. The only trouble is that those Bolsheviki seldom leave their rooms except to eat. And then I'm obliged to wait on table."

I nodded, a little troubled. But it was unthinkable that these treacherous Reds should even dream of bomb-murder in Switzerland. Whom might they desire to slaughter, unless it were the poor, fat Princess? And they would scarcely blow up an entire establishment in a neutral country for the purpose of scattering portions of the Princess over the adjacent Alps.

And yet I began to feel oddly uneasy, now. Of what such vermin might be capable I could not guess, with the frightful example of the two arch-traitors Lenine and Trotzky staring a sickened world in the face,—a world already betrayed twice since its sad history began—once by Judas, once by Benedict Arnold.

Judas would have sold the souls of all mankind: Lenine and Trotzky sold only one hundred and fifty million bodies to the anti-Christ. Things were improving on earth after all.

I said: "Smith is a good man to have here at such a time. He's a wonderfully level-headed fellow. I don't believe we need worry."

"I ought to dislike him. But I don't," remarked Thusis.

"Dislike Smith?"

"He's turned my sister's head!"

"But—good heavens!—if she cares for him——"

"I care for *you!*" she cut in crisply. "But I haven't lost my head or my sense of proportion——"

"I wish you had."

She looked at me in silence almost hostile. Suddenly she blushed furiously:

"I wish I had, too! I care for you as much as my sister cares for Mr. Smith! More! Much more! I'm—I'm quite hopelessly in love! But I don't—don't—forget that—that——"

She shook her head but sat looking at me out of tragic eyes—suffered me to press her lovely hands to my lips, watching me all the while.

"You had better go, Michael."

I laid her hands in her lap. She clasped them so tightly that the delicate nails whitened.

"It will come out right," said I, rising.

"It never will. . . . I—I love you."

At the door I hesitated. But she did not speak. And I opened it and went out.

# XXI

## SUS SCROFA

FOR two exasperating weeks, now, the Schwindlewald pass had remained hermetically sealed with snow, utterly isolating the valley.

It is true that a Swiss airplane had appeared overhead and had dropped several tons of bread which we did not require, and a message couched in hysterical language reminding us that God would protect us while several score of sweating Swiss dug us out.

Personally I didn't care except for the highly objectionable colony of boches with whom I was obliged to share an imprisonment which otherwise would never have bored me.

But the royal circus was a dreadful visitation—kings, queen, lesser fry, and Bolsheviki became almost unendurable, even when, during the first week of our captivity, they flocked by themselves and conspired to their hearts' content.

Had this condition endured, the situation might have been borne with a certain philosophy. But the inevitable, of course, happened: one week of exclu-

sive gregariousness was enough for these people:
they began to bore one another.

It showed first, characteristically, at table. Tino
and spouse, always engaged in continual bickering
to the vast discomfort of everybody, now had it out
in star-chamber proceedings; and the King, badly
battered but jaunty, appeared at table with one eye
partly closed and a mouth so swollen that he could
not comfortably manipulate a cigarette. He explained that he had bumped his head in the dark.
But it was perfectly understood who had bumped it.

King Ferdinand became moody, and his cunning,
furtive features often bore a white, scared expression. He developed, too, a morbid mania for a most
depressing line of conversation—celebrated assassinations being his theme,—and he ransacked the history of all times in search of examples, Eddin Bey
slyly assisting him.

Sluggish livers and piggish feeding probably ac-
counted for the sullen lethargy of Von Dungheim
and Bummelzug. Their ever latent and brutal tem-
pers blazed at absurd trifles, involving usually the
bad manners and lack of respect shown them by the
Bolsheviki, who chattered back at them like enraged
monkeys, terrifying the Princess Pudelstoff who had
never forgotten her "dream."

Admiral Lauterlaus, whose personal habits were
always impossible, now spent most of his time bullying the wretched Secretary Gizzler or, with a tele-

scope such as chamois-hunters carry, 'squatted on the veranda steps and swept the Bec de l'Empereur for "gamps," and heaven knows what else.

Only the Countess Manntrapp and Eddin Bey appeared to retain their good humor. The Turk, a handsome fellow of distinguished manners and gay address, evidently possessed a lively eye for pulchritude. He lost no time at all in paying his sly court to my servants, beginning with Thusis, progressing to Clelia, and ending with Josephine Vannis in the kitchen: and he accepted defeat with such cheerful and humorous alacrity that they all forgave him, I think, and his perfectly frank suggestions that they return to Adrianople with him and honor him by becoming the nucleus for a zenana.

He found, however, a pretty bird of his own vivacious and volatile temperament in the exceedingly bored Countess Manntrapp. And they were often together and apparently having a jolly flirtation, being cleverly aware of each other's character and entertaining no delusions.

Except for these two at table and on the veranda, and except for the companionship of Smith, and now and then an opportunity for a few cautious words with Thusis, those days would have been insupportable for me. A hungry hun is bad enough; an ill-tempered one is worse; but a bored boche!— imagine a penful of them with time heavy on their hoofs!

# Sus Scrofa

The old story—"What's time to a hawg!"—has
no significance among the *Sus scrofa* or the "Bosch
Vark." Bored, the embers of that dull, slumbering
rage glow hotter; the sulky silence is broken by
grumbling, then by quarrels; the blind, senseless instinct to brutalize and rend obsesses. Small wonder
the boche desires a place in the sun where his herds
can spread out from the constricted and common
wallow!

Tino had again appeared at luncheon with the
other eye done in thunderous tints of purple, taupe,
and an exquisite mauve. Parallel scratches adorned
his nose; some of his mustache was missing. But I
must admit he took it jauntily enough, and his bland
explanation—something about tripping over a rock
in the woods—was accepted by all and believed by
none.

The queen, still somewhat pasty and pinched from
the effects of this ritual *in camera*, ate haughtily,
disdainful of what anybody might really think, and
calm in her conviction that the Hohenzollern is responsible to Gott alone for whatever a Hohenzollern
may choose to do.

That she had done plenty to Tino was painfully
visible: but he was in a jocose and waggish humor,
and his barrack-room quips and jests were plainer
than usual. In fact, they became so coarse that
even the Admiral bristled his beard and eyebrows,

sniffing lack of respect for himself in the loud-mouthed levity of the King.

And I was getting madder and madder, Thusis and Clelia being present to wait on table as usual, and I was on the point of making a sharp observation to King Tino, when a sudden burst of applause from the other end of the table checked me. The Countess Manntrapp was speaking. She continued:

"This enforced imprisonment is becoming exceedingly dull for everybody. Why not divert ourselves? Has anybody any suggestions to offer?"

"A mountain party," rumbled Admiral Lauterlaus. "I, in my time, a famous hunter of 'gamps' have been."

"We don't wish to break our necks to divert ourselves," sneered the queen.

"A fishing party!" exclaimed Von Dungheim. "If there is a good big net we can all help draw it and clean out every trout in the stream!"

"Droly," expostulated Tino, "you have such wholesale ideas! Our host might possibly object, you know."

At the very idea of anybody objecting to the destructive wishes of a Prussian officer, General Count von Dungheim glared at me.

"Why not give a baby-party?" inquired Smith, blandly.

"A—a *baby*-party!" repeated Baron Bummelzug

vacantly, in English; "what perhaps iss it a baby-party?"

Thusis, serving me, bent over and whispered in my ear: "Not the sort of baby-parties they gave in Belgium; there are no babies." And she moved serenely to serve the queen, her beautiful face placid and inscrutable.

The Princess Pudelstoff began to clap her pudgy hands excitedly:

"A baby-party! A baby-party! That'll be fun! That'll be great! And we'll have a feed and a spiel——"

"Ach wass!" shouted the Admiral exasperated. "Tell us once what it iss a baby-party, und stop your noises yet!"

But the excited Princess had become uncontrolable, and she began to hammer on the table with her fat fists, shouting:

"A feed and a spiel! For God's sake somebody start something in this hellofa hole!"

Amid her clamor and the ominous roaring of the infuriated Admiral, I tinkled my goblet with my fork and presently secured comparative silence for Smith.

In a few pleasant phrases he explained to them the simple intricacies of the American baby-party.

"I'll come!" cried the Countess Manntrapp, delighted.

"I also!" echoed Eddin Bey.

Tino was visibly enchanted at the prospect, and he clapped King Ferdinand on his elephantine back exultingly:

"We'll go as twins!" he cried. "This is most agreeable to me! Eh, Sophy? I'm half dead for a bit of a frolic! Everybody must come. Nobody is to be excused. Desperate cases require desperate remedies. Ennui is what is killing us; diversion is what we need!"

He was pounding the breath out of King Ferdinand who began to cough and dodge and blink wildly at everybody out of his little wild-pig's eyes, when I stood up giving the signal.

"The party," announced Smith, "is for to-night! There will be games, a dance, and a supper. All are politely invited!"

"My God," said Secretary Gizzler to me, rubbing his bony hands together, "to what foolishness does noble company resort in order that ennui may be escaped."

The Princess Pudelstoff overheard him:

"Crape-hanger!" she said, giving him a vigorous dig in the ribs which almost disarticulated his entire and bony frame.

The majority, however, trooping out to the veranda where they could teutonically enjoy their coffee and cognac "im grünen," appeared desirous of engaging in the proposed diversion.

Even the queen deigned to inquire of me whether

there was, in the house, material with which to construct a pair of ruffled panties for her husband.

Only the Bolsheviki remained aloof, chattering and mouthing together and waving their soiled fingers at each other and, presumably, at the bourgeois world in general.

Later, Smith came into my room whither I had retired to resume my series of poems to Thusis,—a rather melancholy occupation yet oddly comforting, too.

"Why the devil," said I, "did you suggest such a party?"

"I don't know. It occurred to me. I'm rather tired of their wrangling."

"But a *baby*-party!"

He laughed: "You see how they take to the idea. Anything to dissipate this sullen, ugly atmosphere. It gets on my nerves."

"Are *you* going?"

"Certainly."

"In costume?"

"Of course."

"Good heavens, Smith! I didn't think you had it in you to frivol."

"Why—I don't know," he said, smilingly. "I'm intensely happy."

I eyed him gloomily: "Yes," said I, "no doubt you are—winning the affections of the girl you wish to marry. By the way, has she been civil enough to tell you who she really is?"

"No," he replied cheerfully.

"Do you mean to tell me you are engaged to marry a girl who refuses to disclose her identity?"

"Exactly."

"How the devil is she going to marry you? Under an assumed name?"

"That is for Clelia to decide."

*"That,"* said I, "is a most remarkable view to take of the situation."

"Why? I am in love. I dare believe she cares for me. It makes no difference to me who Clelia may be. That she is Clelia is enough—enough that she will be my wife. And when a man stands for the first time inside the gates of happiness with the girl he loves—what an ass he'd be to bother her about details!"

This was a totally new and unexpected Smith, to me. I never dreamed it was in him.

"Don't you agree with me?" he inquired.

I nodded doubtfully.

"Wouldn't you accept Thusis as she chose to offer herself?" he insisted.

A pang shot through me:

"Good Lord, yes!" I said. "I'd marry her if she were a beggar or a convict or the least creature of her sex. I'd never ask a question; I'd take thankfully and happily what she offered. You are right,

308

Smith—wonderfully right. If you love, love! If you don't, worry!"

"Quite right," he said; "it's either love or worry; the genuine article doesn't admit of both. If you really love you are satisfied; if you worry it isn't love—it's merely something resembling it. Love is specific; there are sub-species and varieties, none the real thing. The acid test of love is contentment; baser metal dissolves in trouble, and the sediment is worry. I——"

"Oh, shut up!" I burst out, nervously; "you're too darned eloquent on the subject. Besides," I added with a perfectly new and-instinctive suspicion, "you're so confoundedly contented with yourself that I believe you have begun to guess the identity of Clelia, and that it pleases you enormously!"

He reddened.

"*Have* you any idea who she is?" I insisted.

"A vague idea."

"And that vague idea pleases you?"

"It does," he said with a shy sort of grin.

That was too much for me. "Go to Guinea!" said I, resuming my pen and paper and paying him no further attention.

Clelia came for orders, sweet and serious in her garb of service. Again I laid aside my poem to Thusis.

"I am glad," said I, camouflaging my melancholy

309

with a sprightly allure, "that you have renounced kidnaping kings and have decided to kidnap Mr. Smith instead."

She didn't seem to think it was funny. The newly engaged lack humor.

"Josephine," she said with dignity, "suggests this supper-card." And she handed me the written sheet.

"Fine!" said I. "Stuff 'em till they're unconscious and we'll have peace."

At that she laughed.

"Josephine desires to know what time the party is to begin," she said.

"It begins with dinner, Clelia. They all come in costume. After dinner they play games. Supper at midnight. Then they dance—God help them."

"The Bolsheviki, too?"

"That's another breed of cat," said I. "I haven't the faintest idea what they intend to do. All I know is that they're not coming to the party. So give them a table by themselves in their rooms half an hour before we dine. Otherwise those chattering apes are likely to spoil the party."

She agreed with me.

After she had departed I began again on my poem called "Nobody Home":

> "She who, risen from the sea,—
> Body fashioned from its foam,—
> Once appeared to favor me,

Now has left me all alone:—
When I call she's not at home;
Silent are the Temple closes
Where her priestess used to roam
Smiling at me, crowned with roses
Underneath the Temple's dome;
So I stand outside alone.
From the dead fire on her altar
Now I turn away and falter:
Aphrodite's not at home.

Goddess born of sun and sea,
Goddess born of sea and sun,
Blue-eyed Venus pity me,
I would wed my Dearest One:—
She denies; and I'm undone!"—

Just here I found myself in difficulties: the verse called for two more words to rhyme with "sun," and the available ones already unused included such words as bun, dun, fun, gun, hun, nun, pun, run, shun, ton, and won—at least these were all I could think of—none among them available for classical purposes.

Much disturbed I sat consulting my Rhyming Dictionary and smoking a cigarette without relish, when a terrific screaming from the Princess Pudelstoff's apartment brought me to my feet and out into the corridor.

The Princess stood in the hallway wringing her hands and almost dancing with rage and fright while, from their doorway across the hall, Puppsky and Wildkatz jabbered at her in apparent fury.

"What the dickens is all this!" I demanded angrily.

"They've got cooties!" she screamed. "I suspected it! I knew it! All Bolsheviki have 'em! Don't let 'em near me! Lock 'em up and turn the gas on! Make 'em take baths! They don't want to, but make 'em!"

"What do you mean?" said I, feeling suddenly ill and pale.

"I mean what I say!" she cried, wringing her jeweled hands. "They've got 'em but we don't have to have 'em! We ain't in the trenches, thank God! No, nor we ain't in Rooshia where them things is family pets! I d-don't want any! I don't want any even from my own brother——"

I strode over to Puppsky and Wildkatz.

"Get into that room or I'll knock your heads off!" I whispered in an ungovernable rage.

They began to chatter at me but thought better of it and fled; and I tore the key from their door and locked it on the outside. Then I went downstairs and out to the stable where I found Raoul and gave him the key.

"You will take a couple of gallons of sheep-dip," said I, still in a cold fury, "and you will go up and fill their bathtub with it, and then you may call me."

"Oh," said Raoul, coolly comprehending, "I can souse them myself, Monsieur."

"Tell them I'll beat them to death if they stir until I permit it," I added. "Also be good enough to burn their clothing and bedding, and fumigate their rooms."

"Give yourself no anxiety, Monsieur," he said, amused.

# XXII

TOWARD the dinner hour excitement in the house became intense as the royal circus fussed and pinned and basted and struggled with its impromptu costumes.

Bells jangled to summon Thusis and Clelia; the Princess Pudelstoff was too fat to braid her own hair; the Countess Manntrapp required basting into her boy's breeches; the Queen, desiring to go as the infant Germania, had pasted tin-foil all over her high Austrian corset, but still it didn't resemble armor, nor did the oval boiler-lid furnished by Josephine Vannis particularly resemble a shield.

Otherwise a blonde wig of tow in two obese braids and a shiny fireman's helmet of 1840 which I discovered in the garret, consoled the queen. To these properties I rashly added an eel-spear; and then, remembering her quick temper, I feared for King Constantine, wondering whether, if fatally prodded, he would name me as accessory after the fact.

As for the men, they continually rang for Raoul who acted as dresser and as messenger between them and Josephine Vannis who had constructed their cos-

314

tumes from odd scraps and from such of their own garments as would serve.

Admiral Lauterlaus was monstrous as a sailor-boy of six; Von Bummelzug, Eddin Bey, Von Dungheim, and Secretary Gizzler were school-lads in socks, bare knees, and denim blouses. King Constantine who, it appeared, rather fancied his own legs, went as a smirking doll in a costume principally constructed out of his wife's underclothes.

But the most gruesome sight of all was Ferdinand as a youthful ballet-girl; and he most horridly resembled an elephant on his hind legs in a stick-out tulle skirt, and his enormous feet, cross-ribboned, went shuffling and flapping to and fro as he waddled about busy with powder and rouge.

Raoul laced his stays and tugged in vain to indent his bulk. It was useless, but we got him into his corsage and left him before a mirror ponderously prancing in imitation of the pony ballet, and singing la-la-la! furtively peeping the while at his own proportions with the unfeigned pleasure of perfect approval.

Really, except for the characters of these impossible individuals, the jolly noise and confusion they made with their preparations and the lively excitement that pervaded hall, corridor and stair, resembled the same sort of delightful uproar one hears at a week-end party in a big country house under similar circumstances.

The queen's bell had been jangling persistently for some minutes when, stepping from my room into the hallway to see whether anybody was answering it, I came face to face with Thusis.

Warm, and delicately flushed with her exertions, she was half vexed, half laughing now as she cast a prudent glance right and left along the corridor before slipping through the door into my room. I followed, locking the door.

"Michael," she began, "the queen says there are not enough women in the party and she insists that Clelia and I find costumes and join. I was furious —and she's making a violent row about it now, insisting, bullying, ordering Clelia about——"

"What! Ordering my servants about!" I interrupted angrily.

"Yes—your servants, Michael," dropping me an ironical curtsey which brought me back to my senses. We both laughed. And suddenly it occurred to me how adorable Thusis would be at a baby-party.

"Why not?" I exclaimed. "Why not drop hostilities for an hour and enjoy the ridiculous? Absurdity always appeals to you, anyway, Thusis," I added, "and the entire situation is so impossible that it ought to attract you!"

"It does," she admitted with that engaging and reckless little laugh I had come to know so well. "Besides, you are my host, Michael, and I am under your roof. So who your ragamuffin-bobtail

316

guests may be does not concern me. Clelia and I
are not responsible, are we?"

"Not at all," said I. "The ignominy of this royal
riff-raff rests upon my shoulders. Anyway, you do
not need to dance except with me," I added reas-
suringly.

"Eddin Bey is rather attractive," she mused, letting her glance rest on me sideways while the innocent pleasure of this discovery parted her lips in a
honeyed smile.

"All right," said I shortly, "dance with him!"

"Michael——"

"Go ahead and dance with him," I repeated,
stabbed by the most ignoble of emotions.

"What an absolute boy you can be," she said. "If
I do this thing at all it is because the tension of
months is becoming unendurable. Reaction from the
tragic usually lands one on the edges of the grotesque. . . . If you had been a girl, Michael, always
sheltered, secure, living a colorless restricted life,
and if you suddenly were cast upon your own feet
with the accumulated responsibility of your race on
your shoulders,—and if, in the very middle of your
first years of liberty and opportunity you suddenly
found this wonderful world flaming like hell all about
you, and all its inhabitants at each other's throats,
and all delight in living turned to hate and fear—
and if you concluded to take your fate into your
own hands and run away from authority, and, in

your own way, fight the good fight for God and King and Country,—and if the strain became, for an hour, too great—wouldn't you react—perhaps to the verge of folly?"

"You bet I would, sweetness," said I, taking her lovely hands in mine.

"I was a school-girl," she said, "when—it devolved upon me, and upon Clelia, to determine our own futures. . . . The loss of parents is a—bewildering thing. . . . Our mania was travel and education to fit us for—for what we considered to be our rightful future positions in the world. . . . We have been in your country,—I don't mean Chile. We know England and France—God bless them both. Then, owing deference anyway if not perhaps blind obedience to the—to a—gentleman in Italy——"

"The King," I said soberly.

"Yes, the King of Italy. We were expected to return to Rome and defer to him all questions concerning our future. . . . And we ran away."

"Why, Thusis?"

"Because we happen to have minds of our own, Michael."

"And you immediately employed them by concocting a plot to kidnap some kings!" I said. "Oh, Thusis, you are the limit!"

"I know I am," she said naïvely. "A mind that

318

does not range to its extremest limits is a rather dull one, isn't it?"

"It is," I admitted, laughing and crushing her hands between my own. "You are delightfully right, Thusis; you are always deliciously right. I don't know who you are except that you're the lovely and mysterious Laughing Girl. What else you may be I don't know, dearest, but you are doubtless somebody or the King of Italy wouldn't bother his clever head about you and your sister."

"He *does* bother, I am afraid," admitted Thusis, smiling. "I'm sorry we've been obliged to annoy him. But it couldn't be helped, because we differed, politically, with the King of Italy. And we ran away from Rome to prove to him that our conception of world-politics was right and his was wrong. And we expect him, some day, to be very grateful to us—because we really are, Clelia and I, two of his most loyal subjects."

She spoke so frankly, so earnestly, that I dared make no jest of what she said.

However, I think she saw a glimmer in my eyes, for she flushed.

"Nothing," she said, "is sacred to a Yankee. Let me *go*."

"Shall I tell you what is sacred to a Yankee, Thusis?" said I, retaining her hands.

"No!"

"I'll tell you all the same: liberty of mind!—lib-

319

erty within law!—liberty within the frontiers of conscience."

"Then you do not deny these privileges to me?"

"They *are* yours, Thusis. No man can deny essential rights and liberties."

"You believe I have a right to act as my conscience dictates?"

"Absolutely."

"To run away from authority?"

"If your mind approves."

"And—and devote my life—risk it—to free my native land and restore to my sovereign what once belonged to him?"

"Naxos?"

"Yes."

I said gravely: "If, in your self-dedication to this work there be no ulterior motive;—if you undertake this unselfishly, and with a heart clean of all personal ambition—then, Thusis, I say, go on! . . . And I am at your service."

Twice she started to speak, and hesitated. In her clear eyes, so intently, almost painfully fixed on mine, I saw she was fiercely pondering my words. Her intense and youthful seriousness in her concentration held me fascinated. And for a little while neither one of us stirred.

And it gradually began to appear to me that what I had said to her had suddenly opened to her young and ardent eyes a totally new view of some things in the world with which she had, perhaps, believed herself thoroughly familiar.

She turned from her absorption; and now she was presented to me in profile with downcast eyes and bitten lip, and a least relaxation of her slender figure which had been so straight and rigid.

It was becoming evident that she had nothing further to say to me,—no reply to make to what I had rather ponderously propounded as an ethical axiom.

But, as responding to the restless pressure, I released her hands, she turned back and stood looking at me out of painfully perplexed eyes—eyes that lacked no courage, either, yet doubted, now, almost wistfully.

Then, not speaking, she unlocked my door and went out.

Smith knocked at the doorway communicating between our apartments, and came in at my absent-minded invitation.

"Of course *you're* not in this, are you, Michael?" he inquired.

"We weren't asked. Besides, there are too many men now, and the Queen wants Thusis, Clelia, and Josephine Vannis to serve dinner in costume and join the party afterward."

"Are they going to do it?" he asked, surprised and amused.

"I don't know. . . . Tell me, Smith, whom do you suspect Thusis to be? I can see you have some theory concerning Clelia—some idea. Haven't you?"

"Yes, I have."

"Would you care to share it with me?"

"Yes. But I can't."

"Could you tell me why you can't?"

"I think I may tell you that much. The King of Italy requested me to maintain silence in the possible event of my discovering the identity of Thusis and Clelia. I am here on the King's service, with certain definite orders. I shall scrupulously observe these orders. Among these is his request concerning the identity of these two charming young girls."

"Just one thing, then. *Have* you discovered the identity of Thusis?"

"No."

"Of Clelia?"

He reddened. "Yes, I have," he said. "Or rather she has confirmed what I had begun to suspect."

"Clelia has told you who she is!" I exclaimed.

"She has."

"Isn't that disobedience of orders?"

"She told me before I could stop her. I never dreamed she was going to tell me. It came out—like a bolt of lightning—while I—I was—slipping over her finger that ring I used to wear——"

"*She* wears it!"

"Yes. She was glorious. She———"

"And she's going to marry you?"

"Yes, God bless her."

So I wrung his hand in silence and strove hard not to let any comparison of his situation and mine taint with the slightest trace of bitterness my happiness in his good fortune and my cordial recognition of it now.

Thusis was not mentioned between us. He didn't say "buck up, old chap," or "go in and win," or any insincere thing of that sort, for I felt that he believed my case to be hopeless.

Presently he returned to his room and closed the door. And I sat down at my table and produced pen and paper with a view to further poetry—my only form of relief from grief.

But rhymes evaded me; and finally I gave it up and rested my head on both hands, unhappy, unsatisfied, feeling that I was a failure, and always had been one.

After all what could such a glorious young thing as Thusis see in an interior decorator from New York?—a profession into which had minced all the lady-like young men and lisping sissies in Manhattan!

Perhaps, after all, the profession was all right, but the people who practiced it were weird and incompetent. And as for me I was perfectly aware that I had no taste, no color sense, no glimmering idea of composition.

Doubtless my artistic and financial success had been due to my utter incapacity.

I proceeded to masticate the cud of bitterness.

Ï had been masticating longer than I realized for the light in the room was already growing less when a knock came at my door; and I shoved my unuttered verses into the drawer and grunted out, "Come in !"

It was Thusis, transfigured, sparkling, mischievous, audacious. And she was the most beautiful thing I ever saw.

Her magnificent ruddy hair, unloosened, framed her face, its upcurled, burnished ends falling to her waist.

Otherwise she was an exquisite French doll in knee-skirts and sash and all over pale blue ribbons.

"I'm going to have a good time if I do murder to-morrow, Michael. Do you like my costume? Really? That is so sweet of you! You always are the most satisfactory of men! And you should see Clelia! She's like me only her ribbons and sash are primrose. She is really charming."

"Thusis," said I, "you and Clelia shall sit at table and Smith and I are going to turn waiters! No!" as she exclaimed in protest, "let's be logical in our grotesqueries! This little world of ours here in

Schwindlewald is already absurd enough with you
and Clelia waiting on table. Let's turn it completely upside down and stand it on its head."

She finally consented, forced by my gay ardour,
and, I think, mischievously pleased at the prospect
of protest from the Queen.

All over the house, now, I could hear snatches of
loud laughter as my Teutonic guests began to gather
and visit one another in their costumes. Thusis
fled; and I opened the door and broke the news to
Smith.

"Get into your evening duds," I added, "and announce dinner. We're all going stark mad and I'm
glad of it."

So I dressed, and found him ready when I was;
and we went downstairs into the large lounging room
where Raoul was fitting disks into the music-box.

He laughed when we told him our intentions, and
then we went into the kitchen and informed Josephine Vannis. That stately Juno condescended to
smile on us. She was rather tremendously impos-
ing as a baby with bonnet and stick-out skirts—as
though somebody had decked out a masterpiece of
Praxiteles.

Retiring, Smith murmured: "Only the Parthe-
non possesses such awe-inspiring symmetry; only
the Acropolis could vie with her. Did you ever see
such superb underpinning in all your life?"

Stunned by such stupendous symmetry I admitted that I never had. And we went away to announce dinner.

But it was not until the noisy company were gathered in the dining-room that the Queen perceived the two empty chairs and began to realize my intentions. And she came to me and made angry representations, refusing to be seated on the right of a servant, or, indeed, to suffer servants at all at table, and saying that if she chose to admit my waitresses to the dancing hall, it was because such privileges sometimes were graciously permitted to the peasantry who never misunderstood such condescension.

"Madame," said I, "my housekeeper, Thusis, sits in my place at table this evening. And if, madame, you are so deeply concerned about it, comfort yourself with the explanation that in my housekeeper you behold your host; she is my vice-reine, or viceroy, or vice-regent—whatever you like best, madame! She represents me! In her you see embodied the inviolable authority of the master of this house wherein you are a guest! However, madame, if you prefer to be served alone in the bar, I will have a table set there for you——"

She almost spat at me; and Thusis entered, her hand linked in Clelia's.

I think the royal circus was stupefied by the beauty of these two young girls. A rather frightful silence reigned for a moment; then the Countess Manntrapp clapped her jeweled hands and sang out in her clear, soprano voice: "Brava! Bravissima! They are beautiful, our little waitresses!"

Eddin Bey removed his red fez and, swinging it by the tassel, gave three hochs.

Then, instantly, the cheers broke out everywhere: I gave Thusis my arm; Smith offered his to Clelia; and we seated them amid shouts and the waving of napkins, the queen's eyes glittering like twin daggers all the while.

Such an uproar as Smith and I served the soup! Gurgles, gulps, scraping, sucking sounds arose from feeding Teutons. The fish produced a frightful clatter of knives and forks, and the Princess Pudelstoff cut her lip with her knife but stuck a patch on it and joyously immersed it in gravy.

They—the kings and admirals and generals were drinking too much; I noticed that in the din. And toward the wrecked climax of the dinner when everybody was offering everybody else tinsel bon-bons, and people were pulling snapping-crackers with one another, I sent Raoul out to start the music-box; and Josephine Vannis emerged all clean and fresh and scented to join the revelry.

Her appearance awed us all; again I felt that innate reverence for the prodigiously beautiful, that awe for things superbly Greek. Her effect upon the two kings, however, was pronounced. The wild-pig eyes of Ferdinand became fixed and vitreous for a full minute; King Constantine's orbs bulged. Both

made straight for her when Thusis gave the signal
to rise; and I saw the exasperated Queen staring at
her spouse and fingering a large, sharp, jeweled pin.

But I went into the dancing room and took command without loss of time; and Smith followed with
a bottle of wine and a roast chicken—our own dinner
which we intended to discuss while supervising this
party and keeping the music-box busy.

"Silence!" said I, hammering on the glass lamp-
shade with my fork. "The party begins, like all
children's parties, with children's games. 'Going to
Jerusalem' will be the first game played!"

"How is that played?" demanded several at once.

I instructed them gravely; and presently Smith
and I, eating our dinner beside the music-box, beheld
our guests in their baby costumes marching around
and around a row of chairs and, at a given signal,
falling into the unoccupied seats with squeals and
shrieks and bellows of laughter.

They tired of that, presently, and I laid aside my
chicken and glass of claret and, rising, instructed
them in the game called "Oats-peas-beans." They
listened attentively, but Thusis and Clelia appeared much disconcerted when further revelations
on my part disclosed that it was a "kissing" game;
and they both withdrew, firmly declining to play it,
much to the dissatisfaction of Eddin Bey and Tino.

So Thusis and Clelia came over to where Smith
and I were installed, and, while we resumed our

dinner, they cranked the music-box in which I had inserted a disk containing the immemorial air of "Oats-peas-beans."

We then became pleased observers of royalty and nobility in baby clothes, hands joined, walking very seriously in a circle in the center of which stood the Princess Pudelstoff, and singing in unison and with all their might:

*"Oats-peas-beans*
  *And barley grow,*
  *Though you and I and nobody knows*
  *Where oats-peas-beans*
  *And barley grow!"*

*"Thus the farmer sows his seed!*
  (All made motions of scattering something.)
  *Thus he stands and takes his ease!*
  (All with hands on hips.)
  *Stamps his foot,*
  (All stamp)
  *And claps his hand,*
  (All clap.)
  *And turns around to view the land,*
  (All turn.)
  *While waiting for a partner!*
  *While waiting for a partner!*
  *So open the ring*
  *And choose one in*
  *And kiss him when you get him in!"*

329

The singing ceased; the Princess Pudelstoff giggled; then, to his dismay, she pounced upon Eddin Bey, almost throttled that handsome Moslem in her enthusiasm, and gave him a resounding smack amid screams of laughter and roars of approval.

And then the game waxed fast and furious: Eddin Bey chose the Countess Manntrapp and kissed her delicately and courteously; she chose King Constantine, but merely saluted his cheek, much to his exasperation.

Then Tino held the ring, waggish, jocose, bantering everybody with their expectations. But though the queen eyed him commandingly, furiously, he swaggered over to Josephine Vannis and soundly kissed that classic memorial in animated Grecian marble.

The Teutons behaved rather grossly; King Ferdinand ranged the ring like a liberated wild hog and presently charged the object of his osculatory intentions—Josephine.

Probably nobody dared kiss the queen, but such respectful abstention seemed to please her none the more, for presently she hissed something into Tino's ear, and he chose her into the ring with an agility born of terror.

Once there she glared at everybody and then, with a sneer, selected Tino again, and the game, promising to become a monotony and a deadlock, I rose and, waving a leg of the chicken to impose silence, proclaimed that the games had ended and that dancing would now begin.

Raoul inserted a fox-trot of sorts; and the next instant everybody was footing it.

"Raoul," I said in a guarded voice, "did you souse those Bolsheviki in sheep-dip?"

"I did, sir."

"What did they do?"

"They made an agonizing noise, Monsieur. I fear it was, perhaps, their first bath."

"Go up and dip 'em again."

"All Bolshevikdom will shriek," he said, grinning.

"Let it for a change. It's set all the world scratching. Let Bolshevik Russia do a little shrieking, now that she feels the boche biting her worse than her native cooties! Get some more sheep-dip and de-louse that pair of things upstairs."

He went away, laughing.

# XXIII

**F**OR a while the dancing was lively and good-humored hilarity reigned.

The Tzar of all the Bulgars had imbibed enough wine to dull, if not to obliterate that continual desire of his to slink into corners and peep out at a hostile world bent on his assassination. Only when somebody spoke to him too abruptly behind his back did the customary symptoms blanch his face and set his wild eyes roving and his big nose wrinkling like a boar which winds an enemy.

He was having as good a time as such a person can ever have; and toward supper time his exhilaration incited him to attempt a waddling sort of Bulgarian dance with the Countess Manntrapp—an amazing exhibition of mammoth movements on his part; and a sort of infernal and fascinating grace on the part of the lithe Countess.

Dancing with Thusis, I hastily led her out of their way, and everybody else stood in the circle, the center of which was pervaded by Ferdinand and his lively vis-à-vis.

Which performance presently stirred Admiral

Lauterlaus from a somewhat beer-sodden lethargy, and he emitted raucous sounds of protest. But Baron Bummelzug began to snap his fingers and stamp and caper in imitation of the *schuplattl* of the Bavarian peasantry; and all the boche, except the Queen, imitated him and seized partners.

Eddin Bey came to ask Thusis, and he was so faultlessly polite and so gay and graceful that she cast a saucy glance of dismissal at me and accepted him.

It was quite all right, of course, but it depressed me a little, particularly because Clelia had inexorably refused everybody except Smith.

Now there is a very beautiful Grecian dance supposed to be the triumphant dance executed by the Ten Thousand when they caught sight of the sea; and it is called "The Sea-dance."

Tino, rather drunk, climbed on a chair, shouted for attention, and informed the company that he was about to perform this celebrated dance.

But when we all gave him room he jigged around a while like an intoxicated soldier's drab, and, remarking jauntily that he had forgotten it, offered ten thousand drachma to anybody present who could dance the Sea-dance of the Ten Thousand.

He was rather vulgar about it, too, digging into his pockets and pulling out fistfuls of hun gold, and loudly demanding that somebody should attempt to win it.

I glanced instinctively toward Thusis who, her dance with Eddin interrupted, stood in the circle opposite me.

Her gray eyes were brilliant, her cheeks delicately flushed, and the shock of thick ruddy hair fairly glittered, every silky thread afire with the gleam of molten gold.

She looked at me with the sweet, reckless audacity of a spoiled child; then she laughed and said something to Clelia. I saw the latter go to the music box, select a record, start it; and the haunting air called The Sea-dance floated out.

Then Thusis seemed suddenly to melt into motion; her slim feet scarcely touched the floor; head, arms, slender body, were all part of a single and exquisite motion flowing from one soft curve to another.

You could have heard a pin drop in the room; and I did hear one—a big jeweled affair, that clattered to my feet.

As I stooped to recover it the queen said hoarsely in my ear:

"Who is that girl?"

I turned; she snatched the jewel and dug it into her hair.

"That girl, madame, is Thusis, my housekeeper."

"Fiddle," retorted the queen. "She's something else, too,—or once was. The first time I noticed her it occurred to me that I'd seen her somewhere.

What was she—a celebrated dancer?—before she became your *housekeeper?*"

The queen's nasty insolence froze me.

"I am not," said I, "as familiar with celebrated dancers as your husband is—and the various men of your immediate family."

That I had penetrated her incognito did not appear to disturb her as much as my inferences concerning Tino and the Kaiser and that degenerate nest of reptiles, her nephews.

A white, pinched expression came into her frosty face and her eyes flamed.

"I thought you were a Yankee," she said.

"A Yankee from Chile," said I, bowing.

She looked clean through me at Thusis.

"I've seen that woman somewhere," she said without emotion. "I'll recollect where, presently."

But my eyes and attention were now focussed on the lovely Thusis and I paid no further heed to this bad-tempered Hohenzollern.

Never have I seen such an exquisite dance, such grace, such loveliness. As for the boches, when Thusis ended her *Dance of the Sea*, they were like a herd of cattle galloping around her and bellowing their satisfaction.

Tino, drunk and prodigal, began to throw handfuls of gold at Thusis, and, enraged, I caught him by the collar and jerked him onto a chair.

"Where the devil do you think you are—in the

335

Coulisse of the Opera?" I cried in his partly deafened ear.

But he only grinned and wagged his head and attempted to fish more gold out of his pockets. But
now his thrifty wife interfered and she ordered Secretary Gizzler to pick up every coin. Then she
hissed something into Tino's ear which seemed to
galvanize that partly soused monarch so that he
found his feet with alacrity and suffered himself to
be led aside by his tight-lipped spouse.

From time to time during the festivities I had
heard distant significant noises indicating that upstairs the Bolsheviki were not enduring sheep-dip
and imprisonment with resignation.

Once I had slipped away to the corridor outside
their quarters, but, when I made my presence known,
Raoul from within calmly assured me that the de-
lousing was progressing successfully and that he
did not require my assistance.

Russia, forcibly scrubbed, had put forth agon-
ized howls; and now, Russia imprisoned, was bat-
tering at its door and yelling murder.

Now and then, a hun noticed the noise and inquired concerning its origin, but I always turned on
more music and they soon forgot in the din of the
dance.

Thusis had resumed her dance with Eddin Bey;
Smith and Clelia were dancing. I said to Raoul,

who was starting to crank the music-machine: "I'll just step up and quiet those Bolsheviki."

They were raining blows upon their door when I arrived. I rapped sharply.

"What do you want?" said I.

They gibbered at me in Russian.

"Speak English!" I insisted.

Perhaps Puppsky was so excited or so demoralized by his first bath that he forgot he could speak English.

I tried them in Italian: "Whata da mat'?" I inquired pleasantly. They chattered back at me like lunatic squirrels.

"What the devilovitch is the matsky?" I shouted, incensed at their stupidity. "You listen to me! Your clothes are being boiled and you've got to stay where you are! Stop your noise, Puppsky!"

And off I went to inspect the big wash boiler in the kitchen where, lifting the lid which had been the queen's shield, I was gratified to observe the garments of the Bolsheviki simmering nicely.

"It is not the only vermin that Germania's shield covers," said I. And much pleased with my *jeu d'esprit*, I poured in another bottle of sheep-dip and returned to the dance salon where supper was now being served at little tables.

As soon as I entered the room I felt trouble brewing. The inevitable hunnish reaction had set in. A tired boche is an ugly one; an intoxicated hun may

become either offensively sentimental or surly and
ingeniously bestial. And now they were about to
become surfeited huns, heavy with wine, heavier with
food. I did not fancy the looks of things very much.

The queen alone appeared to be perfectly sober;
the others were engaged in that sort of half insolent
raillery always provocative of a row, shouting German pleasantries at one another from table to table,
lifting slopping glasses, cheering, singing and leer-
ing at the ladies.

Bummelzug demanded that the music-box play
"Deutschland über Alles," but the disk was non-ex-
istent.

Von Dungheim, who exhibited an inclination to
weep at any mention of Germany, asked in a hoarsely
saturated voice for a folk-song. And Raoul turned
on two; and the huns sang first "*Du bist wie eine
Blume,*" which shattered them sentimentally so that
loud sobs punctuated the "*Lorelei*" which, of course,
followed.

Then Ferdinand, one arm around the Princess
Pudelstoff, and a chicken wing in the other hand,
lifted a voice choked with food and attempted a
Bulgarian folk-song—something about the "Kara
Dagh" and "Slivnitza"—but presently lost all recollection of what he was doing and challenged everybody to extemporaneous rhymes in praise of his native land.

Nobody obliged.

"Too stupid!" he' remarked thickly. "Nobody clever enough to rhyme *'Bulgarian'*—eh, mine host?" looking around at me where I sat shielding Thusis from the playful attentions of King Constantine who was attempting to pinch her.

"Of course," said I, " *'Bulgarian'* rhymes with *'vulgarian'*; but that's obvious." And I smiled at the Tzar of all the Bulgars and offered Thusis a bon-bon.

She looked at Ferdinand, at Tino, at the queen: suddenly she threw back her head, and that lovely, childlike, silvery laughter rippled through the Teutonic din.

There was no scorn in her laughter, only the delicious, irresistible gaiety of a young girl face to face with the excruciating. And there is nothing on earth more innocently insolent.

Every Teuton head was turned toward her in stupefied displeasure; fishy, fixed, pig-like eyes stared at this young girl who dared condone an insult to Bulgaria with her fresh, impulsive laughter.

Suddenly behind me there was a brusque movement; I heard Tino protest that his foot had been trodden on; and, turning, I saw the queen excitedly rising from her place.

"I know who that woman is now!" she said in a voice as sharp as a blade. She pointed at Thusis like a vixen from the markets:

"That's The Laughing Girl!" she cried. "Look at her! Anybody can recognize her now from her photographs!"

Thusis colored crimson and shrank from the brutal publicity against my shoulder, staring wide-eyed at the hatefully sneering visage of the queen.

"The celebrated Laughing Girl!" repeated the queen mockingly; "Mr. O'Ryan's *housekeeper*, gentlemen—and our guest at dinner! And what does our German chivalry and nobility think of that insult launched at us by a Yankee inn-keeper?"

"Be silent, madame!" I said sharply. "If you don't know how to conduct yourself I shall request your husband to remove you!"

Then it came, the boche deluge!—a herd of huddling swine on their feet, all grunting at me, enraged, clamoring, waving their arms. And in the midst of the guttural uproar a thin, high voice pierced all sound and dominated it—the sniffling whine of Secretary Gizzler.

Possessed by a sort of cringing exaltation, he rose to his thin, splay feet, and pointed a meager finger almost in the shocked face of Thusis.

"That is the Duchess of Naxos!" he squealed.

At that Thusis was on her feet, white as a slim sword-blade, and her gray eye charged with lightning.

I rose, too, incredulous, astounded.

"Thusis, Duchess of Naxos!" piped the excited

voice of Secretary Gizzler. "She and The Laughing
Girl are one! I know! I was in the Intelligence!
I procured that photograph so that if this woman
ever gave our fatherland any trouble she could be
easily recognized wherever she might be!" He beat
his temples and glared at Thusis: "Stupid! Stupid!" he squealed; "why did I not recognize her at
once! Why did not a single German present recognize the chief mischief-maker in Greece!—the insti-
gator of revolt!—the pupil of Venizelos!—the enemy
of their majesties King Constantine and Queen
Sophia!—the plotter who aided in their downfall!—
Thusis, Duchess of Naxos!"

The huns seemed thunderstruck; Thusis, very pale,
swept them with insolent cool eyes.

All at once King Ferdinand got to his feet and
loomed up like a bad dream.

"Naxos! Where is Naxos?" he demanded.

And when Secretary Gizzler would have answered
him: "The man's mad," he said heavily; "there's
no such place."

At that I saw Thusis's face flame; but the boche
all around her burst into a roar of ironic laughter.

"Let the fatherland tremble!" bellowed General
Count von Dungheim. "Naxos declares war!"

"Look sharp!" shouted Admiral Lauterlaus, "or
we'll have Andorra invading us."

"And Monaco, too!" growled Bummelzug. "*Gott*

*in Himmel!* If Naxos defies us through her Duchess we're as good as lost!"

"I tell you!" shrieked Secretary Gizzler, "that it's no laughing matter! That girl *is* the Duchess of Naxos! And the other—her sister—look well at her, gentlemen!—she is Duchess of Tenedos!"

"That belongs to my country!" cried Eddin Bey, laughing, "the island of Tenedos. I sincerely hope the Cyclades are not in revolt! But if they are I'm very glad so charming a lady is to own one of them."

But his attempt at a good natured diversion made no impression on the huns; and Gizzler, venomous and quivering, held the floor and kept his weak, vicious eyes on Thusis.

"It was the Ægean League that exiled the King and Queen of Greece!" he said. "*She* made that league!—that woman standing there—Thusis, Duchess of Naxos!"

"It isn't a Duchy!" cried the queen, choking with fury; "it's a Greek Island!"

"It's a Venetian Duchy and belongs to Italy, madame," I said calmly—having read up on it in the Encyclopedia since I had fallen in love with one of its inhabitants.

At that the queen turned on me like a fury.

"You lie!" she said.

I tried to control myself:

"Naxos is a Venetian Duchy, belonging to Italy,"

I repeated. "I am happy and proud of the priv-
ilege of acknowledging the restoration of Naxos to
Italy—and I salute its ruler—Thusis, Duchess of
Naxos!"

And I lifted the white hand of Thusis and touched
it with my lips.

"There's conspiracy here!" shouted Tino, very
drunk, and vainly attempting to stand up. "We're
all tangled up in treason here! We're in the web of
the Ægean League! What are these people doing
here, anyway!—all these Yankees and Duchesses
running about underfoot——"

A hiccough terminated his activities and he slid
up against his spouse who shoved him away, her eyes
flashing.

"That lying Yankee," she began, almost beside
herself, "has set a trap for us here!"

At the word "trap," King Ferdinand, drunk as
he was, got up hastily and started toward the door.

"You'd better defend yourselves!" he shouted.
"I've got pistols in my room——"

His voice ceased: Raoul blocked his way:

"Stay where you are," he said, smiling and cool.
And placing a powerful hand on King Ferdinand's
chest he shoved him backward onto a chair. Then,
to my surprise, Raoul slipped a pair of automatic
pistols from his side pockets and cast a merry glance
around him at the company.

343

"The first man that moves," he remarked, "is not likely to continue the movement."

The dead silence which fell over everybody was startling. Raoul, resting gracefully on a table with one leg on the floor, looked about him as though immensely amused. Then, as we awaited further developments, his countenance assumed a thoughtful expression—and he absent-mindedly hummed aloud his favorite air:

"Crack-brain-cripple-arm
You have done a heap of harm——"

# XXIV

RAOUL looked up, thoughtfully, playing with his pistols, and said to King Constantine in an unaccented and conversational tone:

"After all, who were you to rule Naxos?—you cheap, treacherous, yellow dog!"

That partly cleared the king's muddy mind and he lurched to an upright position and began to take notice.

"You sold Greece to the boche," continued Raoul in his serene, even voice, toying idly with his pistols. "What else you did—what else you are—is a trifle too vile to repeat aloud——"

He turned and looked at the Tzar of all the Bulgars whose ungainly bulk as he sat on his chair was now agitated by visible tremors:

"Murderer and coward," mused Raoul aloud. "Every time you hire your gun-men to kill an enemy you hurry away to establish an alibi, don't you? You cheap peddler of duped people—you made a rotten bargain this time, didn't you? When your treacherous pal, Tino, betrayed Serbia, you swindled your own people, didn't you?"

He shrugged, dangled his pistols, glanced at Giz-

zler,—or rather *through* Gizzler as though the
wretched creature were not there,—and his eyes encountered the interested jet black orbs of Eddin
Bey.

Both smiled, Eddin in the face of death; Raoul
with the generous grin of a man who recognizes in
his enemy a peer.

"Eddin Bey," he said, still smiling, "the Osmanli
fight fairly. Ask the British Tommy. . . . And
your fool of a Sultan is dead. And what do you
think of affairs at present?"

"They are not any too gay," replied Eddin Bey,
laughing, "especially in the Alps."

The half smile on Raoul's face flickered and faded:

"You're about done for, you Turks," he said
quietly. "You bet on the wrong horse, too. And
now Enver Pasha keeps running to Berlin to ask why
the all-highest doesn't make him Khedive of Egypt
as he promised. And Taalat is scared, and the
butcher Djavid is in the dumps. Oh, I know it was
not you Osmanli that set the Kurds and Bashi-Ba-
zouks on the Armenians. That butchery of a million souls, men, women, children, babies, was conceived by the Berlin government and superintended
from the Yldiz Palace."

Raoul turned and looked contemptuously at the
Germans:

"You square-heads," he said, "have achieved one
thing, anyway. Never before in history has a na-

tion been indicted, and it was supposed it could not be done. But it has been done in your case. And for the first time also in history an entire race is spoken of and known to civilization only by a revolting nick-name—*boche!*

"Do you know what it means? There have been disputes concerning the origin of the term *boche*. The French say it means a stupid fellow—a clown; the Belgians think that it is a vulgar term for 'blockhead.' But I shall tell you what it really does mean: it means, in South African Dutch, an unclean and degraded species of wart-hog; and it has been in use for fifty years!"

He lifted one pistol and sat idly twirling it around his fore-finger.

"I know why you came here to Schwindlewald," he said, "to put *that* back on the throne of Greece!" —he nodded toward Tino.

"In Berne you live luxuriously and wastefully in the midst of famine. You eat as usual; your bread is white; there are no restrictions for you in the matter of food amid a hungry people. You maintain a court there with flunkies, stables, motor-cars —every necessity and luxury which is now forbidden by Swiss law and by the law of decency you violate daily!"

He looked at the queen:

"Your effrontery, madame, is of course, in keeping with Hohenzollern tradition. But things are

happening now—*now*, madame,—at this very moment! And I'm wondering just how long the Swiss
are likely to endure your behavior in Berne."

He sat silent after that for a little while, twirling his pistols and whistling softly to himself:

"Crack-brain-cripple-arm——"

Suddenly Eddin made a quick motion and Raoul
shot the leg off his chair letting him down with a
crash.

The startling crash of the pistol-shot brought
them to their feet.

"Sit down!" said Raoul sharply, "or it will be a
living leg next time; and the time after that a wooden
head!" He sat watching Eddin getting to his feet
with a shame-faced laugh:

"No use," said Raoul in a friendly voice, "it can't
be done, Colonel."

"I notice it can't," remarked Eddin, laughing.
"Well sir, you have entertained us very pleasantly
with your historical inappropos. Is there to be a
denouément perhaps?"

"Did you expect one?"

Eddin shrugged: "A firing-squad, possibly. But
of course I don't insist."

Raoul shook his curly head: "No, Colonel Eddin;
no firing-squad. No Turkish atrocities, no Bulgarian murders, no boche bestialities." He turned
contemptuously on Constantine:

348

"You laid plans in Berne to entrap the leaders of the Ægean League. You forged instructions sent to me by Monsieur Venizelos. You attempted to foment an uprising in Naxos because you foresaw the trouble it would bring between two of the Allied powers—between Italy and Greece!

"Also you conceived and encouraged a plot to attempt the capture of yourself and your wife because you believed that Greece, although now rid of you, would resent such an attempt; and that chivalrous America would be shocked at the kidnaping of a woman—even such a notorious one as your Hohenzollern wife."

He eyed him for a moment: "You *are* the cheapest back-stairs scullion who ever grafted, Tino," he said. "But remember this little couplet the next time you go gaily grafting:

"'Grecian gift and Spanish fig
Help the fool his grave to dig!'"

"That's the motto of the Ægean League!" burst out the queen in a white hot fury.

"It is, madame," returned Raoul, pleasantly.

Then he placed the other foot on the floor and got up leisurely from his seat on the table.

"You're all free to go," he said carelessly.

A moment of suspense, then the boche herd scrambled to its feet and rushed for the nearest exit. And

Raoul came over to where I stood beside Thusis with Smith and Clelia beside me.

"All their weapons are locked up in the cellar," he said, laughing; "let them look for them. Also I have all their documents packed up. We're through with them," he added, smiling at Thusis.

But there was a thunder cloud on her white brow:

"Are we not going to secure and crate the kings, Raoul?" she demanded. "Do you and Josephine fail me, now?"

"Duchess," he said smilingly, "news came to-night —a real communication from Monsieur Venizelos."

"*How* could it come?" I asked.

"The Pass is open," he replied serenely. "And," turning to Thusis, "so is the road to France. And we should travel it this night unless we wish to see our papers taken from us and our persons subjected to arrest by these somewhat singular Swiss gendarmes."

"What did Monsieur Venizelos say?" insisted Thusis, tears of disappointment and vexation shining in her gray eyes.

"The letter is here,"—Raoul touched his breast pocket—"at the disposal of her grace the Duchess of Naxos——"

"*Tell* me!" cried Thusis, angrily, "and let my 'grace' go to the devil!"

"Monsieur Venizelos warns us of Tino's forgery. We are *not* to touch these kings: we are *not* to proclaim Naxos an Italian Duchy and you its hereditary ruler."

There was a painful silence.

Very slowly Thusis turned and looked at me. And I remembered then what I had said to her about the purity and unselfishness of justifiable revolutions.

And now I realized that part of this revolution in Naxos was the restoration of an ancient Duchy and of a family as ancient, embodied in this young girl before me.

At that moment Tino came lurching into the room followed by the queen, and presently by the majority of the huns in the house-party.

"Somebody has been through my luggage!" he barked. "Now I'm damned if I put up with that——"

Raoul still held one of his pistols in his hand and Tino's bloodshot eyes fell on it.

"Oh, very well," he said, turning on his heel.

The queen, pallid and ghastly with fury, faced us a moment:

"You'll all pay this reckoning!" she whispered,— "every one of you!"

"Madame," said Raoul gaily, "the Pass is open. And really very wonderful news has come through. But I'm afraid you don't like Yankees, and it won't interest you to hear that the Yankee General Pershing has wiped out the St. Mihiel salient, and the guns of Metz are saluting the event."

"Lies!" she retorted; "Yankee lies!" She bit her lip, glared at us all, turned her Hohenzollern back on us. Behind her stood the huddled huns, sullen, enraged, baffled in their headlong rush to find weapons for avenging Prussian "honor."

They were quite helpless although outnumbering us; and they seemed to realize it.

Raoul, watching them, passed his pistols to me and walking coolly in among them and shoving the Admiral and Von Dungheim out of his way, went to the kitchen. Josephine had wrung out the disinfected garments of the Bolsheviki. But they were still steaming when Raoul unlocked their door and flinging the clothing at them, bade them dress and depart.

"The Pass is open," he said. "It's a summer night and you won't take cold. Get into those things and get out of this house! And," he added, "you ought to be obliged for what I've done to you."

When Raoul came back the huns had retired to their several apartments; Smith and Clelia stood by the window whispering together; Thusis was absently looking over the letter from Monsieur Venizelos; and I leaned in the doorway gazing out at the high stars above the disfigured Bec de l'Empereur.

"Nature pulled his nose and twisted it, too," murmured Raoul, passing me. Then he said aloud:

"It really is not healthy for us here any longer.

352

[The Swiss gendarmes will arrive in the morning. I have held the wagon that penetrated the Pass. It's waiting for us. So if you'll be kind enough to pack your luggage——"

"Are you going?" I asked, appalled.

"We must," said Raoul gaily. "And I regret to say that I think you and Mr. Smith had better come with us."

. I shrugged my shoulders.

"It's too bad to have done this to you," said Raoul, "but we couldn't very well avoid it. You had better cross with us into France until this blows over. The boche are sure to raise a terrific row; and the Swiss are mortally afraid of invasion. So if you remain you'll be annoyed—held for examination—possibly imprisoned. But they won't confiscate your estate: you know too much about the Swiss Government's cognizance of these hun conspirators, and their use of neutral soil."

I scarcely heard him; I was looking at Thusis who stood bending over the music-box and studying the disks lying there.

"Could I help you to pack up?" insisted Raoul.

"Thanks; I shall remain here," said I quietly.

[At that moment the door burst open and Puppsky, his clothing still steaming in spots, rushed in upon us followed by Wildkatz in similar and vaporous attire:

"I been robbed!" yelled Puppsky. "All my papers und evertings it hass been robbed me alretty!"

Raoul shot a contemptuous glance at the chattering pair of Reds: "I haven't bothered about *your* papers," he said.

"Did I say you done it! No, I did not say you done!" shouted Puppsky. "I see this here Countess hanging around by the room of comrade Wildkatz. What for iss she in this, I ask it? She iss who, perhaps? I think she got my papers also comrade Wildkatz he also believes it——"

"Go and ask her!" said Raoul bluntly.

When they were gone Smith turned from the window where he had been whispering with Clelia:

"It's quite *en règle*," he said coolly. "The Countess Manntrapp is in the employment of the Siberian government. She came here to get what she wanted and report on these Reds. She left for the Pass an hour ago, on foot."

The unseen web in the center of which I had unwittingly stood for so long suddenly became partly visible to me.

Raoul laughed. "It's really a pity," he remarked to me, "that we can't catch and box up these kings and take them along with us. But Venizelos says no; and he's always right. So we had all better pack up and be on our way."

He went off whistling the "Crack-brain" song. Presently, without noticing me, Thusis turned from the music-box and walked over to where her sister was standing; and I heard her say something about dressing.

I turned away and went silently upstairs to my room, and, closing the door, seated myself.

The baby-party indeed was ended.

# XXV

I WAS still sitting there when somebody knocked, and, supposing it to be Smith, I said, "come in."

Thusis entered, and I rose. We looked at each other in silence, then I set a chair for her by my table and she dropped onto it as though tired.

She wore a dark hat and a dark gown which I had never seen. Also she was gloved, another phase hitherto unfamiliar to me. And her beauty almost hurt me.

"You are not going with us?" she asked in a low voice.

"No."

"Why not?"

"There is no reason why I should go."

"You are not afraid to remain?"

I forced a smile.

"You choose to stay here in this house all alone with these huns?" she persisted.

"What else is there to do? Besides, they'll leave to-morrow."

"And then you'll be utterly alone here."

I nodded, smiling.

"Won't you come with us as far as France?"

I thanked her.

"Why won't you?"

"I think I'd be rather lonelier in France," I said lightly, "than I might be here."

"Will you be lonely?"

I did not answer.

When I glanced across the table at her again she had unpinned her hat. I waited; but she tossed it from her onto my bed.

"Why do you do that?" I asked.

"I shall not leave unless you do," she said serenely.

"That's nonsense! I am in no danger!"

"I should be, if I left you alone here."

"In what danger?"

"In danger—of falling a prey to—grief—Michael."

My heart almost stopped: she was looking down at the gloves which she was slowly stripping from her wrists:

"Danger of grief," she repeated, "of lifelong sorrow—for leaving you—here—alone. . . . Because, once, I gave my heart to you. . . ."

"You were only Thusis, then," I said, steadying my voice and senses with an effort.

"Am I less, now, in your eyes?" She lifted her head and looked at me.

"You are the Duchess of Naxos."

She smiled faintly: "What was it you once said to me about revolutions?—about the necessity for purity of motive and absolute unselfishness for those who revolted against tyranny?"

I was silent.

"Michael?"

"Yes."

"How can I incite my people to revolt unless my motives are *entirely* free from selfish interest?"

"Are they not?"

"Why do you ask me? You know that I would be Duchess of Naxos if my country regains its freedom under the Italian crown."

"Has that influenced you?"

Her candid, sweet gaze met mine: "I think it has."

And, as I said nothing, "I hadn't quite considered it in that light," she said. "I thought my motives were pure. Besides, I really am hereditary Duchess of Naxos—if ever there is to be such a Duchy again." She laughed a little. "A phantom ruler in a phantom realm. It must amuse you, Michael."

"It may all come to pass," said I.

"No."

"Why not?"

"Monsieur Venizelos does not wish it. Nor does the King of Italy. Also I am afraid that Naxos is really quite contented under the Greek flag, now that

Constantine is exiled and because, moreover, that same flag flies beside the flags of England, France, and Italy. . . . No, Michael, there will be no revolution now in Naxos; no Duchy, no Duchess. . . . And," she rose and looked at me, and stretched out one fair hand, "come into France with me, Michael. . . . I can't leave my heart here with you unless I stay here, too. . . . I can't become disembodied and float off to France leaving heart and mind and body and soul here—in your arms—in the arms of the man I—love. . . . Can I, dear Michael?—*Can* I—my dear lover?—my dearest—my beloved——"

Her fragrant, flushed face was close against mine when we heard Smith's trunk banging in his room and Raoul's voice: "Easy, *mon vieux! Mon dieu,* but it's heavy, your Norwegian-American luggage!"

"Darling!" she exclaimed in consternation, "you're not packed up! Quick, Michael! I'll help you——"

"Thusis, I don't want this junk! Do you know what I am going to take with me?"

"What, darling?"

"My poems to you; the portrait of the Admiral; and my photograph of The Laughing Girl. . . . And nothing else whatever."

I picked up the photograph from my dresser as I spoke and slipped it into my breast pocket.

"Are we to start housekeeping with the portrait

of the Admiral and your heavenly poems of which
I never before heard?" she exclaimed, enchanted.

"Not housekeeping," I said smiling, and drawing
her into my arms.

"Aren't we going to keep house, Michael?" she
asked, her surprised eyes uplifted to mine.

"After the war," said I.

For a full minute she stood gazing at me. Then:

"I understand." And she offered her lips for the
first time to any man. And for the first time I kissed
her.

"Yes," said I gaily, "I join Pershing. Or the
Legion, if the Yankees won't take a Chilean——"

Smith rapped loudly on my door:

"Is Thusis there?"

"She is," said I.

"Did she persuade you to come with us?"

"She did."

"Good business!" cried Smith. "Is your luggage
ready?"

"It is."

I handed Thusis my poems, unhooked the portrait
of the Admiral, and tucked it under one arm.

Thusis pinned on her distractingly smart little
hat, turned, flung both arms around my neck.

"There may be the deuce to pay for this in Italy,"
she whispered. "Oh, Michael! Michael! I adore
you!"

Half way down the corridor a door opened and the queen's head in curl papers was thrust out. When her hard eyes fell on us she stiffened for an instant, then the celebrated Hohenzollern sneer twitched her features:

"Your *housekeeper!*" she hissed.

And Thusis threw back her beautiful head and the silvery laughter of The Laughing Girl filled the house with its exquisite melody.

"Oh Michael, Michael!" she said, "they'll be the death of the world after all—the boche!—for we'll all perish of laughter before we're done with them!"

And we went gaily on downstairs, my poems clasped to Thusis' breast, the Admiral's portrait under my left arm, and the lovely little hand of Thusis in mine—for ever, God willing—for ever and a day.

(1)

THE END